Acclaim for

R E S I S T A N C E

"Supe   love
and l   plic-
ity an   horrors   lies."

"From   the
reader   . . .
Resista   bed-
early,   ead-
ing ex

"In be   arks
on a c   . In
Resista   om-
mitmer   nas-
tered.   war
to its a   oti-
cism

"Reminiscent of Helen MacInnes's *Assignment in Brittany* and Erich Maria Remarque's *Arch of Triumph*. . . . Here's to Ms. Shreve."
— *New York Times Book Review*

"Anita Shreve's perceptive novel relates a simple story set in terrible times in a clear, dispassionate voice. . . . Her respect for her characters is striking, as is the meticulous attention to detail. . . . I reached the last chapter with hungry eyes, wanting more."
— *Los Angeles Times Book Review*

"Shreve is an intelligent, powerful writer."
— *San Francisco Chronicle*

"Touching. . . . The monumental events of World War II provide a vivid, terrifying backdrop to what is essentially a tender but tragic love story. This is war on an intimate scale."
— *Hartford Courant*

"A touching tome from a skilled pen."
— *Booklist*

"Shreve's prose is as gentle and dignified as the affair she describes."
— *Atlanta Journal & Constitution*

"Realistic, vivid, and gripping. . . . Shreve is a skilled storyteller."
— *Washington Times*

RESISTANCE

RESISTANCE

A NOVEL

Anita Shreve

BACK BAY BOOKS

LITTLE, BROWN AND COMPANY

Boston New York London

First Paperback Edition

The characters and events in this book are fictitious. Any similarity to real persons, living or dead, is coincidental and not intended by the author.

Library of Congress Cataloging-in-Publication Data

Shreve, Anita.
    Resistance: a novel / Anita Shreve. — 1st ed.
        p.   cm.
    ISBN 0-316-78999-2 (HC) 0-316-78984-4 (PB)
    1. World War, 1939–1945 — Belgium — Fiction.   I. Title.
PS3569.H7385R47   1995
813'.54 — dc20   94-39269

10   9

Printed in the United States of America

For our fathers who flew in the war

AUTHOR'S NOTE

This novel is entirely a work of fiction, yet it would not have been possible without the help of the following individuals: Marlyse Martin Haward, Andre Lepin, and Rosa Guyaux, who shared with me details and anecdotes about Belgium during World War II; John Rising, Chief Pilot of the Collings Foundation, who checked over the flying sequences for me; George Cole, who took me up in his plane; and, in particular, Mable Osborn, who gave the seeds of a story. I would also like to thank my editor, Michael Pietsch, and my agent, Virginia Barber.

Finally, a necessary word about the Belgian surnames. I have used, for the most part, surnames that were or are prevalent in southern Belgium. Just as the novel is fictional, however, so are the names that are attached to the various characters. I mention this because the period about which I have written is a sensitive one, and my use of certain names is not meant in any way to confer honor upon, or castigate, any Belgian families.

RESISTANCE

10 November 1993

Gentlemen,

INAUGURATION OF A MONUMENT
TO YOUR FLYING FORTERESSE B 17

On Thursday next December 30, our association will inaugurate
a monument in rememberance to your aeroplane fallen down on
1943 december 30th at the Heights nearly our village.

It consists in a marble block extracted out of our village quarry
on which a stele with the following inscription will be fixed.

*

<u>Homage à nos alliés</u>

Le 30 décembre 1943 vers midi s'écrasa à 500 m d'ici la
forteresse volante américaine Woman's Home Companion

<u>Equipage</u>

Pilote: Lt. T. Brice
Co-pilote: Lt. W. Case
Navigateur: Lt. E. Baker
Bombardier: Lt. N. Shulman
Ingénieur: J. McNulty
Ass. Ingénieur: E. Rees
Radio: G. Callahan
Ass. Radio: V. Tripp
Mitrailleur: L. Ekberg
Mitrailleur: P. Warren

Delahaut, le 30 XII 1993
*

With this letter, we would like to invite you and your wife to be
present at the inauguration. It will be a pleasure for us to offer you
a lodge in Delahaut.

If you are still in contact with the other members of the crew,
please will you make them known they are also welcome. Send us
their address so we can invite them officially.

Meanwhile, Gentlemen, please agree our best rememberance.
Jean Benoît

December 30, 1943

THE PILOT PAUSED AT THE EDGE OF THE WOOD, WHERE already it was dark, oak-dark at midday. He propped himself against a tree, believing that in the shadows he was hidden, at least for the moment. The others had fled. He was the last out of the pasture, watching until they had all disappeared, one by one, indistinct brown shapes quickly enveloped by the forest.

All, that is, except for the two on the ground, one dead, one dying. He could no longer hear the gunner's panicky questions. The cold and the wound had silenced him, or perhaps the morphine, administered by Ted's frozen fingers, had dulled the worst of it. Dragging his own wounded leg through the battered bomber, Ted had reached the gunner, drawn to him by the pitch of the man's voice. He had separated the gunner from the metal that seemed to clutch at him and pulled the man out onto the hard ground, still white with frost even at noon. The wound was to the lower abdomen, too low, Ted could see that at once. The gunner had screamed then, asked him, demanded, but Ted looked away, businesslike with the needle, and whispered something that was meant to be reassuring but was taken by the wind. The gunner felt frantically with oily fingers for the missing pieces. The pilot and the navigator had held his arms, pinned him.

Possibly the gunner was dead already, he thought at the edge of the forest. There was too much blood around the body, a hot spring that quickly pooled, froze, on the ground. The other man, the rear gunner, the man who was undeniably dead, dragged also to lie beside the wounded, had not a scratch on him.

Ted slowly tilted his head back, took the air deep into his body. As a boy he had shot squirrels in the wood at home, and there were sometimes days like this, days without color, when the sky was oily and gray and his fingers froze on the .22.

The plane lay silent on the frosty field, a charred scar behind it, the forest not forty feet from its nose. A living thing shot down, crippled now forever. A screaming, vibrating giant come obscenely to rest in a pasture.

He ought to have set fire to the plane. Those were his instructions. But he could not set a fire that might consume a living man, and so they had gathered all the provisions in the plane and made a kind of catafalque near the gunner, whom they had wrapped in parachute silk, winding sheets, the white silk stained immediately with red.

Soon people would come to the pasture. The fall of the big plane from the sky could not have been missed. Ted didn't know if the ground he sat on was German or French or Belgian. It could be German, might well be German.

He had to move deeper into the wood. He hesitated, did not want to leave the plane. He felt, leaving it, that he was abandoning a living thing, an injured dog, to be dismembered by strangers. They would take the guns first, then the engines, then every serviceable piece of metal, leaving a carcass, a dog's bones.

Gunmetal bones. A plane picked clean by buzzards.

One's duty was to the living.

Ted might have aborted. He was allowed to abort. He knew the mission was not a milk run, that they were going into German territory, to Ludwigshafen, to the chemical plant. And he had felt unlucky without Mason, his navigator, whom he had found drunk in a hotel room in Cambridge with his English girlfriend. When Ted had entered, the room had been heavy with the smell of gin. A bottle was nearly empty on a side table. Mason had looked at Ted and had laughed at him. Ted had thought then, abort. A missing navigator was a bad omen. They had flown eleven missions together, had sometimes come under heavy fire, but there had been no serious injuries, no deaths. Abort, he tried to tell himself; but at dawn, when the thin, wintry light had come up over the landing field, and he'd looked at his plane, he could not make the decision to abort. Mason was replaced. A capable man but a stranger. Together they had pinned the arms of the gunner, looked into each other's eyes.

But had the missing piece of the crew fatally altered the mix, in the same way that an error in the mix of the fuel, too rich or too thin, could also be fatal? Had unease over the missing navigator made Ted hesitate even a second when he should not have hesitated, or made him act too quickly when he *should* have hesitated? Had his belief in bad omens clouded in some indefinable way his judgment? Case, his copilot, was right. They should have ditched. But he couldn't, and it was no use pretending he could.

Twigs crackled. Ted tried to stand, leaned against the rough bark. He had dragged himself out of the clearing, his right leg wounded inside his flight suit. When he stood, the pain traveled up his thigh. He embraced the tree, his forehead against the bark. A sudden sweat broke out on his face from the pain. He bent over quickly, heaved onto the frozen leaves. He might have saved a needle for himself, but he was afraid that he would crawl into the forest and freeze to death while he slept. He knew he had to move deeper into the wood.

Today was his birthday. He was twenty-two.

Where did the gunner's dick go? he wondered.

He turned to look at the plane once again, and from his full height he saw what he had not seen before: In dragging himself to the edge of the forest, he had made a path in the frost, a path as clear and distinct as a walkway shoveled in snow. He heard the first of the muffled shouts then. A foreign voice. He dropped to the ground and pulled himself away from the pasture.

———

The boy reached the Heights before Marcel. Jean dropped his bicycle, his chest burning. He gulped in the icy air and stared at the plane on the dead grass. He had never seen such a big plane, never. It was somehow terrifying, that enormous plane, unnatural here. How did a machine, all that metal, ever get up into the sky? He approached the plane cautiously, wondering if it might still explode. He heard Marcel behind him, breathing hard like a dog.

Jean walked toward the bomber and saw the bodies, the two men in leather helmets, one man wrapped in a parachute. The white silk was bloody, drenched in blood.

Jean spun and yelled at Marcel: "La Croix-Rouge, Marcel! Madame Dinant! La Croix-Rouge!"

Marcel hesitated just a moment, then did as Jean had asked, unwilling yet to see exactly what his friend had seen.

When Marcel had gone, Jean walked slowly toward the plane. For the first time since he'd seen the giant, smoking surprise drop suddenly from the cloud cover, he could breathe evenly. He was chilled, the sweat beginning to freeze inside his pullover. He hadn't thought to fetch his coat before racing out of the school to head for the Heights.

When he reached the plane, he looked down at the bodies. Both of the flyers had their eyes closed, but the man wrapped in blood was still breathing. Beside the two men was a pile of canteens and brown canvas sacks.

Jean moved away from the men and began to circle the plane.

The plane was American, he was sure of that.

The bomber rested deeply on its belly, as if partially embedded in the ground, the propellers jammed and bent under the wings. The wings were extraordinarily long. The tail seemed to have been ripped apart, to have stripped itself in the air, and there were dozens of holes in the fuselage, some of them as large as windows. There were markings on the plane and a white, five-pointed star.

Jean walked to the front of the plane. Perhaps, he thought, there were men still trapped inside the cockpit, and for a moment he entertained the fantasy of rescuing them, saving their lives. The windshield had been shot away. Jean climbed onto the wing and peered into the cockpit. He looked at the debris and glass and smashed instrument casings. He tried to imagine himself behind the controls. He hopped off the wing then, and walked around the nose to the other side of the plane. Below the cockpit was a drawing he couldn't quite believe and beneath the drawing were English words he couldn't read. If Marcel had been with him, Jean would have pointed to the drawing, and the two boys would have laughed. But alone, Jean did not feel like laughing.

Slowly he circled the rest of the plane and returned to the two men lying on the ground. The man in the parachute began to moan, opened his eyes. Instinctively, Jean backed away. He didn't know whether he should speak or remain silent. For a moment, his own eyes welled with tears, and he wished Madame Dinant would hurry up and get here. What could a ten-year-old boy do for the man in the pasture?

He walked backwards from the plane, his hands frozen in his pockets. And as he did so, he saw what ought to have been obvious to him, but was lost in his eagerness to inspect the plane. Fanning out from the front of the plane to the forest were footprints in the frost — large footprints, not his own. He could see distinctly where the footprints had gone: this trail, and that trail, and that trail — all into the wood, spokes from the plane.

And then there was the one path.

In the distance, Jean heard voices, the murmur of excited, breathless voices scurrying up the hill toward the pasture. Quickly Jean marked in his memory the entry points of the various trails into the forest. Without knowing quite why he was doing this, he began to scuffle over the field, erasing footprints with his shoes. The voices grew louder. His own feet would not be sufficient. He ran to the edge of the clearing, ripped down a fir branch. He whirled around the pasture, sweeping the frost from the grass.

———•———

Antoine was ahead of him, limping with remarkable speed up the cow path. How could such a fat, ungainly man move so fast? Henri wondered. His own chest stung with the effort. He didn't want to find this plane, didn't want to see it.

Just minutes ago, in the village, he and Antoine had been

drinking at Jauquet's. Thinking to make something of a noon break, not quite a meeting, talking about the leaflets, drinking Jauquet's beer, not as good as his own. And then the plane dropping out of the sky as they sat there in the Burghermaster's small, frozen garden. Dipping and wobbling as they watched, three of its engines trailing dark plumes, creating an eerie charcoal drawing. He wanted to cover his head; he thought the plane would fall onto the village. The bomber barely missed the steeple of St. Catherine's, and Henri could see it had no landing gear. Excitement and fear rose in him as he watched the plane lift slightly and then fall, and then lift again to disappear over the Heights. Waiting for the explosion then, watching for billows of smoke from the field. In silence they had waited seconds. Nothing had happened.

American, Antoine had said.

How long since the plane had crashed? Nine minutes? Eleven?

The others approached the clearing just ahead of him. Thérèse Dinant was first, walking so fast she was bent forward in her wool coat, retying her kerchief under her chin against the cold. Behind her, Jauquet was puffing hard to beat her into the pasture. Léon, a thin man with steel glasses and a worker's cap, couldn't take the hill, was falling back. And schoolboys, running, as if this were an outing.

He heard exclamations of surprise, some fear. He turned the corner and took it all in at once: the broken plane, the bodies, the scarred ground. From habit, he crossed himself.

Not a crash, but a belly landing. The smell of petrol, the thought of fire. Thérèse kneeling in the frost. Taking the pulse of a man wrapped in a parachute, speaking constantly to him in a low voice. She raised the wrist of another man beside the first, but Henri could see, even from where he stood, that the man was dead. It was the color of his face.

Dinant looked up and ordered stretchers and a truck. Girard, who worked with Bastien, the undertaker, ran suddenly from the pasture.

More people arrived in the clearing. Twenty, twenty-five, thirty. The villagers surrounded the plane, climbed onto the wings. Schoolboys rubbed the metal of the engine cowling with knitted gloves as if it were burnished gold. They peered down under the wings to marvel at how the propellers had bent in the landing. A distance was kept from the wounded and the dead, with Thérèse watching over them, except that some of the men gave their coats to be piled over the wounded man to warm him.

Henri meant to give his coat. He couldn't move.

Women — farmers' wives, shopkeepers — inspected canvas sacks, exclaiming over the provisions. The chocolate, he saw, was taken immediately. Later, he thought, after the bodies had been removed, the sacks would be picked clean.

There was activity inside the plane. Paper and instruments were spilling from the cockpit. He saw Antoine beckoning for him to come closer. Henri stood with uplifted hands to receive the salvaged goods. He didn't want to see what the instruments were, what the papers said. It was always true: The less you knew the better.

How long until the Germans came to the clearing? Minutes? An hour? If they came around the corner now, he would be shot.

Turning, he saw Jauquet with schoolbags he'd comandeered from the children. How did the Burghermaster know which children could be trusted? Antoine climbed out of the plane and over the wing. He slid to the ground, helped to pack the sacks.

I'll wait two hours, then go to St. Laurent. Jauquet speaking, puffed up with the mission. To tell the Germans was what he meant. Standard procedure in the Resistance, Jauquet said knowingly, though privately Henri wondered how the man could be so sure, since this was the first plane ever to fall precisely in the village. Jauquet expansive now, explaining the risk: If the Germans found the plane before they were officially told, Jauquet's head would be in a noose. But more than likely, Henri thought, the Germans were eating and drinking at L'Hôtel de Ville in St. Laurent, as they did at every noon hour, and had probably had so much beer to drink already they hadn't seen or heard the plane. It was meant to be a joke: The Belgian beer was the country's best defensive weapon.

He saw a boy by the front of the plane now, gesturing to another, looking up at something on the nose. The boys' eyes widened. They whispered excitedly and pointed. "La chute obscène," Henri heard them say.

Stretchers were arriving on a truck. Thérèse would take the flyers home, tend to the wounded. Bastien would come for the dead man. If the wounded man lived, he'd be put into the network before the Germans could find him.

The village women maneuvered in toward the sacks. More people at the pasture, gathering closer to the plane, as if it were alive, a curiosity at the circus. Fifty now, maybe sixty. Schoolgirls in thick woolen socks and brown shoes stood on the wing and crawled forward to peer into the cockpit. There was nervous giggling. Their laughter seemed disrespectful to Henri, and he was irritated by the girls.

Beside him, Antoine's voice: We'll hide the sacks with Claire, convene a meeting in the church.

Henri turned with a protest, the words dying on his tongue. Not with Claire, he wanted to say. Antoine's face a wall.

We've got to find the pilots, Antoine insisted quietly. Before the Germans do.

Henri, with the heavy sacks, nodded as he knew he must. It was beginning now, he thought, and who could say where it would end?

———•———

When she was alone, she sometimes stood at the window near the pump and looked across the flat fields toward France. The fields, gray since November, were indistinguishable from the color of the farm buildings, stone structures with thick walls and slate roofs. On cold days like this, she could not always tell where in the distance the fields met the sky. She liked to imagine that in France, if she could go there, there would be color — that it would be like turning the pages of a book and coming unexpectedly upon a color plate. That was the image she had in her mind of crossing the border, a drawing of color.

She drew from the pocket of her skirt a cigarette and lit it. She stood at the window, looking out, one arm across her chest, the other holding the cigarette. The smoke wafted in a lazy design around her hair in front of the glass. This was her third already, and she knew she must slow down. Henri was good about the cigarettes. He seldom failed to come by them, no matter how scarce they were in the village. And the bargain she had made with him, one bargain of many, was that she would smoke no more than the five on any given day.

They had brought her an old Jewish woman this time. The woman had escaped the Gestapo by hiding in her chimney for two days and nights. The woman's son, who was a doctor in Antwerp, had designed the hiding place for his mother in her home because her shoulders and hips were so narrow, even at seventy-five, that she could fit inside the chimney. When the Gestapo came before dawn, the old woman ran directly to the chimney and climbed to the foot braces her son had made for her. She stood in the chimney in her nightgown, her feet spread apart on the braces. She regretted that she had not embraced her husband in the bed before each of them had jumped up and fled. She listened with fear as the policemen searched her home — once, twice, three times — and finally found her husband, who had also been a doctor, in his hiding place in the basement. It was all she could do to keep from crying out to him, so that now, in her sleep, the old woman often cried out to her lost husband: *Avram . . . Avram . . .* And Claire, through the wall, lay awake at night listening to her.

When the old woman's legs could stand no more, she slid from the braces and tumbled onto the damp hearth. She was found in the dirty fireplace, blackened beyond recognition, by the tailor's son, who had come to see if anyone in the doctor's house had survived the raids. The tailor's son at first thought the old woman had been burned alive by the Gestapo, and he vomited onto the Persian rug. But then she called out her husband's name — *Avram . . . Avram . . .* — and the tailor's son carried her to his mother's house. The tailor's wife bathed the old woman and put her into the network. It was unclear to Claire how long she had been traveling. The woman's story was told to Claire by the man who had brought her to the house. The old woman herself had very little to say.

Madame Rosenthal was upstairs now, in the small attic room that was hidden behind the false back of the heavy oak armoire. The armoire had once been part of Claire's dowry. Henri had fashioned a door in its back that opened onto a small crawl space behind; and he had made a window in the slate roof, so that some light was let into the hiding place. If one day the Germans decided to climb onto the roof, the small opening, sealed with glass, would be discovered, and Claire and Henri, too, would be taken away and shot. But the window was hidden behind a chimney stack and not visible from the ground.

Madame Rosenthal was the twenty-eighth refugee to stay with them. Claire remembered each one, like beads on a rosary. Barely had she and Henri heard of the fighting in Antwerp before they learned that Belgium's small army had been no match for the Nazis. Even so, she had been unable to believe in the reality of the German occupation until the first of the refugees from the north had arrived at their village in May 1940. They stopped in the square and asked for food and beds. It seemed to her now that important lines were drawn, even in those first few weeks. Some of the residents of Delahaut had immediately come into the square and taken the displaced Belgians into their homes. Others had silently closed their doors and shutters. When, in that first month, Antoine had come into the kitchen of their house to ask Claire and Henri to join him in the Maquis, Claire had seen at once that Henri, on his own, might have closed his shutters. But Antoine was persistent. Claire had languages and the nursing, Antoine had pointed out. Henri had looked at Claire then, as if the languages and the nursing might one day be a danger to them both.

Their first family was from Brussels, the father a professor at the university. There were six of them in all, and Claire made up pallets in the second bedroom. That night, in the kitchen, she asked Henri if they should flee themselves, but Henri said no, he wouldn't leave the farm that had been his father's and his father's father's.

Then we have to make a hiding place, she said. There's going to be a flood.

Claire turned away from the window and laid out the white sausage made with milk and bread, the sausage that had no meat that she had made for her husband's noon meal. There was also a runny white cheese and a soup made from cabbages and onions.

She had grown thin from the war, but her husband, inexplicably, had grown bigger. It was the beer, she thought, the thick, dark beer Henri and the others made and kept hidden from the Germans. There were barrels of it in the barn, bottles of it in the cellar that sometimes popped or exploded. The beer was strong, heavy with alcohol, and if she drank even one glass, she felt peaceful almost immediately.

Earlier she had crawled awkwardly with her tray into the attic space and given the old woman some of the soup, holding her narrow shoulders with one arm, feeding her with a spoon. The old woman was extraordinarily frail now, and Claire did not see how she could be moved, how she could withstand a move. But the Maquis would want her out, across the border to France within the week. The network had arranged it, and there would be others who would need the attic room. More than likely, Claire thought, the doctor's wife would die in the attic.

She put her apron on again and prepared the coffee — a bitter coffee of chicory that no amount of sugar, if they had had sugar, could sweeten. At least, she thought, it was better than the coffee they'd had last month — a nearly undrinkable coffee made of malt. She moved back to the window and watched for her husband. She didn't know where he was or even if he would be back. He had left the barn more than an hour ago. He hadn't stopped to tell her why.

In the morning, he'd gone to the barn as he always did for the milking. They had had seventy cows before the war began; now they only had the twelve. The Germans had taken the rest. Henri spent most of his days tending the tiny herd and repairing simple farm machinery — a difficult task since parts were nonexistent. He had to fashion his own parts, design them, hammer them, from old pots or kettles or buckles, anything that Claire could spare from the house. Once he had taken her ladle, a pewter ladle with a long handle that she had brought with her to the marriage, and they had fought over the ladle until her anger had subsided. He had needed the ladle more than she had; it was simple.

She didn't like to think of what it must be like each day

for Henri in the barn. Perhaps he had been drinking from the barrels already, and she wouldn't blame him. The air was frozen and raw, and sometimes it was colder in the barn than it was in the fields.

Behind the barn, they had the one truck, which they never used. There was no gasoline for the Belgians, but Henri had kept the gazogene, for emergencies. Surprisingly, the Germans had not taken the truck for themselves, although the soldiers sometimes commandeered it for a week at a time. Delahaut had escaped the fate of some towns. The Germans didn't billet there. The accommodations in St. Laurent were better.

Claire removed the brick from behind the stove and retrieved her book. That December she was reading English. Sometimes she read Dutch or Italian or French, but she preferred reading in English when she could get the books. She liked the English words, and liked to say them aloud when no one was in the house: *fox-glove, cellar, whisper, needle.* She could read and speak English better than she could write it, and she was trying to teach herself this skill, though she had to be careful about leaving any traces of written English or the English books themselves in the house. She wished she could read in English to the old woman upstairs, but the woman's first language was Yiddish, to which she had retreated from the Flemish. Together they could communicate only in German, which seemed to distress them both.

She sat down at the oak table and held her book open with her crossed arms. The book had been given to her by an English gunner who had had to parachute out of his plane and who had broken his collarbone when he landed near Charleroi. She remembered the gunner, a thin, spotty-faced boy who'd been at school when he'd been called up. He was ill suited to be a gunner — you could see that at once — a reed-thin boy with a delicate mouth. In his flight suit he had two books, a prayer book and a volume of English poetry, and when he left, he gave the book of poetry to Claire. He said he'd already read it too many times, but she suspected that was not quite true. She wondered where the boy was now. She was seldom told the fate of the people who passed through her house, often never knew if they made it to

France or to England or if they died en route — shot or betrayed. She knew the beginnings of many stories, but not their endings.

The world is charged with the grandeur of God.
It will flame out, like shining from shook foil. . . .

She liked the few poems by Gerard Manley Hopkins the best, even though she could not understand them very well. She took pleasure from the sound of the words, the way the poet had put the sounds together. Often she didn't even know what the words meant. She thought she knew *shook,* but she wasn't positive. But *foil?* Yet she loved the sound of *shining from shook,* liked to say this aloud.

She felt then, within her abdomen, a downward draw and pull, a signal that soon, before nightfall, she would begin to bleed. Reflexively, she crossed herself. She shut her eyes and whispered a prayer, words of relief more than of faith. Although she was careful during the time she might conceive, putting Henri off with a sequence of subtle signs — a slightly turned head, a shoulder raised — she could never be quite certain, absolutely positive. She did not want to conceive a child during the war, to bring a child into a world where one or both parents might be taken during the night, where a child could be left to freeze or burn, or might be cruelly injured by the planes overhead. The very air above them had been violated. She herself had seen the dirty smudges and the lethal clouds. She was not even sure she would have a child after the war. Sometimes she thought that the weight of the stories that had passed through her house had filled her and squeezed out that part of her that might have borne a child with hope.

She needn't have been so worried this month though, she thought to herself. She counted. It couldn't have been more than four times. Henri was often gone late into the night with the Maquis, and she sometimes thought that the war, and what Henri himself had seen and heard, had affected her husband as well.

For skies of couple-colour as a brindled cow;
For rose-moles all in stipple upon trout that swim. . . .

She had tried to imagine England, but she couldn't. Even when the English boys told her stories of home, she could not bring the landscape into focus. And the stories were often confusing: Some were of stone cottages where, in the boys' memories, the gardens always bloomed, even in the winter; and others were of city streets, narrow streets of cobblestones and darkened brick houses.

The sound of bicycles rattled on the gravel drive, startling her. Claire swept the English poetry book onto her lap under the table. Henri and Antoine Chimay entered the kitchen. Each of them was carrying children's schoolbags. Henri was breathless.

"Claire."

"What is it?"

"A plane."

"A plane?"

"Yes, yes. A fallen plane, in Delahaut."

"English?"

"American."

"American? Any survivors?"

"One is dead. One almost dead. There might be eight others."

"Where is it?"

"On the Heights. The others are probably in the wood."

Henri and Antoine lay the schoolbags on the table.

"We need you to hide these," Antoine said.

Henri looked at his wife as if to say he was sorry. "The barn is best," he said instead.

Henri was flushed — from the effort of the bicycle ride or his agitation, she couldn't say. He was older than she; he would be thirty-two in the spring. The features of his face seemed to have broadened with age as they often did in the men of the village. It was as though, in face and body, Henri had finally filled out to the shape he would retain as a man throughout his lifetime — stocky like his father, barrel-chested, his shoulders round and solid. He had thick brown hair the exact color of his eyes. A V of hair, like a tail feather, fell forward onto his forehead. She had begun to notice that there was a tooth to one side of his mouth that was darkening. She wondered if it caused him pain; he never complained.

"I have to go now," he said. "I don't know when I'll be back."

Claire nodded. She watched as her husband and Antoine left the house and remounted their bicycles. She hid the book of English poetry behind the brick. She put her coat on and lifted the schoolbags into her arms. Upstairs, through the floorboards, Claire thought she could hear the old woman crying.

—————•—•—————

Darkness between the trees, a false night. It was somebody's birthday in the kitchen. His mother was at work in the courthouse, and his father was not yet home with the stink of meat in his skin. A song from somewhere. From the children's faces leaning toward the candles. And Frances, who had made the cake, bent over him so that he could smell her warm breath at his cheek and whispered to him in the din: A wish, Teddy. Make a wish.

When he cried as a boy, it was Frances he went to.

The ground was hard marble. From time to time he heard a distant shout, a call, a branch cracking from a tree. The cold made the branches snap, like fire did.

He had dragged the leg, a dead soldier, how many feet — a hundred? a thousand? No sun to tell him his direction, the compass button smashed. He could be headed into Germany, out of Germany, no signposts on the trees to mark the way.

When he broke his arm, falling from the tree, it was Frances who sat with him, played gin endlessly at his request. Frances who was tall like himself and had his face, but misaligned. His mother sometimes whispered that Frances would never marry.

His lower leg was stiff and swollen. The knee would not bend. He wondered if a kind of rigor had set in.

He would have liked a cigarette. Wasn't that what they gave the dying?

If he wasn't found, he thought, he would die before morning.

Yet he was terrified of being found. An unfamiliar helmet. The muzzle of a gun pressed against the skin under his chin.

On Stella's porch there was a swing. It was last night or last month, and she sat beside him in a thin cotton dress. Her skin was tanned in the hollow above her breasts, and her legs were bare beneath the skirt. He thought, oddly, of a girl on a bicycle, with bare legs, falling, scraping her knees. She was a girl, still, even then, on the porch. Was that why he had hesitated? The skirt billowed out like a parachute and hid her legs.

That was his nickname when he was a boy. Teddy. Frances called him that. Stella called him Ted.

His hands had frozen into cups. He dragged himself on his elbows. Inside his flight suit, there was a photograph. He lay back, exhausted. Perhaps he would sleep or had slept. He fumbled with the zipper of the flight suit with his frozen fingers, but they did not work. Inside there was a photograph of Stella.

The sky above the trees was the color of dust. Sometimes there were pallets of oak leaves, and they helped him slide. He wondered, when he heard a distant voice, if he should shout for help. There were procedures. What was the procedure for freezing to death in the wood?

It was 1936 or 1937. He forgot the year. Matt, his younger brother, in a rage, running up to his room, Ted's room (Teddy's room then?), and destroying all the model airplanes, hung on delicate threads from the ceiling, each wooden model laboriously assembled and painted, the models bought with money Ted had earned in the fields, the planes made and collected over many years. From below, Ted heard the sound of rage, feared the worst, then went up into the devastation in his room. Splinters and tangled threads, broken wings on the bed. A thousand hours smashed. He made a vow then never to speak to Matt again, ever, and he hadn't until the morning the train came to take him off to war. He stood on the station platform, shivering with his mother and his father and with Frances, who was weeping openly, wishing the train would come, dreading the goodbyes. Then he turned, said to Frances, I'll be right back.

He sprinted the distance, easy for him, he had won the 440 at the state championships and gone off to college on the strength of his legs. He ran past the farms and the farmhouses, the sun just coming up over the fields at dawn, raced up the steps of his own house, white clapboards with a porch, once a farmhouse, now just a house like the others at the edge of the small Ohio village. He found Matt in bed still.

He shook his hand. He said goodbye.

What was the row about? He couldn't remember now. A silly row. And Matt had been just a kid.

He wondered if he would ever run again. Walk again. Would they take the leg?

Who was *they*?

He had seen the young men with the trousers folded and neatly pinned, passing through, going home. Warnings of what was out there.

But you didn't think of that. You drank gin made from grapefruit juice, 150 proof, and hoped they didn't wake you in the middle of the night while you were still drunk.

Anything to escape the fate of his father. The village butcher. His hands in the entrails of animals. Dead flesh always under his fingernails. The stink of meat never left him. Or did Teddy simply imagine that?

His father drank Seagram's. All night.

Ted came to, realized he had slept. Or had passed out. The pain came in waves. He wished his leg would freeze altogether, go totally numb like his fingers.

Where were Case and Baker and Shulman? Case had a shot-up arm, Shulman had been limping badly. Tripp had had blood on his flight suit. Were they found, lost, dead?

It was a toss-up now between a cigarette and a glass of beer.

The thirst had announced itself suddenly. Not a good sign. He propped himself up on his elbows, looked at his leg. There was blood soaking the leg of his flight suit. He couldn't move his foot or feel it.

Were there cigarettes inside his flight suit? He couldn't remember. They might as well be diamonds in a safe. With Stella's photograph.

Her photograph was like all the others he had seen. Creased, worn at the edges. The creases skimmed across her neck.

Why, on the porch the night before he left, why had he not taken her hand, led her away from her house?

Something in him had hesitated.

Foolish, he thought, lying on the frozen ground, these moral quandaries. Hadn't there been thousands of men making love that night, simply to say they were alive?

He imagined his hand sliding up Stella's bare leg, under the parachute skirt.

Was it possible there were people on the ground when he gave the order to jettison the bomb load? It looked like farmland, endless fields, but the cloud cover was so thick he couldn't really tell, except when he came in low, and saw patches of field. The bombardier said it was just field. There wouldn't be people on frozen fields in December. Couldn't be.

He should have kept one canteen.

He drifted, dreamed of parachute silk. He was unwinding a woman and she was smiling, looking at him. He was on his knees, unwinding, but there was so much silk, endless layers . . .

He came to sharply. He had heard something, he was sure of it. Footsteps. Not in the dream.

He propped himself up, lay perfectly still. The sound was faint, not a crackle, but a soft step. There. He heard it again. Coming toward him from the pasture. He could see no one through the trees.

He looked around quickly, searching for cover. If he could hide, he could see who the footsteps belonged to before revealing himself. There was a tangle of brambles twenty feet away. It was dark enough that he couldn't see inside it. He dragged himself as fast as he dared, not wanting to make any noise. The brambles were hard, thorny. He turned, went in flat on his belly.

No voices. Only one set of footsteps.

Closer now. Definitely closer.

He wondered if he should pray. They joked about it; they called it foxhole religion. Men long out of practice, straining to remember words, fragments, sentences, get it right.

He thought he saw a figure.

The Focke-Wulfs were everywhere. The fight field was exploding, smoking. A B-17, cut in half by flak, the nose spinning, tumbling out of control, the tail floating, drifting as in flight, and in the tail, the gunner was still firing . . .

Ekberg screamed. His hands were frozen to the guns. The screaming of the men and the screaming of the plane. The noise, deafening, vibrating, was in the head, in the bones.

Was it possible, going home across the Channel, nearly out of fuel, to bounce the waves and make it? Peterson had claimed it.

A German had miscalculated the clearance, collided with a bomber. The fighter cartwheeled, plummeted, away from them toward the ground.

FWs at twelve o'clock. Count the parachutes. Where did the gunner's dick go? Parachute silk stained with blood. It was Frances who raised him, and he said goodbye to Matt. He was on his knees now, unwinding a woman, and she was smiling up at him. But there were layers, endless layers . . .

———•———

When the boy returned to the clearing, there were fewer people, an impending sense that soon the Germans would be there. No one wanted to be near the plane when the Germans discovered it. Jean had gone back to the school for his coat and dinner sack and had come on foot this time, not wanting a bicycle, however well hidden, to be traced to him. If he were caught in the wood, trying to find or help the Americans who had fled the plane, he would be sent away to the camps. He was sure of that.

He slipped into the wood unnoticed, at the point that he had memorized. In the pockets of his jacket, he had hidden bread and cheese and a small bottle he filled with water. The word had gone out that all children were to return to their lessons at once; those who did not would be punished. He could imagine the round red face of Monsieur Dauvin, his teacher, his skin becoming even more blotchy with his fury when he noticed Jean's vacant desk. He had told Marcel to say that he was sick, but he knew such a lie soon would be found out and would probably compound his punishment. He ought to have said nothing to Marcel, for now Marcel, too, would be caned.

He knew the wood well. He doubted any boy in Delahaut knew it better. His own house, his father's farm, abutted the wood to the north, and even as a very young boy he knew the forest as a safe place to be. Each day after school he walked among the beeches and oaks, observing new growth in the spring, the feathery green buds, the white lilies pushing up from the ground. He fished with Marcel in the spring and in the summer, and he had respect for the forest in the winter. He knew that a man or a boy lost in the wood in December would die there.

The path was easy to follow, too easy. The body had matted the dead grass, broken small twigs from bushes. He had to find the flyer soon, or the Germans almost certainly would. The path was too exposed, and he had no time now to destroy the traces.

What he would do when he found the man he didn't know. He pictured himself giving the flyer bread and cheese and water, and then leading him to safety. His imagination was suddenly excited as he envisioned helping him to escape to the French border, shaking hands with him like a grown man. But when he thought about this hard, doubts began to cloud his mind. Where could he offer the man shelter? He thought of his own barn, and then felt the hot flush of shame on the back of his neck. At school, some of the older boys had begun to whisper, in his hearing, "le fils du collabo," the son of a collaborator.

He learned about his father at school, when the taunts began, and at first he did not understand. When he asked his father what was meant, his father was silent. He told Jean that a war was a man's business, not a boy's. Later, Jean discovered, by watching and by listening, that his father traded for profit with the Germans, that the Germans ate bread from his father's soil and meat from his father's barn. It was as bad, thought Jean, as selling machine parts or even secrets. What did the product matter? It was one thing to have your animals taken by the Germans, as had happened to many in the village; quite another to sell for money. Sometimes the shame was almost unendurable. He had thought of running away from home, running away from school — but it was winter, and where was he to go? Even if he were to make it to France, which he imagined he could easily do, what then? How would he stay alive? Who would take in an extra boy, another mouth to feed? Mightn't he be spotted by the Germans and sent to the camps? And besides, he couldn't leave his mother. The thought of his mother weeping inevitably ended these reckless reveries.

He had come nearly three hundred meters from the clearing. He knew this part of the wood especially well. Not far from here was a pool that in the summer was filled with trout. It would be frozen now, a sheet of black ice. He wondered where the trout went — deep into the mud? He thought of the comfort and safety there. He had skates when he was younger and used to skate on the black ice at the pond, but he had outgrown them. He knew there would be no more skating for some time.

He stood still in the forest. He thought he heard a sound, a sound unlike any other. The soft brush of leaves. His stomach clenched. He badly needed to urinate. He should have done it earlier — too late now; he would be heard. He stepped cautiously forward, each footfall as deliberate and as quiet as he could manage. He stopped, listened. He could not hear the swishing sound anymore. He waited. He walked forward about ten meters, and then, unbelievably, the trail seemed to end. Confused, the boy stood near a tangle of bushes. Instinctively, he looked up. Had the man climbed an oak tree? Had he seen him coming? Suddenly he was frightened, and he wanted to protect his head. He should not be here. At the very least, he should have brought Marcel.

The need to relieve himself was urgent. Where had the path gone? He investigated the area where the trail had abruptly ended, searching for its continuation. Perhaps the man had stood up, was walking now. It would be impossible to track footprints in the dim interior light of the forest, Jean thought.

And then, turning in exasperation, he saw what he had come for. The sole of a boot at the end of the brambles.

The village was just outside Cambridge, the land flat for miles, flat and wet, the soil reclaimed from the sea. All that late fall, since October when he'd arrived, he'd taken a bicycle and ridden the roads and lanes of the countryside, where one could see in the distance, if it was clear, the next village and the next, their steeples rising, an uneventful landscape, a perfect landing field.

They'd taken the village, a massive invasion, farmers' fields now lined precisely with Nissen huts, pneumonia tubes, everyone coughing in the night, from smoke or cold, it seemed to matter little. That night, the night before the twelfth mission, he and Case had lain across from each other in their bunks, each propped up on an elbow, each smoking, talking edgily, wondering, speculating, endlessly speculating on the target, the weather, how deep the penetration, how thick the cloud cover. Case was nervous, high-strung. He sometimes boasted of his pitching arm, claimed that before the war he'd been tapped by the Boston Braves, but there was something in the way he said this, the eyes a bit evasive, that made Ted doubt his story. After missions, Case would get debilitating headaches that left him nearly lifeless in his bunk. Ted thought it more difficult for Case than for himself. Less to do as copilot, more time to think about what might be headed their way. Case could not sleep, and that night neither could he. They smoked, and Case talked about his girlfriend back home, and about the Braves. Case never slept before a mission, and Ted had lost his navigator. Ted sometimes thought that if ever they had to bail out over Germany, Case might, with luck, pass for a German — with his high flat brow and his pale, almost colorless hair. In the dark the two men could hear the coughing. One man moaned, cried out in his sleep. Case looked at Ted, said, *Shulman*. The pilot nodded. In the morning, between them on the floor, there was a pile of butts a foot wide.

Earlier that evening, after word had come down about the mission, Ted had gone to look for Mason, the only member of the crew he'd been unable to locate easily. He'd looked in the aero-club, the post exchange, the mess hall, even the chapel, then given up the search, thinking the navigator would return before the briefing at three A.M.

Each night before a mission, Ted took a shower in the outdoor stall, the water brutal, ice below his feet. It was a ritual, a superstition, a down payment on thinning luck, in the same way that Tripp wore his torn scarf, and McNulty carried a deck of cards with five aces. Returning to the hut, shivering from the icy water and still wet inside his long johns, Ted heard Case say, within his hearing, almost but not quite taunting him, that Mason had gone to Cambridge. Ted dressed, then got on his bicycle and rode in the winter dark to the hotel where he knew Mason often met his English girl. The pilot's hair froze along the way and melted in the lobby. The man at the front desk deferred to the aviator's wings and, against the rules, let him up the stairs. Ted knocked on the door and opened it. In the bed, a woman was naked. He remembered thin red hair, a mottled color to her skin. There was gin on the table, the real stuff, not GI alcohol. Mason was drunk, but the pilot knew it was fatigue that had brought him to the hotel. They called it fatigue, a gentle name for blowing all your circuits, an inability to get back into your plane when your chances of coming home alive were only one in three. When Mason had heard about the impending mission, he'd left the base. In the hotel room, he told Ted he knew he'd be court-martialed, stripped of his wings, but he added drunkenly from the bed that he didn't give a flying fuck, and then he laughed. Ted began a protest, stopped. You couldn't crew with a navigator who had fatigue, who was drunk.

He'd thought then, superstitiously, *abort*. But he hadn't.

On Christmas Day he had a meal with an English family. He brought chocolate and fruit for the children. There was a girl there, a young girl, no more than twelve, with a round face, and short hair parted at the side, a bowl cut on a face that wasn't pretty but reminded him of Frances. And he had felt in the small brick cottage, with the gristled joint on the table and gaudy paper decorations hung from lamps and doorways, a pang so deep he'd nearly wept. He'd steadied himself with long swallows of hot tea from a china cup.

There had been no missions since before Christmas, and when there were no missions, there was tedium. They played cards, they went to the pub. They waited for the mail. They walked out to their planes and talked to the mechanics. Sometimes the weather grounded them for days, and the lull made the men touchy. When they went, that early morning, to the briefing, there was a tension in the room Ted hadn't felt so keenly before. He showed his pass to the MP. Later, when he dressed for the mission, he would leave the pass behind, and take only his dog tags and his escape kit with its evasion photo and a handful of foreign currency. And every man on the ship, he knew, would carry something else as well. A lucky coin. A photo of a woman. Cigarettes. A camera. Small paper books that fit inside a pocket and were made of wartime paper that sometimes crumbled, disintegrated in your hands.

The weather would be terrible. They already knew that. Walking from the hut to the briefing room, each man had searched the night sky for a star, the briefest slip of a moon, some ghostly break in the cloud cover. But the dark that early morning was impenetrable. Ted thought that if they went at all, they would have to corkscrew up, break free of the clouds. Forming up was sometimes catastrophic. He knew of planes colliding in the fog, exploding, spinning to earth when they weren't a thousand feet in the air. A lost squadron dragging through another in the thick cloud, the carnage devastating. Senseless death, as if any death made sense.

Case worked a toothpick; Shulman behind him was humming. Glenn Miller. "A String of Pearls." Shulman was from Chicago, a welder, like his father before him, he had said. He had bad skin and small, tense eyes. Mason had been a drummer with a band. He played in dance halls in New York City. Sometimes in the pub, he had entertained them with wooden sticks made from a pointer he'd stolen after a briefing, then whittled and sanded. Watching his hands fly over the barroom tables, you could imagine yourself in a supper club, at a table on the floor, listening to a solo and drinking pink gin with a woman in a red dress, although Ted had never actually done this. In the briefing room, Case was opening packs of gum and methodically putting the dry sticks into his mouth, one by one. His foot was jiggling. Despite the cold, the sweat had started already, tricking down the copilot's temples.

Ted looked at the map, shrouded in the black covering. He wondered how long the thin, red strand of yarn would be this time, where exactly it would lead them. In the room the men were coughing, and you could see your breath.

He remembered the oil-stained concrete below the plane, and the way the dawn announced itself — an almost imperceptible lightening in a field of endless gray. On the hardstand all around him were other planes, other ground crews, bomb loaders, fuel trucks. Beyond that were the barren fields and the trees, and in the distance, the lonely rhythmic chugging of a train.

He let Case take up his parachute pack and flight bag, while Aikins, the ground chief, gave him the 1A. A bolt on the landing gear had been repaired, he read, and he began his visual inspection of the outside of the plane. The B-17, which resembled a piece of hammered metal, had been repaired well enough to fly — but not cosmetically. Countless missions had taken their toll. Paint was scratched to reveal the silver of metal; bullets and shrapnel had left their imprint. The olive paint near the top of the plane was stained with oil from the engines.

At the rear of the plane, the men were putting on their Mae Wests. His crew was young — nineteen, twenty — and discouraged by the heavy losses. They called him "the old man," even though he was only twenty-two that day. If they made it back he would tell them, and he'd get drunk and stay drunk until the New Year. Warren was a farmer's son; Ekberg had worked in a bowling alley. They were strangers thrown together, men you wouldn't gravitate toward back home. Once in a while, if it worked, there were friendships.

Ludwigshafen. He rolled the name on his tongue. Synthetic fuel and chemicals a hundred and twenty miles into Germany, a plant near Mannheim. In the briefing room, the squadron commander had dimmed the lights, and they had all studied the reconnaissance photos — searching among the gray shapes for the targets they were to hit, small rectangles that looked different from the rest. Every briefing ended the same way, with the time-tick and a worn and dreary message: If they didn't do it, someone else would have to.

He walked forward past the waist to the left wing and to the engines. He looked for nicks or cracks in the propellers. One of the ground crew was polishing the Plexiglas nosepiece and saluted him. Ted hoisted himself up into the plane for the interior check. And it was with that gesture, as it always was, that he began to feel uneasy. Not because he was afraid — he was, like all the rest of them — but because he didn't want to be in command. He was a good pilot, maybe even a very good pilot. But he knew he didn't want the responsibility of all those lives behind him. He'd hoped for reconnaissance work when he'd signed up. He'd wanted to be alone.

Case was in the cockpit, his face already white and doughy. He'd be better once they were airborne, Ted knew. It was the waiting before each sortie that put him on the edge.

A pilot was supposed to love his plane, but Ted didn't really. Not love it, actually. He'd heard the other pilots speak of their planes as if they were the women they named them for — *Miss Barbara, Jeannie Bee, Reluctant Virgin* — caressing them before a mission, kissing them wildly if they made it back. But to Ted, the bomber was a machine that might malfunction and sometimes did — a machine with which it seemed he had barely made a grudging truce in the eleven missions before. He respected the plane, and the men who had to climb inside it, but when the mission was over, he was always glad to leave it behind.

The two pilots were in a five-foot cube. All around them — to the front, sides, behind them on the ceiling, and even on the floor — there were controls, switches, levers. In a B-17, flying was a purely relative concept, he thought, more an engineering operation than a defiance of gravity. In about twenty minutes he would be called upon to perform a complex series of maneuvers in heavy machinery 26,000 feet above the earth, in temperatures of sixty degrees below zero, while German pilots were shooting at him. You weren't supposed to think about it.

Shulman was in the nose; Warren would soon crawl into a fetal position in the ball turret; Ekberg was in the tail. Baker, the new navigator, was quiet with the unfamiliar crew. In the radio compartment, Callahan and Tripp were razzing Rees, who had vomited on the last mission — from fear or from the lousy food on base, the pilot hadn't known. Rees had a large nose, a slipped grin, the grin a defense against the unthinkable.

You puke again, I'm sending you to Ludwigshafen with the load.

Rees leaned toward Tripp, faked a heave.

Fuck off, Rees, Tripp said, pushing the gunner away.

Case, you got any gum?

Case was opening his third stick in as many minutes. He had another one behind his ear. Ted went over the checklist once again, to steady Case's nerves.

Intercooler. Check. Gyros. Check. Fuel shutoff switches. OK. Gear switch. Neutral. Throttle. Check. De-icer and anti-icer, wing and prop. Off. Generators. All set to fire up.

And then he heard it through the radio. The ceiling had lifted just enough over the target. They were going up.

Once, in October, he had really flown a plane. A brigadier general needed to be ferried to another base, and Ted, who had completed his third mission just the day before, was asked to take the job. The plane was a gift from God — a single-engine Tiger Moth that lifted from the runway like a bubble. He wondered who had owned it before the war. A titled playboy with a huge estate? The day was clear, no haze on the horizon, a strafe of thin white cirrus high above them. He made the ferry to Molesworth by the book, the general saying little, Ted even less. But when the man saluted him from the ground, Ted knew he had the plane to himself.

He'd bumped, like a toy, over the Molesworth airfield and hit the smoother surface of the runway. All around him were empty hardstands, waiting for planes that might or might not come back. He saw the Nissen huts, the emergency trucks, the wind sock stuttering toward the east. A mechanic on the wing of an injured B-17 stood to watch him and gave him a wave. Ted opened the throttle. As if sprung, the plane began moving fast. He bounced lightly on the runway, gathering speed. The bouncing stopped. The ride turned silky.

He banked immediately for a turn. Outside his window, the earth pulled away to reveal a stitchery of green and brown and gold, with bits of water glinting in the sun. He saw a tractor plowing, a dog running behind. He could smell the fertilizer on the ground. In another pasture there were sheep, and beyond them, the abstract shapes of hay bales. At the periphery of his vision he was aware of the Nissen huts, the hangar, the wooden control tower — tiny shapes now, of little consequence. Indeed, nothing on the ground seemed to have any consequence at all.

He flew over the village with its pub and church and narrow terraced houses. He followed a dirt lane out to a stone cottage and was rewarded by a reflection of sun from a top window. The sky was a rich navy, the sun glare almost too bright against the nose of the plane. He hit a pocket of turbulence, was buffeted, fell a hundred feet. To the south was a charcoal stain — London, he suspected.

He dove suddenly and went in low over a field of rye to gather speed. He nosed the plane straight up and was pinned against the back of his seat. He climbed into a long, high loop, and for a second, at its apex, he hung motionless, upside down, a speck suspended over the countryside. He fell then into a run out the other side that physically thrilled him. He banked, turned, cruised in an invisible figure eight. They taught you this in flight school, then put you in a thirty-five-ton bomber you were lucky to get off the ground. He was soaring in a barrel roll over the countryside on a day as fine as England had seen in weeks, and he felt, for an instant, free. Free of Case and Shulman and McNulty and the sleepless nights. Free of the pneumonia tubes and the rotten food. Free of the fear of death. Free of the war itself. He had told himself, after the hell of his first mission, that he'd never get into a plane again once the war was over. But on that day — drifting in a slow roll out toward the horizon — he felt, for a moment, the exaltation of flying. A faint whiff of exuberance passed like a mist through his chest, close to his heart.

When the plane stalled, it fluttered and fell like a fledgling that had not meant to leave the nest. He could feel the lightness of the air beneath him, the way the plane began to list. The right wing dipped, and the dip became a spin. He let it go, losing himself in the spiral. He flirted with the spin. But when he knew he had run out of altitude, he put the plane into a steep dive to pull her out and up.

He was a hundred feet from the fields. He'd be grounded if anyone had observed and reported him. He could see the spires of Cambridge in the distance. He began to climb then, as high as he could push the plane. He wanted to take himself aloft — away from the earth.

Case's cheeks were vibrating with the plane. They waited for the takeoff flares. Over the intercom, the pilot asked for position checks. Ekberg, in the tail, sounded drunk. How had he not noticed that before? They would be the second plane behind *Old Gold,* the lead ship painted garishly to identify it in the air — a gaudy duck with its dull flock behind. Twenty planes, and they were number two.

Ted looked at his mission flimsy, passed it over to Case. On it were the code words and the details of the mission. It was made of rice paper; if they went down, Ted was supposed to eat it. He saw the flares then, gave the thumbs-up sign to the chief on the ground to pull the chocks, closed the window. He taxied out of the hardstand and got into line on the perimeter track. He could not see over the nose and had to use the edge of the taxiway for a guide. Already the noise inside the plane was deafening. He thought sometimes he minded the noise the most, and that if there was a Hell, it would sound like the interior of a B-17. He ran up the engines to test them. They were loaded to the limit, with five thousand pounds of bombs and twenty-six hundred gallons of fuel; it was always a guess as to whether they'd make it off the ground. He thought of Shulman in the nose, watching the rush of the ground beneath him.

Old Gold left the runway; Ted gunned the engines. The noise, which before had seemed unbearable, now became monstrous. He knew that behind and below him the men were praying: Get this sucker off the ground. That's right, he thought, get the bomber off the ground, and then do it, if you're lucky, thirteen more times. The runway ended, and they were up into the soup.

The RAFs called it the milky goldfish bowl. Ted climbed in a

spiral over the beacon, looking out for a shadow in the mist —
another groping B-17 that might stray too near. At 10,000 feet, he
gave the order for oxygen and put on his own mask. Twenty seconds without oxygen could be fatal. Squeeze the pumps, he reminded them; don't freeze your spit. He added, as he always did,
to keep the glove liners on, no matter what. The gunners sometimes stripped them off in the heat of battle in order to better
manage the machinery, but at high altitude, fingers would freeze
on gunmetal and have to be ripped off. It would be so cold the
navigator wouldn't be able to make a note with a pencil; lead froze
at 20,000 feet. Icy air blasted through the openings in the waist
where the gunners stood. Most of the men were plugged in, their
electrical suits keeping their bodies functioning. But Ted, after
he'd burned his leg on his eighth mission because of a frayed wire,
had decided to stay with the sheepskin. They all wore their Mae
Wests, but few of them could perform their jobs with their parachutes on their backs. They kept them nearby, hanging on hooks.
When they hit the flak, he'd give the order for the flak jackets.
Rees would stand on his as he almost always did. On a mission
with another crew, Rees had seen a Luftwaffe Junker rake the
bomber's belly. The left waist gunner was shot from below. The
blast had made a hole two and a half feet wide, and the dead man,
to Rees's horror, had simply fallen out the bottom of the plane.

The engines were straining in the climb. At 14,000 feet they
broke into the clear.

From the Channel to the rally point, he rotated with Case
every fifteen minutes, a tactic he had learned to prevent Case from
seizing up on him. Fly the plane close to the others in the formation, but not too close. Scan the sky for the fighters you knew
would soon be out there.

Over the intercom, he could hear the chatter. Idle chatter
20,000 feet over the Channel. You were still alive if you could talk
to your buddies, joke around. The words played along the surface
of the tension, skittering here and there from the nose to the tail.

Those cold-storage eggs weren't any better than that pow-
dered shit. You'd think they'd give the condemned a decent break-

fast. Even prisoners get treated better. Shut up with that condemned shit, McNulty. You'll jinx the plane. Listen, Callahan, it's
simple. You accept you're dead already, what's the problem? Enjoy
the ride. Christ, I hope we don't have to bail out. My chute's
fucked up. The wires are out in my boots. My feet are freezing.
You sure? I'm positive. Hey, Warren, give me your boots. No fuckin'
way, Ekberg. We go down, I'm coming back to haunt you. Man, I
love comin' up over those clouds. I couldn't stand to live in this
country. How do they stand it? Day after day after day, nothing
but rain. What's the matter with *I'll Be Home?* Is she throttling
back? No, she's caught in the turbulence. How many of us are up
here? I dunno, twenty-five, thirty? Boy, am I ever going to let loose
tomorrow night. They're bringing the girls all the way from Cambridge for the party. None for you, Shulman, you're married. Nineteen forty-four. Can you believe it? You think the war will end in
'44? Listen, Rees, I just wanna stay alive in '44. Think we can
manage that?

Ted listened to the chatter, scanned the skies. The fighting,
he knew, could sometimes be a thing of such beauty it took your
breath away. The graceful arc of a fighter that had put its armored
back to you, even as it glided down and away, out of sight, out of
range. The flashbulb pops from silver planes that came at you
from the sun. The way a B-17 seemed slowly to fall to earth with
great dignity, as though it had been inadvertently let go by God.
The odd inkblots against the blue, floating curiosities twenty feet
wide and filled with exploding steel. Long white contrails in formation, road maps for German fighters. A plane, severed at the
waist, that made your heart stop. Count the chutes. And breaking
radio silence, shouting wildly at the doomed crew to bail out, bail
out. It was the worst thing you had ever witnessed, and when it
was over there was no place to put it. No part of you that could
absorb it, and so you learned to transform the event even as it was
happening, a sleight of hand, a trick of magic, to turn a kill into
a triumph.

Right waist to pilot. *Harriet W.* is off to the right.

Roger, right waist. Tail gunner, what have we got back there?

Tail to pilot. Our wingman is about three hundred yards back and down off the right wing. Two other 17s about a quarter mile out to your right.

Thanks, tail gunner.

Ball turret to pilot. Contrails.

Roger, ball turret.

Ted thought of Warren in the turret. Five, six, nine hours in as cramped a position as Ted could imagine. A view straight down with nothing but the earth below you. And if the turret jammed, which it sometimes did, the gunner was a prisoner then and had to endure whatever fate dealt him: the plane hit and going down with no chance to bail out; a belly landing in which he would be flattened. The worst position in the crew.

Left waist to pilot. The wing ship has peeled off. Looks like she's aborting.

Roger.

Tail gunner to pilot. We have another formation at three o'clock high.

Thanks. Keep your eye on them.

Over the Channel, he heard Shulman give the order to test fire the guns. There were bursts of fire, and Ted could smell the smoke passing through the flight deck.

Right waist to pilot. We've lost another ship. She's feathering her prop.

Navigator to pilot. Enemy coast.

Roger. Pilot to all crew. Flak jackets.

He remembered they had just rendezvoused with the escorts, and that his back was hurting from the ceaseless vibrating of the plane. He could smell, he thought, the peculiar acrid scent of the radio emanating from the compartment. And then it was Rees who yelled, or maybe it was Ekberg in the tail. No, it had to have been Rees, and they were hit, shockingly soon, the concussion so severe Ted bit his tongue, and his mouth filled with blood.

The intercom and the skies exploded.

Bandits three o'clock high. Jesus Christ. Shit. Where're the goddamn fighters? FW at twelve o'clock level. Bursts of machine-gun fire. We're in the fight field now. Fuck, my gun is jammed. I saw him, he was hit. He was smoking. Holy Christ. The plane was pummeled, buffeted. White bursts of flame. The escort fighters with them now. Beautiful — look at that. An FW made a pass in front of the cockpit, guns blasting. Knock the pilot out, disable the plane, that's the ticket. *Lady-in-Waiting*'s taken a hit, sir. Jesus Christ, they've severed the wing. She's going down. Count the chutes. Stay in formation. The sun was in his eyes. A hit, a blow that could break a spine. But he didn't know from where. Right waist, call in. Tail, call in. Where's the hit? Just above the bomb bay, sir. Four minutes to the Reich. The navigator, Baker, reporting calmly, plotting coordinates, what was he writing with, for God's sake? Ball turret to pilot. A 17 in the low squadron on fire. Left wing on fire and diving away. Fighters! Three o'clock level. Son of a bitch. There was blood splattered on the windshield. Case was screaming. He was hit in the arm. Case was scrunched down below the instrument panel. Behind him, Rees was laughing maniacally. I got one, I got one. That's only a probable, Rees. Shit no, I got him, no probable about it. Case, white-faced, was vomiting. Tripp, get up here with a tourniquet. Case has been hit. Jesus Christ. We're on fire, sir. Tripp tearing bandage cloth with his teeth. Callahan with the fire extinguisher. Shit, the little friends are turning back. Stay in formation. The sun was in his eyes. The squadron was on its own now.

Jerry, from the east, always had the advantage. Ten Me-109s out of the sun. Oh my God, look at that. Jesus, they're hitting the high squadron. We've had it now. Hail Mary, Mother of God . . . They're cutting them down like flies. B-17s — hit, exploding. Falling in front of his eyes. Ted dove suddenly and steeply. Everything loose in the plane hitting metal. The gunners pinned against the bulkheads, lips flattened back over their teeth. No one could speak. Then pulling out, leveling off, climbing again. Jesus Christ, what was that? A near miss with a falling Fortress. Bring her up. Rejoin the formation. The Me's going for the low squadron now. My gun is jammed. He couldn't identify the gunner. Left waist, call in. The German fighters pulling away. Dull whoosh of flak. He could smell the cordite. They must be near the target. Flak jackets and helmets. They didn't have to be told a second time. Panic, pounding, the shrapnel like a shower of marbles on the metal skin. Screaming in the intercom. Two of the guns had frozen.

Old Gold was dropping back.

What?

There was Baker to talk to, and Shulman in the nose. Is she hit? I don't think so. You see a fire? Nothing I can see. Losing altitude? Maybe a little. Break radio silence? I can't. Why wasn't *Old Gold* calling him? Why wasn't *Old Gold* telling him to take over the lead? The radio shot out? Possibly. His orders were to follow the lead. He had to do it, throttle back, break formation. Would the others follow? This was suicide. He broke silence then. Had to. *Old Gold,* this is *Woman's Home Companion.* Do you read me? Silence. Come in *Old Gold.* Are you hit? Silence. He was angry now, yelling. *Old Gold,* son of a bitch, what's going on? Silence. The radio was out. The lead plane was losing altitude now, but why?

Old Gold banked slightly, and they saw it.

Her fuel was pouring out, a splash of pale ink across the sky. The plane was dropping faster now. They saw the chutes. One, two, three. They waited. Four . . . five . . . They waited. Only five. The plane, a thousand feet below them, dipped its wing and lurched onto its back.

For a moment, there was silence over the intercom.

Navigator to pilot. Sir, we're sitting ducks. You've got to get us out of here.

Case was bent over at the waist. We can make it to the Channel, Brice. We can ditch. For Christ's sake, don't go down here.

Bombardier to pilot. We've got to rejoin the formation.

Ted throttled up, pushed his plane as hard as he dared. The navigator plotting coordinates, trying to calculate how long they had to rejoin. Ted fixing the mixture; they'd lost precious fuel of their own in the fuckup. Scanning the skies till his eyes burned. They were all doing it. Without the formation, they were as vulnerable as a baby. Someone over the intercom was crying. He couldn't make out who. Case still bent over, his head below the instrument panel, retching again on the floor.

Ted looked up. The sky was ablaze — theatrical and wondrous. He thought he had never seen so many fighters. They were silver, sparkling in the sun. He had in his mind the image of hunting dogs with a fox.

Ripping it to shreds.

There was screaming on the intercom. Right waist to pilot. The tail's been hit, sir. A crack, a new vibration in the controls — severe on the rudder pedals. The control cables were damaged. Losing altitude. Put the nose down to avoid a stall. Pilot to rear gunner. Check in. Silence. Rear, check in. Silence. Left waist, check on Ekberg. Callahan moving toward the tail. Left waist to pilot. We've been hit bad. Pieces are flying off the tail. And Ekberg? I dunno, sir. Not a scratch on him. I can't see any blood. Concussion? I think so, sir. OK, pull him into the waist. Get back to your gun. Another hit and another. Everything falling. Everything pummeling. The instrument casings shattered. A direct hit on number-four engine. Feather the propeller so it won't bash and tear the engine cowling. Then a terrible scream. It's Warren, sir, in the ball turret. The screaming filled the intercom.

Jockey around. Evasive acton. Bandits everywhere. So close he could see the bladders of their oxygen masks pumping in and out fast, like his own. Another engine hit. Let's get the hell out of here. Baker was yelling now. He didn't know where they were. Pieces of the fin peeling off in the slipstream. Ted dove for cloud cover, banked, turned west. They were losing altitude and fuel. Number two's on fire. Case screamed again, We can ditch in the Channel. Head for the Channel, you son of a bitch. No we can't. We have wounded. It would kill the wounded. Screw the wounded, Brice. That's only two. There's eight others of us here who will get picked up. Get Warren out of the turret. Can't see the fighters, sir. Couldn't see the ground either. The cloud was a gray protective blanket — but lethal in its way. Bombardier, drop your bomb load, but do it over a field. The bombs were armed, sir, at the IP. Get rid of them now, bombardier. This is an emergency. He waited for Shulman to push the toggle switch to Salvo. Left waist to pilot. Just seen a piece of the stabilizer come away. Ted was fighting to control the rudder, losing altitude fast, trying to keep the plane level. He heard a whoosh — the bomb bay opened. The plane was close enough to the ground that they could feel the concussion. In the breaks, it looked like farmland, but the clouds were thick, the sky gray. Who could tell? Two thousand feet. Could he make it to the Channel? One's duty was to the living. But how could he take two men to certain death? Pilot to all crew. Throw everything out you can. We're going in on our belly. He saw a village in the distance. Pilot to navigator. Where are we? Don't know, sir. Fifteen hundred feet. Beyond the village a plateau, maybe a field. A thousand feet and falling. Pilot to crew. Assume positions for crash landing. Eight hundred feet. Pilot to left waist. Is Warren out of the turret? Yes, sir, but he's hit real bad. Beside the pilot, Case was crying. You can make it to the Channel. Five hundred feet. He was over the village, dipping, rising slightly, the engines straining. Get as far west as he could. Please God, let us make it to the pasture. He could see the field now. Maybe it was enough to land. A belly landing would slow them down. If it didn't, they'd hit the trees. Baker, still reporting. Two hundred feet. They were losing fuel. Sir, do you read me? Sir, do you read me?

He heard the screaming in his ears. Vibrations threatened to disintegrate the plane, snap a wing. He fought to keep the bomber level. He saw the steeple of the church, a pasture. Cows stumbled in the unspeakable roar; a horse reared. The wing dipped, and he righted it just as they came in. He felt the sharp hit, the first bounce, the second, the skid on the belly. There was frost on the grass.

And finally there was silence.

———•———

Inside his jacket, the boy began to shake. It was not the fear or the cold; it was instead, this time, the brambles, the gray sky, the fallen plane. It was as though he had never been, until this moment, in the war itself. It was one thing to imagine finding an American flyer in the wood, quite another to be staring at a soldier's feet. The man must be dead, Jean decided. He sank to his knees, crawled around to the other side of the brambles. He stared at the tangle in the gray light, afraid to find what he was searching for.

Jean saw the face — scratched, with blood on it, lying on one cheek, eyes shut. The face was pink still; the American did not look like the dead man beside the plane.

"Hullo," Jean tried, his only English, his voice cracking.

The pilot opened his eyes. Even in the dim light, Jean could see their color — a translucent green, the green of the sea glass that his mother kept in a box on her bureau. He had never seen such eyes on anyone before — the only color in the dun forest.

Jean whispered urgently in Walloon, "I am Belgian. You have fallen on Belgian soil."

The American looked intently at the boy.

Jean, shaking violently inside his jacket, tried again. He spoke, but this time he accompanied his words with gestures. Pointing to himself and to the soil, then again, then once more, repeating the word *Belgique* over and over. Insisting.

The American was motionless, except for his eyes scanning Jean's face.

The boy removed the cheese and bread and the bottle of water from his pockets. He mimed taking a drink. Jean could not reach the American through the brambles, however. He had somehow to get the man out. But how? Did he dare touch the injured leg?

As if in answer, the American began a slow slide backwards, on his belly, until he had released himself from the tangle of thorns. Jean moved on his knees to meet him at the other side of the bushes. He watched as the American rolled over and lay flat on his back, staring at the treetops. The effort seemed to have exhausted him.

Jean opened the bottle of water, cradled the American's head at an angle so the man could drink. The leather at the back of the American's head was cold to the touch. Jean's hand was shaking so badly he was afraid he would spill the water down the soldier's chin and neck. The American propped himself up on his elbows then, took a long swallow. He said an English word the boy could not understand.

The American pulled himself to a nearby tree, managed with his wrists to make it to a sitting position. Careful not to touch anything that might be injured, Jean gingerly held out the bread. The American — pilot? gunner? navigator? Jean couldn't tell — took the bread in cupped hands, angled it with his wrists and bit into it. The loaf, however, was tough, and the American had no strength in his wrists, no grip, to pull it free. Jean reached in and steadied the bread for the American, feeding him. He saw that the fingers of the man's hands were stiff, unbending, the skin an unnatural and waxy white.

The American chewed, swallowed, spoke again. Jean could tell by the inflection that the words formed a question, but he could do nothing but shake his head.

"Can you speak French?" the boy asked very slowly. This time the American shook his head.

The boy asked again, though the likelihood was improbable, "Do you speak Dutch?"

The American seemed not to understand.

Fearful that the tentative link between them might now be severed, with no words left to share, Jean pointed to his own chest. "Jean," he said.

The American nodded. He pointed to himself. "Ted."

Jean wished he were smarter. As he fed the American the bread and cheese and water, he tried to figure out how to convey his plan — a plan that had to be executed quickly, or the Germans would find the American. The frustration of being unable to speak made him want to cry. Wildly he pointed to himself, to the northern edge of the forest, and then made an arrow with his fingers that returned to the brambles.

The American studied the boy. He said something in English, shook his head, indicating he did not entirely understand.

Jean tried again.

"Germans," he said, pointing to the trail the soldier had made, leading to the pasture and the plane. But the American stared blankly at him.

"Ted," Jean said urgently, pointing to inside the brambles.

The American nodded.

"Jean," Jean said. He again pointed to the north, then back. He repeated the gesture. In exasperation, the boy said in French, "Hide yourself. I will return for you." And the American seemed to catch in the sentence a word that sounded familiar.

"Return?" the aviator asked slowly.

Jean, too, heard the word in his own language. He nodded vigorously and smiled, nearly exultant.

The flyer began to smile too, then suddenly blanched with pain. Jean looked at the leg, at the flight suit, which in his attention to the man's face and eyes he had missed. One leg of the flight suit was covered with blood, dried brown blood. Jean felt lightheaded, dizzy.

"Quickly," he urged the American, pointing to the brambles. "Quickly."

The tone of the boy's voice, rather than the word itself, seemed to reach the American. Carefully, he lowered himself, used his forearms to pull his body into the hiding place.

Jean studied the hidden American. The Germans would find him, just as Jean had, he was sure. Unless he could outwit them.

He scooped up handfuls of pine needles and bark and dried leaves and buried the American's protruding feet in mulch. But that wouldn't be enough.

The extra minutes his idea would take were critical, Jean knew, yet it had to be done.

The boy retraced the matted trail, running until he was fifty meters from the pasture. He could hear voices, though he could not make out the words or even their nationality. He began to destroy, backwards toward the bramble bush, and as best he could, the existing trail. But when this proved impossible — the matted grasses would not rise up; the broken branches could not be mended — he devised another plan and was momentarily excited by his own cleverness. He made other paths, diversionary spokes, leading out from the central hub. In a kind of madness, he dragged himself on his back, bending branches and twigs, scuffling leaves with his feet. He tried to calculate the odds that the Germans would enter the forest at the correct point and then would choose the precise spoke to the American.

He surveyed his work.

Whatever else happened, he told himself, he had at least done this.

Turning north, he bent his head to protect it, put out his arms, and scrambled at a near run through the forest. It was December, and darkness came early.

———•——

The bicycle shuddering, the tire nearly flat. Shit, why hadn't he paid attention to the tires earlier? People in doorways, hanging out of windows. A plane in the village, fallen from the sky like an omen. Head down, keep the head down, blend into the stone, look inconspicuous. Antoine should slow down; people would notice they were racing. Antoine in the kitchen with Claire. Antoine stank of pigs. He was ugly with his pink face, his small eyes, and that greasy, thin, white-blond hair.

Claire in the kitchen. Did she know he had been drinking in the barn before he'd gone into town? Her breasts in her rose sweater, the way she stood with her arms folded under them. If she died before he did, he would remember her that way. And the way she was able to make a meal out of nothing. It was a trick, a gift she had. Like her silence, the quiet of her. She was from his mother's side of the family. Sometimes too quiet. Though he'd rather have that than what Antoine had got himself — a shrew with a high-pitched voice. That terrible whine. You could hear it all the way to Rance. How did the man stand it? Maybe it was why Antoine had been so quick to go with the Maquis. Get away from the old woman.

The brakes squealing from lack of oil. A dull ache up the back of his neck from the beer. Heavy, flat beer; maybe it was going bad, that's why he had the headache. How many bowls had he drunk? He wished he hadn't, but who knew a plane was going to fall out of the sky?

The drink took the edge off the cold, made the hours move. The drinking was illegal, the beer contraband, all, that is, except for the weak beer that tasted like cat piss that they let you have in the cafés. All the real alcohol was supposed to go to the German front. But Henri, like Antoine and Jauquet, made his own beer and then kept it hidden in the barn.

Every morning the same routine: the bread, the awful coffee, the fricassee that no longer had any bacon. Then the frigid air of the barn, where he pretended he had work to do. When the war was over, if it ever ended, the farm would be exposed for what it was — a ruin. Nearly sixty head of dairy cattle gone, the Germans would get the rest before the winter was out. His father's legacy — his father's father's legacy — slaughtered. He'd keep the house, get a job in the village, maybe Rance or Florennes. But what was there to do? What could he do except make repairs to nonexistent machinery?

But nothing would ever be the same again, so what was the point of worrying? Who knew what would be left when the Germans were through with them? He'd known nothing would be the same since the day Antoine had come with the news Belgium had fallen, and then had asked him to join the Maquis. You couldn't say no. If you were asked, you had to join. He didn't like to think too long about what might have happened to him if Antoine hadn't asked. Ride the war out is what he'd have done. And there would have been some shame in that. If he had any motivation, and it wasn't much, it was that when this goddamn war was over he wanted to have done the right thing. Not the same as wanting to do the right thing. Not like Antoine. Not like Claire. With her nursing and her languages.

The truth was, say it, he was scared, scared shitless every day they had a Jew or an aviator in the house, scared just to be in Antoine's presence. He'd heard the life expectancy of a Resistance fighter was three months. Then how had he and Antoine made it so long? And didn't that mean their time was up? You knew you would be caught one day, shot. It was the only way you could get out.

When Antoine had asked, Henri had known he couldn't say no.

Léon now. Léon had courage. Léon had nothing left to lose. His son dead in the single week of fighting when the Germans had trampled over Belgium. Léon, angry, still grieving, but too sick for heavy work. He waited at the Germans' tables at L'Hôtel de Ville and listened to the talk, sometimes brought Antoine messages. Léon with his steel glasses and his workers' cap. It was a wonder the Germans hadn't killed him already. He looked like a Bolshevik.

Henri didn't want to find an American flyer. He didn't want to have to hide an American flyer in his attic. If the Germans caught him at this game, he would be shot, and the American would be given a beer.

Shit, it was cold. The cobblestones made his teeth hurt. The sky the color of dust. Days like this, the cold seeped in, stayed through the night. You couldn't get rid of it no matter what you did. A young girl in a doorway. Did she wave at him? Was that Beauloye's daughter? The girl in dark lipstick. How old was she, anyway? Fifteen?

Antoine parked his bicycle behind the church. Henri did the same. Antoine knew how to look around and see everything without moving his head. They would go in separately, Antoine first, then a minute later, himself. Smoke a cigarette, lean against the wrought iron railing, stub it out, sigh, curse maybe, as if you were thinking of having to go home to a woman like Antoine's wife. The heavy wooden door squeaked open. The gloom was blinding.

Shivering already. Fear or cold? He didn't know. He swore the stone was wet. High stone, a small candle flickering in the distance. He touched the water in the font, crossed himself, genuflected. He moved toward the altar, genuflected again, slipped in next to Antoine, Léon just beyond them.

Base Ball. The words said precisely in English behind him. Emilie Boccart. It was the cigarettes, that voice. He didn't turn, but he wanted to. She was what, forty, forty-five, and still he wanted a look at her. Long, low-slung breasts; her nipples would be erect in the cold. Her coat was open, he had seen her from the back coming up the aisle. If he turned, he could look at the outline of her breasts through the cloth of her blouse. She was Jauquet's lover. Jauquet, who had a wife and five children.

It's a game. An American game, she said. Léon coughed.

Then Léon whispering to Antoine, so that Henri could hear

too. And any minute the words could change to a prayer. Emilie would be watching, begin to pray in an audible voice. Hail Mary, Mother of God . . . A simple signal.

Lehouk found two of the Americans already. One has a wound to the arm. The other's in shock, no memory of anything, not even his name. They've already been taken to Vercheval.

And the wounded man from the plane? Antoine speaking.

With Dinant. She's keeping him. He's too badly hurt.

Antoine angry now. She was told . . .

Léon raising a hand. There's no persuading her, Chimay. I tried.

The other?

With Bastien.

Where's Jauquet?

St. Laurent.

Telling the Germans, Henri thought, shifting his weight.

Again the hoarse voice behind him.

He's afraid he'll never play *Base Ball.*

Who's afraid?

The man with the broken arm. He says he's a *Base Ball* player.

We don't have much daylight, Antoine said. We've got to cover the woods.

I'll go. A thin voice from behind and the left. Dussart. The boy with the missing ear. An accident in the quarry. Pale and thin and blond, the hair grown long to cover the bad ear. He volunteered for everything. A wild streak in him that bore some watching. If it hadn't been for the war, Henri thought, the boy would have fled Belgium, gone to Marseilles, Amsterdam.

Dussart. Then Henri. Then Dolane, another dairy farmer. Van der Elst, the butcher. Van der Elst hid Jews above the shop. Once he had been raided, but his wife, Elise, had sent the refugees over the roof to Monsieur Gosset.

Any other planes? Antoine again.

No, just the one. The pilot was trying for the Heights.

Antoine considered. Antoine could kneel only on the left knee, the right injured in an accident with explosives. A tiny candle in a red glass. Jesus hanging from the cross, the blood in exaggerated drops on the Saviour's side. As a kid, it made him ill. The smell was mildew, he was sure of it. Even in the summer, the place was damp.

Emilie, tell Duceour and Hainaert. Léon, go back to the hotel.

I can't.

Why not?

I sent Chimène this morning to say I was sick.

Tell them you're better.

Léon coughing and rising. His breath making small puffs on the frigid air.

Antoine turning now to Henri. Can you take another? He meant in addition to the old woman from Antwerp. Henri nodded. The old woman was going to die anyway. Maybe even today. A scuffle of shoes behind him. Emilie, Dussart, Dolane leaving. He heard the sharp report of high heels on the stone floor; he loved that sound. It was worth the Mass on Sundays.

The candle still flickering. Who had lit it? Emilie for herself? For them all? For the children she never had? For her sins with Jauquet? Would he and Claire have children? Four years and nothing. He didn't understand it. Was there something wrong with his seed? With Claire somewhere deep inside her? There'd been nothing like that with anyone on his side of the family; his mother had reassured him. They waited in the pew. He couldn't pray. If he prayed, it would be *not* to find an American flyer. To go home and have his noon meal instead. To go to bed.

But probably he should pray, he thought. Pray to be relieved of his fear. To want to do the work he was given. To have courage like Antoine did, and not hate this war so much. He blew on his hands to warm them. Antoine farted quietly. Antoine was a pig. And a hero in the Maquis. He had blown up a bridge. Killed two German soldiers with his hands.

Henri waited his turn, the last to go but for Antoine. He wished now he could eat. He would probably not get food until late tonight. Antoine said a word. Henri rose, slipped along the pew. His own boots caused echoes in the sanctuary. Outside, the light, though muted by thick cloud cover, hurt his eyes. He looked all around the square. The members of the Delahaut Maquis had already disappeared into the gray stone.

Sometimes, when his father slaughtered his animals, when his father sold to the Germans not just the grain, but also the meat, Jean saw, in the barn, the odd bits left on the filthy table, odd bits crawling with maggots. A sight as sickening as anything he had ever witnessed, and now, with the barrow, with the dark seemingly sinking through the tall beeches like fog or cloud, that was the image Jean had of the forest. His forest, crawling with maggots, the Germans with their high black boots and revolvers, searching for the Americans.

The route Jean decided to take was an old hunter's route, and he doubted the Germans knew of it, though they could stumble across his path and demand to know what he was doing in the wood with a barrow. And if they went to his father, to query him about his son and the forest, his father would tell them of the hunter's path — not visible from the perimeter, but not so overgrown it couldn't be used to gain access to the interior of the forest without losing one's way. Even so, Jean didn't think anyone knew the wood as well as he — not even his father. It had been, for years, his playground; now it was his home, a place to which he could escape the unhappiness and shame in the farmhouse where his parents lived.

Steering the barrow was sometimes more difficult than he had anticipated, and occasionally Jean left the trail when two straight oaks refused to let him pass. He was not at all sure he would be able to make his way back with the American, but several months ago, in the summer, he had carried a large sow from Hainaert's farm to his own. Could the American possibly weigh more than the sow? he wondered. The man had seemed lean inside the sheepskin, tall but not heavy. Jean remembered clearly the American's face — the eyes still, not afraid, nearly smiling when he and Jean had hit upon the word they shared — and changing just the once, going white from the pain. He didn't want to think about that pain, or the cold of the forest floor, or the odds that when he arrived at the bramble bush the American would still be alive. He didn't know which he feared more — to find the American dead, or to find him gone, taken by the Germans.

He heard a voice, the crack of footsteps on dead wood. He stopped, dared not even set the barrow down. In that position he tried to quiet his breathing, to control the panting from his heavy exertions and his fear. He thought he heard the footsteps move closer, though the voices were still only mumbles, and he could not make them out. The fast settling of night, which before he was cursing, now seemed a gift. In these moments between daylight and evening, the wood, he knew, became an illusory and mystifying landscape, its geography shifting even as you observed it, a tree in the near distance vanishing, then returning, shadows taken for bushes, bats flying faster than the eye could catch them. In his old gray coat, a worn and oft-patched coat he used to hate to wear to school, he might not be seen in this light, even from only ten meters. He waited until he was certain the footsteps had moved away. He knew that soon the Germans would return with torches.

He scrambled more quickly now, aware that the temperature was dropping fast. When he arrived at the place where he had left the American, he settled the barrow on the ground and knelt beside the bush. He felt more than saw the flyer's feet, his hand reaching below the mulch cover to find the heel of a boot. When he touched the boot, the man shifted his foot slightly, and Jean let out his first sigh of relief.

"Jean," he said quickly, not wanting the American to be alarmed.

At first the man did not move, but then, after a time, Jean saw in the dim light the slow slide from the brambles. The American pulled himself free, tried to make it to a sitting position. Jean reached for his shoulder, held him upright with his weight. Jean pointed immediately to the barrow. The boy had worried about the logistics of this part of his scheme. If the American himself was not able to climb into the barrow, the entire plan would collapse. Alone, Jean couldn't lift a grown man.

Slowly the American turned, dragged himself over to the barrow. On his stomach, with his forearms, he pulled his weight up and over the lip of the bed of the barrow — a fish flopped upon a deck. Jean tried to help by hooking his hands under the man's armpits and pulling. The bouncing of the leg must have been excruciating — the American bit hard on his lower lip. When the flyer had made it as far as his hips, he rolled over. He used his elbows to pull himself back an inch or two and stopped. Jean hopped out of the barrow and with all his strength lifted the long handles. There was the possibility, he knew, that the wooden poles would break free of the barrow, but miraculously the barrow lifted. With the tilt, the American slid, tried to sit up against the barrow's back. Jean, bending his head and shoulders as far to the side as he could, mimed for the American to lie down. Stray branches in the dark could tear across the American's face.

In the dark, the boy trusted to all the years that he had played there, all the times he had come along this path. Once he ran into the thick trunk of a tree, and the American, unable to stop himself, cried out in pain. Apart from that collision, and several agonizing moments when the barrow became wedged between two trees, the trip was easier than Jean had hoped for. At the edge of the forest, Jean set the barrow down. His arms trembled from the strain. He couldn't cross the open field with the American, even in the darkness, until he was certain no one was in the barn.

He didn't stop to explain to the American what he was doing. The flyer would not move or speak, Jean was certain, and would know by now that Jean intended to hide him. Running silently across the frozen field, Jean reached the barn, lifted the heavy beam that fastened the door. He winced at the squeal of the hinges, waited for the sound of footsteps. When there were none, he looked inside the barn, satisfied himself that no one was in there.

Where before in the wood the barrow seemed to make no sound of its own, the thuds across the rutted field were thunderous in the boy's ears. The journey of a hundred meters seemed to take an hour. He set the barrow down outside the barn door. Again he endured the squealing of the hinges, wheeled the American inside.

There was a soft movement and the lowing of cows — not a

sound, Jean knew, that would alert anyone in the house. He wheeled the American to a long trough that held mash for pigs in summer, potatoes in winter, and was empty now. Truly frightened by the audacity of his plan, and by the proximity of his own house, not twenty meters away, Jean moved quickly. He reached for the American's arm, tugged him slightly toward him. He took the arm, ran the large hand along the edge of the trough so that the American could feel the shape and perhaps understand the plan. The flyer seemed to, inched himself forward, rolled, hooked his good leg over the side of the trough. Holding the man as best he could, Jean helped guide him out of the barrow and into the trough. When the American finally fell inside it, the thud seemed to Jean the loudest sound he had ever heard.

Earlier in the day, Jean had emptied the trough of potatoes. He knew he would again have to fill the trough with potatoes to cover the American. He reached for the flyer's hand again, made him touch a potato, but he didn't know if the man had any feeling in his hands. He placed a potato near the American's face, on the off chance the man might be able to smell it. But there was no more time for explanations.

Carefully, Jean placed potatoes in the trough, positioning them as gently as he could around the pilot's face and legs. The man made no sound, no protest. Knowing the gaps between the potatoes would allow the man to breath, and hoping to provide some protection from the cold, the boy filled the trough to its top, hid the sack with the remaining potatoes underneath a pile of hay. He moved toward the door, anxious to be gone from the barn, but hesitated at its threshhold.

Making his way back to the trough, he bent low over the spot where the pilot's head was. Jean's lips brushed the skin of a potato.

Return, he said in English.

His father hit him such a blow he spun, knocked a chair on its back. His world, a shrinking world inside the kitchen, went momentarily black, then spotty with bright lights. His upper lip was split over his teeth, and when he put his hand to his mouth, his fingers came away with blood. He didn't dare to move or speak.

He couldn't be exactly sure what the blow was for, and he knew it was always best to wait, to keep silent. Nothing enraged his father more than a protest or a challenge.

"Monsieur Dauvin's been here. Says you weren't at school. Not from noon on," his father yelled from the sink. Artaud Benoît picked up his lit cigarette from the table, took a quick drag, held it between his thumb and forefinger. How had his father known he would come through the door at that precise moment? Jean wondered. He'd have been waiting, and in the waiting he would have become drunk. Even from across the room, Jean could smell the beer. There were unwashed bottles under the table.

"You weren't at that plane, I'm hoping. No son of mine."

No son of mine, Jean thought. He put a hand on the tabletop to steady himself. His legs felt weak. He desperately did not want to fall. The oilcloth on the table was worn, threadbare in places from his mother's scrubbing. A single bulb hung from the ceiling, illuminating the room, casting harsh shadows on the wallpaper, the stove, the marble mantel with the crucifix and the bottle of holy water. The boy's dinner, which his mother had put out for him, lay congealed on a plate on the table. The thought of his mother, who would have gone up to the bedroom, made his chest tight.

"And your mother, lying to the teacher for your sake, telling him you'd come home sick. Weeping afterwards, not knowing where you'd got to."

Jean stood as still as he could, despising his father for the show of false sympathy for his mother. He kept his breathing deliberate and measured. He dropped his eyes to the stone floor, a floor his mother swept and washed every day.

"I hope to Christ the Germans didn't catch you at that plane. I got problems enough without having to explain for my son. Next you know, they'll be thinking you're a Partisan. And you know what they do to Partisans."

It was not a question. His father took a deep pull on his cigarette. It was poorly rolled, and bits of tobacco fell onto the floor. "Don't you stand there like a stone, or I'll give you another one of these."

Jean did not look up, but he knew a fist had been made.

"I know you were in the wood. I can see by the sight of you. You see any of the Americans?"

Jean shook his head.

"Don't lie to me, or you'll be no son of mine. That's what you were looking for, isn't it? You think this is a game? It's a game that'll get your neck broken, that's what. You see an American, you tell me. You understand?"

Jean nodded. The blood from his lip was in his mouth. He didn't dare to spit. He swallowed it.

His father picked up the plate that contained Jean's meal, threw it at the stove. The crockery broke against the cast iron. The boy flinched. It was a casual, unnecessary gesture on his father's part, meant to frighten the son, hurt the mother when she saw the broken plate in the morning, if she had not already heard the noise from her bedroom above. Jean knew that if his father hit him again, he'd go down. He had no strength left in his legs. He wasn't even sure he could make it up the stairs.

"I'm not through with you yet, but I'm sick of looking at you."

His father made a dismissive gesture with his arm. Gratefully, Jean left the room, not even stopping to remove his coat.

On his bed, in the small room under the eave, Jean lay fully dressed, holding a sock to his lip to stanch the blood. He had not washed because he'd have had to do so at the sink in the barn, and he could not go back into the barn. Jean had imagined he'd be reported missing from the school, but he had not thought Monsieur Dauvin himself would come to the house. He wanted to go into his mother's room, to tell her he was all right, but he wasn't all right, and she would see and be alarmed — and besides there was again the risk of encountering his father.

He lay on his bed and thought about the flyer. He tried to imagine what it must be like to lie in that cramped trough with the potatoes. He thought about the dark, the smell and feel of the potatoes, the low sounds of the cows. But the more he thought about the flyer, the more worried he became. What if the American froze to death in the trough, died before the morning? And if the man didn't freeze to death, what was Jean to do with him then?

The boy had not planned beyond getting the flyer into the barn, and perhaps during the night smuggling some food and water to the man. But as Jean lay there, the enormity of what he had done began to close in around him.

Something would have to be done before daylight. There could be no stopping now. What had it all been for, if not to save the flyer? But if he waited until morning, his father would find the American and turn him over to the Germans. Was his father right? Had he, Jean, merely been playing a game? Living out an adventure that this time might end in catastrophe?

He wanted to cry. He began to think about the flyer's leg. It needed attention, a doctor or a nurse. What if it became infected and had to be amputated — all because Jean had brought the man to the barn and could not think of a way to get him out? What if the American died of the infection? Could a grown man die so quickly from a wound? And surely there was the loss of blood, too, and shock. In the darkness he saw the American's face. The man who had called himself Ted, who had no use of his hands, who had nearly smiled at their small triumph of communicating a single word.

The boy had said he would return. He had promised that. He had to get the flyer out of the barn before daybreak.

He held the sock to his lip, fighting off sleep. He stared into the absolute darkness of his tiny room. He made his eyes stay open, and he thought. After a time, he listened to the heavy tread on the stairs of his father's footsteps, heard the door to his parents' bedroom open and close.

And when he had thought a long time, he sat up on the edge of the bed, threw the sock to the floor, and pulled his coat around him.

———•———

She was asleep or near sleep, listening still for the familiar sounds of Henri entering the kitchen downstairs. The scuffle of his boots. Water at the pump. A glass set on the table. She had waited up as long as she felt able, but then the chilly air had driven her to bed. Underneath the thick comforter, in her nightgown, she drifted between sleep and waking, wondering what had happened to Henri. She was not especially alarmed; it was not the first time he had been gone the entire night on a mission. But still she wished he had sent word to her somehow. She was concerned for the old woman who lay just beyond her wall, breathing irregularly now, refusing to eat, even to sip broth. Claire had wanted to bring the old woman downstairs, to lay her by the fire, but alone she couldn't manage her on the stairs. Instead Claire had piled blanket upon blanket on the frail body. But it seemed to Claire that she was merely burying the old woman, making it impossible for her to move.

She didn't have much hope for the old woman. Even if Claire could help her regain her strength, the Maquis would want the woman moved through the lines, the space cleared for the next refugee or aviator. Claire didn't even have the luxury of allowing Madame Rosenthal a room in her house. If she suggested it, Henri would tell her what she already knew. Madame Rosenthal was a Jew. A Belgian could not keep a Jew in a house. The punishment would be death for Madame Rosenthal and themselves.

But she was worried for Madame Rosenthal. Even under the best of circumstances, she guessed it would be difficult to make it across the French border, even more difficult to get to Spain. She thought of one story that had filtered back to her. In April, forty men, among them two English aviators who had been sheltered in Delahaut, had made it within twenty-five kilometers of the Spanish border. Ebullient after their harrowing journey, one of the Englishmen, while bathing in a stream, had begun a song in English. A neighbor, an old woman, heard the English words over the wall of her back garden. Tipped off by this collaborator, the Gestapo arrested the two English pilots, as well as the other escapees. Just a morning's walk from freedom, all thirty-two men were machine-gunned over a ditch, into which the bodies fell and were left uncovered as a lesson to the townspeople.

Claire sat up. She thought she heard a knock at the door. A short rap, then silence. A short rap, then silence. Instantly, her skin grew hot. She pushed the comforter off, and, forgetting her robe, ran downstairs in her bare feet to the kitchen. The stone floor was a shock to her body, the cold painful on her soles. She held her arms around her, stood behind the door. The rhythmic rapping continued. What time was it? Three, four in the morning? Had something happened to Henri, and someone had come to tell?

"Who is it?" she called from behind the door.

"It's Jean Benoît," she heard in a quiet voice.

She heard the name, but it refused to register. Jean was a boy, only ten years old. She asked the question again: "Who is there?"

"Madame Daussois," came the urgent voice. "Please, open the door. It's Jean Benoît."

Claire opened the door. The boy was shivering on the doorstep. The icy air blew into the kitchen, and she beckoned to the boy to come inside. She shut the door. In the dark of the room, she could just make out his features. She drew on an old coat of Henri's that hung on a peg beside the door, and lit a candle on the mantel. The sight of the boy made her put her hand to her mouth.

His face was swollen on the side, a dark bruise beginning. His lip was split, and there was dried blood on his chin and cheeks. His coat was filthy, with bits of twigs and bark stuck to it.

"I need Monsieur Daussois," the boy said in a barely audible voice. He cleared his throat.

She studied the boy warily. Everyone knew the boy's father was *collabos*.

"Who did that to you?" she asked.

The boy looked at her, did not answer.

"Was it the Germans?"

The boy shook his head.

"Was it your father?" she asked.

The boy seemed to hesitate, as if making a decision. Then he nodded once quickly. "I must speak with Monsieur Daussois," he said. "It's urgent."

The panic in the boy's voice sounded authentic, but even so Claire knew she must be cautious.

The members of the Maquis were always at risk. Sometimes the treachery was obvious; sometimes it was subtle. The Germans fed their own airmen into the system, men who spoke perfect English and landed on Belgian soil with American or English parachutes. They'd be sheltered, put through the networks, only, at the end, to expose all those who had helped them escape. The men and women who were captured would be tortured to reveal other names. Claire knew of men who'd been blinded or burned with electric prods. And then these men — and women — would be shot, or suffocated, and buried without winding sheets in shallow graves, where animals soon picked their bones. But this method of exposure, she knew, didn't always please the Germans. Sometimes they wanted the individual Allied airmen more than they wanted the networks. The Gestapo began then to infiltrate the networks with one collaborator along the way, one link in the chain, who could deliver, selectively, the most valuable of the allied officers, so as not to cast too much suspicion upon themselves, and thus keep the networks open. After all, who could say for sure at which link an airman had been exposed? Always it was a tenet of the Resistance that each cell know only of the one directly before it.

"Why do you need him?" she asked, eyeing the boy closely.

He gave a long sigh. She could see that the boy was frightened. Frightened and hurt. His lip and the side of his face needed medical attention.

"I have the American," the boy said simply.

At first she did not understand. How could a boy have an American? And then, meeting the child's shy gaze, she understood.

"Where is he?" she asked.

"I have hidden him in my father's barn. He's injured in his leg. I need Monsieur Daussois to help me get him out before my father goes into the barn in the morning."

"Where did you find him?"

"In the wood."

"And no one else knows?"

The boy shook his head.

She stared at the boy. Could she trust him? She wondered immediately how it was that the boy knew to come to her house and not another. This fact alone was alarming — were she and

Henri known already to the Germans? Or was this a ploy, a way to identify a member of the Maquis? Yet she had believed the boy when he'd said it was his father who had hit him, split his lip.

In a small village such as Delahaut, she had learned, it was not possible always to conceal either resistance to or collaboration with the Germans. Certain collaborators were easily known — the Black Belgians, for example, men who wore black shirts and held positions of power within the occupational force, even occasionally replacing a Burghermaster. Then there were the women who went with German soldiers, accepted presents and money for their favors. In Delahaut, there were several, and they were regarded as worse than whores. Claire had seen these women spat upon in the village streets by men and women, and she didn't want to think about what might happen to these women after the war.

But the members of the Resistance, unlike some of the collaborators, had to be extremely careful about inadvertently revealing their identity to anyone. Claire knew Henri and Antoine had taken a risk in removing items from the fallen plane while schoolchildren were able to observe them. But schoolchildren, she knew, more often than not, saw the Maquis as heroic, longed to grow up to fight within its ranks. No, the danger was seldom children; it was instead the men and women who might come to your house, share a cup of ersatz coffee with you by the stove, even express their hatred for the Nazis in your presence, all the while listening for a sound in your home that might be different from all the others.

Suddenly, she understood how the boy had identified her.

The Resistance operated cautiously, trusting as few people as possible, but there were some villagers sympathetic to the Maquis one had to depend upon. Omloop, for example. In Belgium, everyone was rationed. The daily ration per person was 225 grams of bread, three lumps of sugar, two small sausages, and half a kilo of potatoes. But those in the escape lines — the Jews, the Allied airmen, the Belgian boys fleeing the German work camps, the Maquis themselves — had no ration stamps. Obtaining food and feeding this small army was full-time work in itself. The Resistance therefore had to rely on sympathetic shopkeepers who would pad rations from the black market. When Claire went to Madame Omloop's, the shopkeeper, without saying a word, always gave Claire larger portions than her ration book allowed.

"You've seen me at Omloop's," Claire said to Jean.

The boy looked down at his feet. When he looked up, she saw the confusion on his face.

"Monsieur Daussois is not here," she said slowly. "He's out." She left it at that. She looked toward the ceiling, thought of the old woman. "I can go with you," she added. "Perhaps together we can move the man."

Relief softened the boy's face. Claire put on her clogs, fastened her coat, and tied a kerchief under her chin. There was the old truck behind the barn, and the gazogene. Henri had said to use it only in an emergency. Could she get the gazogene to work? Could she and the boy crank the old Ford into life? She could see no other way. She hoped that the old woman would not call out to her while she was gone.

Jean, beside her, told her to turn off the lights and cut the engine while they were still on the lane and out of sight of his father's farmhouse. Quietly they opened their respective doors, got out of the cab. There would be snow in the morning, she was certain. She could smell it on the air.

The boy led, and she followed behind. She did not allow herself to think of the consequences of being caught at this. Occasionally, she had been asked to another house, to a terraced house in the village or to another farm, to nurse an injured airman or to translate. But on those trips, she had gone by bicycle, as almost everyone in the village traveled, so there had been minimal risk. A woman and a boy in a truck in the middle of the night after a plane had crashed in the village would be impossible to explain. Had the truck been spotted on the road from the Daussois farm to the Benoît farm? What time was it exactly, and how long did they have until daybreak? She cursed herself for not looking at the grandfather clock in the kitchen.

She sucked in her breath at the uneven squeal of the barn door opening. Beneath Henri's coat, she shivered in her nightgown. She could see nothing in the darkness of the barn, dared not move forward lest she stumble and fall. The boy touched her gently, and, holding her by the wrist, led her to the interior. She could smell and hear animals, but couldn't see them.

The boy tugged downward on her wrist and spoke to her. She knelt, put out her hands. She was kneeling on something soft, a mixture of hay and dried manure, she thought. Her hands touched the rough wood of a trough, the humpy shapes of potatoes.

She listened to the boy working quickly beside her. Once she heard him say, in a low voice, *Jean*. She was aware of the dull thud of the potatoes falling to the soft ground all around the boy. And then the boy stopped.

He reached for her again, this time for her hand. She let him draw her fingers over the trough and along the surface of the potatoes.

She felt the warmth of human skin, a man's face. And the boy beside her said a name.

December 31, 1943, to January 7, 1944

THE COURTYARD BEHIND THE SCHOOL WAS A BLUR OF movement as boys in ill-fitting jackets and old wool pullovers played hoop and boules and pitch-the-pebble in the few remaining minutes of the dinner hour. Few of the girls had ventured into the cold; most of them had remained behind in the classroom with Madame Lepin, who was teaching them to knit socks for the imprisoned Belgian soldiers in Germany. Jean stood at the top of the steps and surveyed the scene. Marcel, who had been waiting for him to emerge from the school, spotted him first and called to him. At the mention of Jean's name, the other boys halted in their play, watched as he descended the stone stairs. An officially designated punishment, no matter what the offense, never failed to produce curiosity in the boys. Jean walked toward his friend.

"Jean," Marcel whispered frantically. "What happened? What did Monsieur Dauvin do to you?"

Jean held out his hands, where the evidence was obvious. With an effort of will he made his hands remain still. The knuckles were swollen. On the middle fingers the skin had split, and there were slits of blood.

"The stick?"

Jean nodded.

"Better than the caning."

Jean nodded again.

Marcel shook his head. "I didn't tell them," he said, again

65

whispering. "I know you said to tell them you were sick, but Monsieur Dauvin was so angry, I didn't dare speak."

"That's just as well," said Jean. "Then you, too, would have gotten the stick."

"What happened to you, anyway?" Marcel asked. "Where were you all afternoon? Did you find any of the Americans?"

Jean looked beyond his friend to the place where a group of boys were playing boules. They played with a hand-whittled and sanded ball that wasn't perfectly spherical and wobbled in the dirt just beyond the courtyard. No one had asked him why his mouth was swollen or his lip was split when he arrived at school that morning. It wasn't the first time he had come to school in such a state; they knew his father often beat him.

"Jean, what happened to you? What did you find?"

Jean slowly turned his gaze back to his friend. Marcel badly needed a haircut. Tufts of hair grew over his ears. Like his own, the boy's trousers were too short. "Nothing happened," he said to Marcel. "I went back into the woods, but I couldn't find anything. When I got home, Monsieur Dauvin had been to see my father, and so he hit me."

"Oh," Marcel said. He looked disappointed.

Jean tried to put his hands into the pockets of his trousers, but his knuckles wouldn't easily bend. He knew that his fingers wouldn't work properly until tomorrow at the earliest. This was not the first time he had been rapped.

It was, however, the first time he had lied to his friend. But the lie had come immediately, before he had had time even to think about what he might say. Instinctively he'd known somehow that what had happened in the night was not to be shared with anyone. Not just for his own safety, but for Madame Daussois's as well. He could not forget the sight of her standing in her nightgown in her kitchen, nor the strength of her later in the night. She was beautiful. He was sure he had never seen a woman so beautiful, not even Marie-Louise, who was regarded as the village beauty, the village flirt. Marie-Louise stained her legs with walnut and painted a seam up the back in order to fool everyone into thinking she wore silk stockings. Jean was sure that Madame Daussois would never do such a thing. He would suffer a dozen canings for her if he had to.

In the darkness, he and Madame Daussois had together emptied the trough of potatoes, helped the airman to his feet. The American was dazed and weak — barely able to stand. Madame Daussois spoke constantly to the man, whispering English words, so that she might calm him, help him to understand that she and the boy were friends. Jean replaced the potatoes in the trough. When he stood, he could not clearly see the flyer's face, but he could feel the weight of the man, feel the leather and then the fleece of the large open collar of his flight suit. The aviator weighed even more in his heavy flight suit than he would have without it, but Jean knew that it was only the flight suit that had allowed him to survive. He had heard the stories of the flyers who had bailed out of their planes with electric suits, and who had frozen on the fields and in the woods before they could be rescued.

Madame Daussois in her nightgown and her husband's heavy coat, and Jean in his old jacket and hat, had wheeled the airman from the barn to the truck. Together they had lifted and pushed and heaved the man onto the truck bed, as if they were taking a dead animal to market. It was impossible to be silent in this effort, and with each grunt from himself or muffled cry of pain from the injured man, Madame Daussois, and then Jean, had looked instinctively for movement at the farmhouse. When they had the flyer finally in the truck, Jean had walked to the cab. He was about to hoist himself into the passenger seat for the ride back to Madame Daussois's house. It had not occurred to him that he would not go. How else was Madame Daussois to get the airman into her house if not with his help? But Madame Daussois had caught up to him, put a hand on his shoulder. He argued then, whispering as fiercely as he dared, trying to persuade her of his usefulness, but Madame Daussois would not be moved. She didn't look hard, not like Marcel's mother, for example, but she was. Of that he had no doubt now. Not like his own mother, who did not look tough and wasn't. He cringed when he thought about his mother, about the way she was afraid of her own husband.

Madame Daussois had insisted he return quickly to his bedroom. She said that if he was captured, he would not be able to withstand the torture, and in the event, would put them all at risk. For a moment, Jean had hesitated, thinking to defy her, unwilling to relinquish the airman. After all, if it hadn't been for Jean, the aviator would not have been found, might even have died in the night. In fact, Jean thought, he almost certainly would have died, or would have been found by the Germans. He remembered that his nose and eyes were running in the cold as he struggled with his own desires and fears. Finally, he shrugged and pulled away from Madame Daussois, saying not a word. He felt bad about that now. He had walked away from her in a sulk, when he had every reason to be grateful to her for having come to his aid when he had asked her. He wished now that he could go to her farmhouse and tell her that he was sorry for his behavior. He badly wanted to know how the flyer was, if he was still with her, if he had been transferred elsewhere. He had seen the alarm on Madame Daussois's face when she realized that Jean had guessed she was with the Resistance. He wanted to reassure her that her secret was safe with him, that no matter what happened he would tell no one of last night.

He had stood off to one side in the shadows, watching as she turned the truck around in the dark. He remembered the trip from her house to his, when her body had shaken so violently she was barely able to manage the gears or the clutch. The back road they had taken was badly rutted, the ruts frozen into ridges and heaves, and he knew the truck bed, thrusting and shaking over the uneven surface, had to have been an agony for the American. Driving away from Jean last night, Madame Daussois had turned on the lights only when she was a good hundred meters from the place where they had parked. They shocked Jean, their sudden brightness, illuminating each tree, casting harsh shadows that moved, and he felt anxious, as though a search beam had fallen suddenly upon her. He bit the inside of his cheek. He waited until he could no longer hear the motor of the truck before he started up the long dirt drive to his own house.

"Benoît."

Jean turned at the voice. Pierre Albert, a year older than Jean, stood close to him, tossing a wooden ball from one hand to the other. His eyes were narrowed. Pierre's cousin, Jan, had been a saboteur with the Maquis in Charleroi and had been shot by the Belgian SS when caught in the basement of his flat with explosives. Pierre never tired of telling the story, as though the heroism of his cousin conferred upon Pierre an honor he himself had earned.

"You got the stick."

Jean said nothing. Marcel looked anxious. Pierre was a bully, and Jean knew that Marcel was afraid of him.

"For what?"

"You know for what," Jean said, now painfully forcing his rigid fingers into the pockets of his trousers.

"So why weren't you at school?"

"I was sick."

Pierre sucked his teeth. He closed one eye.

"My father says he knows where the Americans are."

Jean said nothing. He doubted that Pierre's father knew where any of the Americans were. Or if he did, that he'd have told his son.

"I saw the plane myself," Pierre boasted.

Again, Jean was silent. He did not remember seeing Pierre in the pasture. Telling Pierre Albert he was a liar, however, would only make things worse.

Marcel shifted his feet, looked as though he would like to join the other boys at pitch-the-pebble. "Come on, Jean," he said.

Pierre turned and sneered. "Where are *you* going?"

Marcel stopped his retreating movement. Pierre looked back at Jean.

"So you were sick," Pierre said.

Jean stood still, didn't answer him.

"You know where I think you were?" Pierre asked, tossing the ball so that, as it descended, it barely skimmed Jean's face. Jean refused to move.

"I think you were sneaking off to St. Laurent to tell the Germans, that's where I think you were."

Jean opened his mouth to protest — this he would not allow! But before he could speak, the bell rang loudly in the courtyard, momentarily surprising him. He heard Marcel's sigh of relief.

Pierre thrust the wooden ball inches in front of Jean's face. Jean heard the hated words as the older boy turned his back and ran. *Fils du collabo.*

———◆———

Claire knelt beside the airman. She took her scarf from her head, opened her coat. In the candlelight she could see the man's face for the first time. He looked oddly peaceful, as though he were merely sleeping. He was twenty-one or -two, she guessed. The light made shadows of the bones of his face, the shape of his mouth. There were cuts on his forehead and cheeks, and his mouth was badly swollen. Briefly, she ran the back of her fingers along the side of his cheek. As she sometimes had for the others, she wondered who might be dreaming of this man even then, which mother, which woman loved him, prayed for him, received his letters, counted the days until he might come home. If he did not regain consciousness — and she felt no certainty that he would — she would never know. She unzipped the flight suit to the middle of his chest, felt with her fingers for the chain. She held his identification disc in her hand, the metal slightly warm from his skin. She dropped the tags to the stone floor. She wanted to scream. The magnitude of the carnage was stupefying. She thought of the boys barely men who died unthinkable deaths far from home; of the men and women of her own country tortured to death simply because of the accident of their birth. No matter how long she thought about it, how deeply it had entered her life, how long it lay in her house, she did not understand how this thing had swept over them, how their lives had been forever altered. And if there ever came a time when she might understand what had happened to the Belgians, to the people of her own village, she would never be able to fathom why young men came from so far away to defend a country about which they knew nothing. Some of the soldiers she had tended had not known before the war that Belgium even existed. They could not accurately locate her country on a map. Belgium meant nothing to them — nothing real, nothing substantial — and yet they continued to come. And continued to die.

Henri returned from parking the truck behind the barn, bringing with him the sharp chill of the frigid night. Claire looked up at her husband from the stone floor on which she was kneeling. Henri's face was drawn, gray, exhausted. There was grime in the creases of his skin. He'd been stunned when, just minutes earlier, he'd bicycled into the gravel drive and found his wife in the truck bed with an injured airman. She knew that he was afraid of this work, that he was afraid of the presence of the foreign airman in his home. And yet he had never turned a soldier or a Jew away. He had never refused a request from the Maquis.

"I'm going for Madame Dinant," he said from the doorway.

Claire nodded. She wanted to tell him to go upstairs to bed, but she knew that was impossible. The airman couldn't be left alone, and Henri would be able to bicycle to Dinant's much more quickly than she could.

"Tell her to bring plaster and morphine," she said. "And tell her . . ." Claire looked toward the ceiling of the kitchen. "Tell her that the old woman is dying."

When Henri left, the room was still. She could hear the clock tick and looked up at it; it read one-fifteen. She removed the pilot's leather helmet and put a pillow under his head. His hair was the color of sand, and matted flat. She examined the rest of the flight suit. One trouser leg, the right one, was soaked in blood near the foot.

Claire stood and removed a pair of long shears from her sewing drawer. She bent over the American flyer. Her hair, unrolled, fell like sheets at the sides of her face, hampering her vision. She made an impatient gesture, swinging her long hair to one side, and, tilting her head just slightly to keep it there, she began to cut the man's trousers, starting at the ankle.

The shears were dull against the leather. Bits of sheepskin, dirty with blood, came away in tufts, and began to make a pile surrounding the man's leg. When she reached the wound, she felt a sudden nausea and had to swallow hard. The skin of his calf down to the back of the ankle had burst open like an angry blossom. As delicately as she could, she picked off dried pieces of fleece from the open wound. She heard a sharp intake of air, looked quickly at the airman's face. The skin had gone gray. He was awake now and was watching her.

"I am sorry if I am hurting you," she said in English.

He shut his eyes briefly, and exhaled slowly, trying to control the pain. The wound was exposed now to the air.

"You are safe now. You are in Belgium," she said softly. She whispered the word again, and then again. *Belgium. Belgium.*

She studied him. The color was not returning to his face. Claire noticed a day's growth of beard. He shook his head slowly. She didn't know if he meant to say they were not safe, or if he did not believe he was in Belgium. His eyes closed again, and he lay back against the pillow.

Thérèse Dinant had not slept since the previous night, but, unlike Henri, she showed no signs of fatigue. She walked noisily into the house, as if all rooms in Belgium were open to her.

"We treat the aviator first," Dinant announced, as though there had never been any question. Claire knew the aviator would be a priority: Save the airmen at all costs. But it was also triage. Tend to those who had the best chance of life.

"What is the man's name?" Dinant asked.

"Lieutenant Theodore Aidan Brice," Claire answered.

"The pilot, then," Dinant said absently.

In the warmth of the farmhouse kitchen, Dinant stripped off her coat, but she kept on her kerchief. Her face was reddened and dry, with fine hairs on her cheeks. She wore a long, black cardigan and gray knit stockings that accentuated her sturdy legs. On her feet she wore a man's clogs. Dinant worked without preliminaries and with dispatch. She had been with the Croix-Rouge and subsequently with the Maquis since its inception in 1940, and lived alone in a small terraced house in the village. She was as large and as strong as a man — larger even than Henri. She was perhaps only thirty, Claire thought, but she was of a type that had looked middle-aged for years.

Dinant injected the airman with morphine, then cut away the rest of the flight suit. She wanted the pilot naked, she explained, in order to make sure there were no other wounds. A bullet wound in the back, under a shoulder blade, might go unnoticed in an unconscious patient. Claire and Henri did as they were told, together undressing the airman, rolling him over for Dinant's inspection. Claire was sweating in the heavy wool coat, but could not remove it altogether. Antoine, Dinant had told them, was coming soon to collect the schoolbags, and there had been no time to put a dress over her nightgown.

Dinant told Claire and Henri to keep the man on his stomach and pin his wrists down, avoiding the hands if possible, but if it became necessary, to sit on the pilot's hands. In a rudimentary English she told the pilot that what she was about to do would hurt, but she would be quick.

The pilot, drifting in and out of consciousness, raised his head and shoulders when Dinant began to treat the wound. Henri held the pilot's shoulders; Claire put her hand to the airman's mouth, and he bit the soft pad at the inside of the thumb. When that moment was over, a moment even the morphine couldn't touch, the pilot's forehead fell down onto the blanket. His skin was a terrible color.

Claire helped Dinant to roll the plasters around the man's calf. The bandage stretched from the sole of the foot to the knee. Only his toes, white and waxy, were exposed.

Her hands covered with blood, Claire became aware of another presence in the room. Antoine Chimay had entered the Daussois kitchen without a sound. Such stealth, even grace, in a large, rotund man was always a surprise, and came, she knew, in Chimay's case, from his years with the Maquis. He wore a dirty woolen coat and knitted gloves from which the ends of the fingers had been removed. Without taking off these gloves, he pulled a crumpled cigarette from his pocket, lit it in the corner. The smell of the tobacco produced in Claire a sharp and intense longing.

"Will he live?" Chimay asked Dinant.

It was a dispassionate question. Claire heard the note of weariness in Antoine's voice. The downed pilot was, for Chimay, merely a package, valuable to be sure, but nevertheless a parcel to be sent to England as soon as possible so that he might return to combat.

Antoine was there, Claire knew, not only to collect the schoolbags, but also to interrogate the airman. He might already have obtained information from the other airmen who had been found, but he would want especially to talk to this officer. When Chimay had as much intelligence as he could gather, he would send a message, in code, back to England, via a radio he kept in a suitcase under the hay in his barn. That message, in turn, would be forwarded to the crew's base. Until the survivors had safely returned to England, however, the aviators would be listed officially as missing in action.

Dinant shrugged, flipped her hand back and forth as if to indicate a fifty-fifty chance of survival.

"The wound is deep. There's tendon damage. He's lost a great deal of blood," she said. "And there may be some infection. How he fares will depend upon how well he can fight that off."

Chimay took a long pull on his cigarette, rubbed his forehead with his free hand. "When will he be able to talk?" he asked.

Dinant looked at the pilot's face, and shrugged. "Difficult to say. He will need the morphine for a day or two, and perhaps after that — "

"We can't wait that long," Chimay interrupted. "I'll return in the morning and try again." He looked pointedly at Claire. "Where are the schoolbags?"

"In the barn, under the feed."

Antoine turned and threw his cigarette into the sink. He leaned both of his hands on the lip of the porcelain. In the candlelight Claire could see only the man's broad back, his hunched shoulders. "The Germans have got two of them," he said with disgust. Claire wondered if Antoine thought himself to blame, that somehow the Resistance had not acted quickly enough.

She did not like to think about what happened to the Allied airmen when the Germans had captured them. She knew they were sent to Breendonk in Brussels, or to similar Belgian prisons in Antwerp and Charleroi. Some were tortured by the Belgian as well as the German SS. Those who survived considered themselves lucky to be deported further east into Germany, to the Stalag Lufts there. Claire had heard about the English pilots at the beginning of the war who had had their eyes put out and had been buried without coffins in the cemeteries near Breendonk. There were members of the Resistance whose ghastly task it was to locate the graves of these unlucky airmen, dig them up, and give them a proper burial. All over Belgium there were graves of unknown soldiers.

Chimay left as silently as he had come. Dinant stood and walked to the sink. She washed the blood from her hands. "You can finish this," she said to Claire. "He needs water and to be bathed. No food until midday. Any sign of infection, send Henri to me at once." She dried her hands on a towel. "The old woman is upstairs?"

Claire nodded. Dinant left the room with her bag, and Henri for the first time that night sat down. Claire suspected that her husband had had nothing to eat since noon.

"I saw the wounded American," Henri said. "The one we found near the plane." His face was ghostly with the memory. He put his head into his hands. "Dinant had him on the table in the kitchen when I went to fetch her. I've never seen . . ."

"Henri, go to bed," Claire said quickly. "You have to sleep. I can manage here, and tomorrow Antoine may come again and need you. Do you want any food?"

Henry shook his head vehemently. "I couldn't eat," he said.

"Then do as I say." Claire had seldom spoken to her husband in such a sharp tone, but she knew that if she didn't he would not move. That he had seen something terrible she did not doubt. Only sleep might put the images at a bearable remove.

Henri rose slowly from his chair. "I'll just sleep on the sofa in the sitting room," he said. "If you need me . . ."

When Henri had gone, Claire rose and washed her hands at the sink. She filled a large kettle with water, set it on the stove. The man on the floor groaned. When the water was boiling, she added it to cooler water she had already poured into a basin. She unwrapped a small bit of soap, real soap, not the black soap made from ashes. She brought it to her nose and inhaled its fragrance. She set the basin on the stone floor.

By the fire, Claire hesitated, then rolled the airman over. He did not seem to waken, but some color had returned to his skin. She cradled his head and washed his face and neck, his chest and the hollows beneath his shoulders. She wet a sponge with warm water and let it run over him, soaking into the towels she had put at his sides. He was more muscular than she had imagined, but his pelvic bones were sharp in the firelight. Gently, she rubbed away the dried blood that had matted the sworls of dark hair on his good leg. She filled and refilled the basin with clean, warm water.

Theodore Aidan Brice. She said the name aloud. A man was in her kitchen, on her floor, and she knew nothing about him except that he had flown a plane and landed in her village. The man might die in her kitchen, and she would know nothing more about him. On the floor beside him were his possessions — a photograph of a woman, his identification tags, his escape kit, a crumpled pack of cigarettes. The flight suit itself, or what was left of it, would be burned or buried. She wondered if he was married to the woman in the photograph — a pretty, dark-haired woman who looked very young. But then she thought not, because he had no wedding ring. One English airman who had thought he was dying had given his wedding ring to Claire to send back to his wife when the war was over. Claire had refused to take it, assuring the airman he would live. She learned, later, that he had died soon after leaving her home. She wondered where this pilot was from — America was so vast. She wondered, too, what he would sound like; she had not yet heard him speak.

The morphine, as always, was miraculous. She had never ceased to be moved by its power, by the way it could transform a face, remove years, give beauty to the wounded. Pain twisted a man's features, made him ugly; but the morphine erased the pain. The American's face in repose was open — not severe, not pinched. She had seen his eyes only briefly — when he was conscious and had looked at her. They were startling, a remarkable sea green with flecks of gold. His mouth was broad, even when asleep, and she had a sudden vision then of what he might look like someday, after his lips had healed. She glanced at the place on her hand where he had bitten her. There were still faint teeth marks on her skin.

"Too late."

Claire looked up from her crouch on the floor. Dinant stood in the doorway. "She's dead," she said. There was little emotion in her voice. Claire imagined that Dinant, who had seen the worst of it, who had tended the boys who had been tortured, had come to see each death as merely another failure.

"I will tell Bastien," Dinant said. "He will come and will know what to do. And when he comes, he will help you and Henri carry the American into the hiding place. Every minute the pilot is exposed here, you are at risk."

In the Daussois kitchen, Claire thought, Dinant was a field officer, clear-headed, her orders precise. The war was being fought in kitchens and attics all over Belgium.

The pilot slept for hours. In the afternoon, Claire climbed the stairs with a cup of thin broth made with marrow bones. There was just enough room in the hiding place for her to sit, her legs folded under her. For some time, she watched the American, watched his eyes move beneath his veined lids, watched his body quiver and twitch, as if in his dreams he were still flying. She watched also the snow that dusted, then accumulated upon, the small rectangle in the ceiling. As the snow thickened, the light in the crawl space diminished, so that it seemed milky in the small room, the pilot's features less distinct. She thought of the old woman, of how she had lain there and died, of what thoughts and dreams she must have taken with her. Hers was a death that must be laid at the Gestapo's feet, Claire thought, as surely as if they had shot her in that chimney.

From time to time that first day, Claire said the pilot's name aloud, to waken him, to summon him to eat. *Theodore.* And when he finally opened his eyes, the broth was nearly cold.

His hands were swollen and stiff and incapable of holding the bowl without spilling it. He was able to lift his head only slightly. She fed him with a spoon. It was an imperfect arrangement, and sometimes the broth spilled over his lower lip and onto his chin.

She used the cloth in which she had wrapped the hot bowl to wipe his face. His thirst was keen. He asked for water when he was finished, but when she returned with the water, his head again lay against the pillow, and his eyes were closed. She waited beside him.

Perhaps she dozed. A shadow moved across the opening to the crawl space.

"I might have been a German," he said harshly. Antoine was standing in her bedroom. He meant the open armoire, the attic room clearly seen. He meant she should be careful not to stay too long inside the attic. She crawled back into her bedroom.

"He's sleeping," she said.

"We'll have to waken him," Antoine said. Claire thought of protesting, but knew that Antoine would ignore her.

She was not certain that Antoine, with his pink bulk, would be able to squeeze into the small opening at the back of the armoire; nor was she sure he would find room to sit beside the pilot once he'd managed to get inside. But as Claire waited just outside, she heard two voices — the crude English of Antoine, who often impatiently called to Claire for a translation, and the barely audible murmur of the American, who tried to answer each question. She heard the words *flak, control cables, Ludwigshafen.* Antoine told the pilot that a man named Warren had died from his wounds, which did not seem to be news to the American, and that men named McNulty and Shulman had been captured by the Gestapo, which was. The rest of the crew, said Antoine, were hidden by Resistance workers in the area. One man's arm had been shattered.

Antoine, satisfied with the interview, wedged himself back through the armoire. When he stumbled to his feet, his face was scarlet with the effort. Claire stood as well. With his bulk and height, Antoine seemed enormous in the small bedroom, his head bent under the slanted ceiling.

"We must move all the Americans through the lines as quickly as possible," Antoine said.

"I'm not sure he — "

"It's too risky here for any of them. The Germans know the pilots are hidden."

Claire looked away.

"We'll prepare a passport. We'll need a new photograph taken."

Claire nodded. The photographs the airmen brought with them were almost always useless, though the airmen never seemed to know this. When the air crews had their evasion photos taken at base, each man borrowed a white shirt and tie for the picture, which was supposed to make a pilot look like a civilian. The difficulty was, however, that since all of the men used the same tie, the Germans could not only identify the bearer of the photograph as English or American, but could tell which bomb group the man belonged to.

Antoine's breath, hovering over hers, stank of old garlic. For a moment Claire had the unlikely idea that he might move her toward the bed. Where was Henri? She was trying to think. She had known Antoine for years, since primary school, but she could no longer predict with any certainty how anyone she knew might behave. It was odd, she thought, how perfectly ordinary people, people who might not have amounted to much, people one hadn't even noticed or liked, had been transformed by the war. It was as though the years since 1940, in all their misery, had drawn forth character — water from the earth where none had seemed to be before. Before the war, she had not known of Antoine's stamina or his intelligence, yet because he had changed so during the war, she could not predict how he might act in other matters as well. She thought also, that had it not been for the war, she might never have discovered that Henri, for all his steadiness, was, in crises, physically afraid.

The American slept long into the afternoon and evening. His face seemed to possess, in his sleep, a curious detachment. Rarely had she seen such detachment on the faces of the other men and women who passed through her house. Too often, the particular horrors each had seen and witnessed, and sometimes been a part of, were reflected in their eyes, etched into the creases of their skin. Even on the faces of the young women and the boys.

The American slept so deeply that day she could not rouse him again, not even to give him the water he had asked for. She thought that perhaps he was hoarding his strength, hibernating through the worst of his ordeal. She had an image of him sleeping all the winter, like an animal, rising finally when the warmth came in late March or April.

But that night, as she lay sleeping in her bed, with Henri snoring beside her, she woke to a terrible sound behind the wall that frightened her. It was the frantic scrabbling of a man buried alive, trying to unseal his casket. She opened the back of the armoire, crawled into the darkness, felt the pilot's hands fly past her body, caught them. His skin was shockingly hot to the touch, and when she stripped off the comforters, she discovered with her own hands that his shirt and the bedding were soaked. His body shook violently next to hers, and he spoke English words and phrases she strained to follow, to understand, but couldn't.

She lit a candle, held it near his face. His eyes were open, but as incoherent and as meaningless as his speech. She called to Henri, told him to bring towels soaked in cold water or in the snow. When Henri, in his long underwear, brought them to the attic room, and Claire laid them on the American's skin — on his chest, around his head and face — the pilot tried to fight her, to peel them off, and Claire was astonished by the man's strength. Henri reached in to hold the American down. Claire spoke to the pilot constantly, in a low voice, repeating her words, a kind of incantation. Henri brought new towels when the pilot's skin had turned the cool cloths warm. The American begged for morphine. Claire put a towel between his teeth, which he bit like an epileptic until she had found the syringe and delivered the salve to his veins.

Claire fed the American cool sips of water, while Henri dressed and went for Dinant. The pilot was quieter now, but not yet sensible. Claire listened to him tell of shooting squirrels in the woods, of airplanes with threads attached falling from the ceiling. Once he seemed lucid and asked her name.

Once again, Dinant came with her medicines and her bag. Without greeting, the woman crawled into the attic and began to cut the bandages open, exposing the source of infection. The wound, a grotesque open sore, had festered. Dinant poured alcohol into the wound and cleaned it. The pilot moaned and lost consciousness. Dinant gave the American a tetanus shot, then fashioned a different sort of bandage, a partial closure held together with bits of cloth tied at strategic places. For days, it seemed, Claire sat with the pilot, who hovered between sanity and madness. The infection refused to heal, but did not travel. Dinant wanted the leg off altogether in case gangrene set in, but Claire, who knew a man with only one leg would not make it through the lines, held the woman off — just another day, she said; just another hour — a defensive line that seemed easy to breach, but proved, in the event, to be impregnable.

A hundred faces hovered over him, and in the crowd he searched for his brother. His brother was thirteen or fourteen and was wearing a red plaid flannel shirt. It was important to find Matt among the faces; there was something Ted had to tell him. But Matt couldn't be there, could he, because Matt had gone to war as well, and in the war had died in the water. The ship, the telegram said, sank in the Pacific when it was hit by a torpedo. The telegram didn't say if Matt was drowned in the darkness, or if pieces of him fell into the water and drifted slowly down, or if, in the ferocious heat of midday, Matt let go of a bit of wood and dove into the coolness of the dark, beautifully colored water. Water and air. They were dying in all the elements.

So Matt couldn't be in the crowd, and in truth, when he opened his eyes, there was no crowd at all, no one by his side. He seemed to be in a small portion of an attic, with the roof of the house slanting about five feet above his head. In this ceiling there was a rectangle open to the sky, through which he saw differing shades of gray, slow movement from one side to the other. Were there clues in this movement, in the color of the sky? He tried to remember where he was, what had happened to him. There had been people with him, he was certain. He remembered a woman, a large-boned woman with a coarse face, who wore a kerchief tied around her head and who treated his leg after the morphine and wrapped it in wet bandages soaked with plaster. He felt the stab of pain, but soon it passed away, and he was floating. And sometime after that he got the fever and began to shiver, and he begged for the morphine again, begged through the wall until the other woman came and put a cool cloth on his forehead and held his hand.

And with her hand clasped in his, he had drifted.

He propped himself up as best he could and lifted the comforter from his body. He saw that he was wearing a man's shirt that seemed to be too wide and yet too short for him, and a pair of trousers that lay loosely around his waist. Raising the comforter even higher, he noticed that the trousers were too short as well and exposed the skin above his left sock. Along the right leg, the cloth had been cut to the thigh to allow for a bulky bandage. He imagined that if he could stand, the trousers would drop from his waist.

When they cleaned the wound, he remembered, the younger woman had had her hair down in the candlelight, as she bent over him, pinning him down. A man's coat had fallen open, and under it was a nightgown that looked ivory in the flickering light. He remembered the shallow *V* of her clavicle, delineated beneath her skin. Her hair — a thick, silky, dark blond — was like a veil that hid her face, and he remembered, in his pain, his delirium, wanting to ask her to reveal her face, and not being able to form even the English words to his question.

But he had seen her face since. It was she who had been sitting by his side, he was certain. He remembered large gray eyes and a wide brow. Sometimes she seemed to be hovering over him, sometimes to be looking away. At other times she read while she thought he slept. The eyes were sad; her face was distinctly foreign. Something in the cheekbones, the shape of her mouth; the mouth, he thought, formed by the words of her own language, by their vowels, so that in repose, her lower lip thrust slightly forward. She spoke an English precisely her own, throaty with a heavy accent that drenched the words and made him think of bread soaked in wine. Interesting words and unexpected: *anguish, supple, garland.* And then words of her own, names he had never heard before: *Avram, Charleroi, Liège.*

Her scent was of yeasty bread and violets. He smelled her scent on her throat when she leaned over him, a scent like the steam of baking bread. He saw the underside of her chin, the white of her wrists when they pulled away from her blouse. She reached across him, and in doing so, she lifted her face. He imagined her skin would feel like kid, soft but with texture. There was within him the faintest stirring of desire. He allowed himself to linger on the image of her body in her nightgown, though he sensed that this lingering would make him anxious. Her hair was cut just below her shoulders, the dark blond a color that changed with the light in the attic room, although most often when she sat with him, she wore it rolled. He realized with surprise that he had not even been told her name, or if he had, he didn't now remember it.

He thought it was a kind of anesthesia, the body's natural anesthesia, forgetfulness and sleep, but now, in the vacuum, questions were forming. What of the plane, and where were the men? Someone was dead, and someone was dying, though it had been perhaps days, and the gunner would be dead by now, he was certain. Suddenly Ted was hot; a film of sweat was on his face and neck. All around him there were German pilots in their planes. Where were Case, Tripp, McNulty? Had anyone gotten away? Had he been told that some had crossed the border into France, or had he dreamed that? Where did the bombs go, and could he have made it to the Channel? Hesitation and indecision. He had to get word back to base. He was in Belgium. He remembered now the word *Belgique*, the boy's voice frantic and insistent, crowded with tears; and the word in English, the woman's voice, low and soothing, pronouncing the name of her country as if the word itself were sanctuary.

———

She came in from the milking, washed her hands at the pump. She had seen to the herd, washed out yesterday's milk cans, poured the fresh milk into clean ones and left them, as she and Henri always did, at the end of the road for Monsieur Lechat to collect in his wagon. Lechat would take the milk to the shops and to various customers in the village. Sometimes, when Lechat collected the milk cans and left off the empty ones, he would leave a small sum of money in a metal box. It was what she and Henri lived on. Since the coming of the Germans and the decimation of their herd, the box held very little.

Henri had been gone since daybreak. He would not tell her where he was going, so that if she were questioned, she truly would not know. When Henri was gone, Claire saw to the chores. Regardless of the course of the war, the cows had to be milked and fed. More important, the appearance of seeing to the chores had to be maintained at all costs. The surest way to be denounced, Claire knew, was to draw attention to oneself. Any break in routine could rouse suspicion.

In itself, the work on the farm gave her little satisfaction. She was not like Henri in this. As a girl, she had not thought that she would spend her life as a farmer's wife. Before the war, she had imagined herself at university, in Brussels. Though she suppose now that she had always known that marrying Henri was inevitable.

In its own way, the coupling had been foreordained since she was in grade school, the two families well known to each other, tied to each other by several marriages and by blood. She and Henri were cousins, distant enough for the church to overlook the tentative blood relation. As though they had known, even as children, that a connection of some kind would be made between them, they had drawn together at family gatherings and at festivals to test each other out, to feel what might or might not be possible. And sometimes, if they met in the street, he would take her for a coffee in the café, and she felt important, in her schoolgirl's uniform, sitting with this man, who was then already, at twenty-one, twenty-two, a presence in the village.

They married finally when she was nineteen and he was twenty-seven, when the war in Europe was beginning. He had taken over his father's farm, and it was thought that Claire was old enough to marry.

On the marble mantel, beside the crucifix and the candles, was a photograph of Henri and herself on their wedding day. Henri, who was not much taller than Claire, wore a dark suit, and his hair had been brushed off his face with oil. It was summer, and in the photograph Henri looked uncomfortably hot. The suit was wool, the only one he owned. Claire had been married in a brown suit. She had sent to Paris for the pattern and had sewn it herself. Her mother had given her the pearl earrings and made the lace collar. No one made lace anymore, Claire thought, at least no one of her own generation. Her mother was nearly seventy-three now. She'd been fifty when Claire was born, the last of eleven children. In the wedding photograph, Claire had her hair rolled at the sides and in a snood at the back, and the hat she had splurged on to match the suit had a veil that covered her eyes. She was holding a bouquet of ivory roses with a satin ribbon that trailed down the front of her suit. Her lips seemed exaggerated with a thick, dark lipstick — as if she had not yet been kissed.

The stove was putting out a good deal of warmth — a heat that was designed to rise and permeate the stone farmhouse. Even on gray days, she thought, the room had a kind of inherent cheer. Wherever she had been able, she had placed color — the green-checked tablecloth; a hand-colored photograph of the Ardennes in spring; a blue glass vase, now filled with dried flowers, on the table. She prepared the bread and coffee to take to the pilot upstairs. It was past breakfast already, and Claire was trying to wean the pilot, who had been floating in a timeless vacuum, onto a schedule.

She set the tray on the floor of her bedroom. Immediately she became aware of a sound she had not heard before behind the wall. She stood a moment and listened. She thought it was the sound of whistling. She could not identify the tune, but it was distinctly a song, not merely another set of meaningless sounds.

She crawled through the false back of the armoire. As soon as she had done so, the American turned his head to meet her eyes, stopped whistling.

"What is your name?" he asked.

Claire knelt motionless, unable, for a moment, to answer him. Though she had been waiting for this, the clarity of his question shocked her. She thought then that all the time she had sat with this man, she had not really believed that he would re-cover. She had imagined instead that he would linger for months or possibly years in a suspended state.

"My name is Claire," she said.

He nodded slowly. "Yes, I remember now."

"And you are Theodore Aidan."

He laughed. "No, just Ted." He looked at the coffee and the bread on the tray as if observing food for the first time.

"Is that coffee?" he asked.

"It's not real."

She made her way to her usual spot beside the pilot's bedding. She wound her legs under her as she always did, but this morning the gesture seemed awkward, and her legs felt too long and un-gainly. Before, she had sat with him with her hair down, in her robe if necessary, giving little thought, no thought, to how she was dressed or how she looked. The pilot, in his transcendent state, had seemed disembodied, not a man actually, but rather a casualty, a patient in the most objective sense, a thing to watch over, a task that defined her days. But now that he had returned to his body, could speak, could ask her questions, he seemed another entity altogether.

For the first time since she had begun tending him, she be-came acutely aware of how crowded the attic room was, of how difficult it was to sit without somehow touching his bedding — with her knee, with her foot. She drew herself together more tightly. She had dressed hastily after waking and had rolled her hair ineptly, thinking it unlikely that today she would see anyone from the village. She had on a gray wool skirt that stopped at her knees, and rode above them when she sat. She was wearing a white long-sleeved blouse with padded shoulders, and over that her apron. She had white socks on her feet and shoes with leather uppers and wooden soles, ugly shoes, work shoes. Her legs were bare. She had forgotten her lipstick. Loose strands of hair hung at the sides of her face. Impatiently, she pushed them away.

"It's ersatz coffee," she explained. "We are not having real coffee since before the war."

She handed him the bowl. She watched as he took it, focused on the task of holding the bowl with both hands, brought it to his lips. He took a small sip.

"It's awful," he said, smiling at his success.

She gave him the dark bread from the tray. He experimented with his fingers, distant tools that were wayward and seemed not always to obey his command. Several of the fingers were bandaged still, and the skin was shedding itself from the pads of the last three digits of his right hand. He could hold the bread when the roll was large, but fumbled with it when he had only a small piece left. She caught it on the comforter, held it to his mouth.

She watched him chew the bread.

"Is this your house?" he asked.

She nodded.

"What day is it?"

"It is six, January."

"Then I've been here . . ." He seemed to be calculating.

"Seven days."

"And all that time . . ."

"You have been here, on this bed."

He sat up sharply. "I have to try to contact the crew."

She pushed him gently on his chest. "Is done," she said. "Your crew is knowing where you are."

"Some of the men in the plane died," he said.

She nodded. "Two. One is dead already when your aeroplane crashed. One is . . . died," she corrected, "in the night of the crash."

"And the others?"

"Two are taken by the Germans. We think to Breendonk first. This is a prison near Brussels. And then after Breendonk?" She held her hands open as though to say no one could be certain where in Germany they might be sent.

He looked away briefly. "Do you know their names?"

"They are called McNulty and Shulman."

The pilot closed his eyes and nodded.

"Is story of your friends McNulty and Shulman," she said.

"When they are first captured, the Germans are offering them cigarettes. But the Americans, your friends, they are turning their heads to the side and not taking them."

The American smiled briefly. "And there was a man called Case. He was shot in the arm. Do you know where he is?"

"All the other men are sent into France, and are now trying to reach Spain. The man you are speaking of, his arm is very badly broken. It is said that he is minding that he will not be able to play *base ball*. Yes?"

The American smiled again. "That's Case. He signed with the Boston Braves just before the war. Bad break."

"Yes, the break is bad," she said, agreeing with him.

"No, I meant, bad luck."

"Ah. Yes."

"We were on our way to Germany," he said.

She nodded.

"To bomb a chemical plant," he added. "I've said this before?"

She nodded. "There is a man here, from the Resistance. He is asking you questions about your plane, to send a missile back to England."

"Message," he corrected.

She smiled with embarrassment. "Message. My English is very bad."

"Your English is very good. And I told him about the mission?"

"Yes."

"Do you know where the bombs fell?" he asked quickly.

She heard the strain in his voice. She hesitated, and he saw her hesitate.

She shook her head. "No," she said, looking down. She saw that there was a light dusting of flour on her apron. She tried to brush it away.

"In the mornings, I am baking," she said.

"Where in Belgium am I?"

His voice had a clarity she had not heard in his incoherent ramblings. Its timbre was different as well — deeper, more resonant than she remembered. "Our village is called Delahaut," she said. "It is in southern Belgium, thirty kilometers from the French border."

"And other people live in this house with you."

"There is only myself and my husband, who is called Henri," she said.

The American seemed puzzled.

"There have been others. From time to time. To help you. To ask you questions."

She would not give him Antoine's name, or Thérèse Dinant's. There was no need for him to know.

His eyes had changed as well. The green had grown clearer, more translucent, as if his eyes, too, had taken on life. His nose was large, square at the bottom, like his jawline. His face was long, much longer and narrower than the faces of the southern Belgians. She liked his mouth. The bottom lip was straight, the upper curved. He smiled often. A good color had returned to his skin. He needed to have his hair combed.

"How bad is the leg?" he asked.

Briefly, she considered how much she should tell him, and decided this time to tell him the truth.

"Is nearly lost," she said. "To the infection. But the woman who is here?" She looked at him expectantly to see if he remembered. He nodded slowly.

"She is saving your leg. There is . . ."

She thought. She was about to say "terrible," but she did not want to frighten him. ". . . a bad scar nearly to your ankle. Yes?"

She meant: Was that all right? Could he stand that?

He shrugged.

She answered his next question before he could ask it.

"And when you are standing, we will see how you are walking."

He nodded.

"But I think, not yet. Not so soon. Not today." She shook her head quickly.

He seemed about to speak, to protest. She reached into the pocket of her skirt, pulled out a photograph. She held the picture out to him. He could not manage so thin a piece of paper with his fingers, so she put the photograph into the flat of his palm. She studied his face as he looked at the picture.

"It is your friend, yes?" she asked.

He nodded. "Her name is Stella," he said quietly. "She's my fiancée. Do you know that word?"

"We have that word."

He handed her back the picture, but she stopped him.

"No, I think is good for you to keep it nearly to you." She took the photograph from his hand and laid it on the comforter. "I would write to her? Or to your mother? But . . ." Claire shrugged. "It is not safe now. You are understanding me? Perhaps not so long after you have left us, I can do that."

His eyes were fixed on hers. "Before we landed," he said slowly, "just before we belly-landed, we had to let the bombs go. I want to know where they fell."

This time she deliberately did not move her eyes from his. "No one is telling me this," she said. "Possibly you left them in Germany?"

"I don't think so. I don't see how. . . ."

"Then I will ask someone if this is known."

"What happened to the plane?" he asked.

"The Maquis, they have removed some of the guns and a machine that . . ." She struggled. ". . . finds the place where the bombs are to be dropping — "

"The Norden bombsight," he said quickly.

"And then the Germans are coming and surrounding the plane, and taking pieces of it, and are very angry because some of the guns are missing. And so they are putting all the villagers in the church and asking them about the guns, but no one is saying anything to the Germans. And now the Germans are watching your plane, but" — she made a dismissive sound — "is only three old soldiers who are watching it, so I think is nothing there of importance."

"What is the Maquis?"

"Is Resistance. Soldiers of Resistance."

"Have you seen the plane?"

She shook her head. "No. I have been here always. But I have heard it pictured to me."

A gust of wind shook the pane of glass in the rectangle, and she looked up at the window. The sky was darker, more oily; the storm would soon begin. Because of the impending storm, the light in the crawl space had taken on a yellowish cast. Oddly, she thought of the Hopkins she had begun before the American came. "For skies of couple-colour as a brindled cow . . ." She wanted to read this difficult poem to the American, to ask him if he knew the English words *couple-colour* and *brindled*. Perhaps later, when he was not so weak.

She looked around at the small space in which she sat and he lay. Layers of old wallpaper were peeling from the walls. She wondered if once, years ago, this attic room had been part of the bedroom, or of another room in the attic.

"There was a boy," the pilot said.

"Yes," she said quietly. "The boy who is saving you."

The pilot nodded.

"But you must not tell any person about him. Yes? Is very dangerous for him."

"I would like to thank him," Ted said.

She tilted her head as if to say *maybe*. "Perhaps we are arranging this."

He was looking closely at her face. She lowered her eyes, unused to such scrutiny. A sudden warmth rose along her throat and lodged behind her ears.

"You've hidden others here as well," he said.

She nodded.

"Who was here before me?"

Claire looked up at him. "There is a woman who is fleeing Antwerp. The Gestapo, they have taken away her son and her husband. When the Resistance is finding her, they are sending her to me to get well, and then I am sending her to France, as you one day will go to France, but she is very ill, and she is dying here."

"Dying? Here?"

"Yes. The night you are coming here. She is died already."

"This is dangerous work that you and your husband do."

She looked away, arranged the bowl and plate on the small tray. "It is not so dangerous as the work the others are doing. I am safe here unless I am denounced. The work my husband is doing is more dangerous."

"What does he do?"

"I do not know. He is telling me very little of his work, because is safer for me to know as little as possible. Is true for everyone. Even you."

"How old are you?"

"I am twenty-four years. Why is it you are asking me this?"

"Just curious. Have you been married long?"

She smoothed her skirt as far as it would go along her legs. "Four years."

"And you don't have any children?"

She shook her head quickly.

The American lifted the comforter a fraction and looked down at his shirt. "I noticed that these clothes . . ."

She smiled. "They are the clothes of my husband. They are fitting you — "

"Pretty badly." He grinned. "I don't suppose you have any cigarettes."

"Yes," she answered. From her pocket she produced a crumpled packet. "Forgive," she said, "but already I am smoking all your cigarettes. These are mine and are not so nice as yours."

She put the cigarette in her own mouth, lit it, then handed it to him. Gently she helped him hold it by wrapping his index finger around it and pressing it close to his thumb. He took a deep drag, exhaled through his nose. He coughed once. "Strong," he said.

The smell of the tobacco quickly filled the small space. She wanted to join him, but she knew that the room would soon become too thick with smoke. She watched him enjoy his cigarette. She brushed away an ash that fell on the comforter.

"Your hands are becoming more well," she said. "Each day I see this. You should not worry about your hands."

"Frostbite?"

She pondered this English word. "You fingers are freezing in the forest," she said. "Is the same?"

"Yes."

"Frost bite," she repeated. "Frost eats the fingers?"

"Something like that."

He reached toward her with the cigarette, held it out to her. She hesitated, then took it. She pulled on it quickly, gave it back to him.

She raised herself on her knees a fraction. She brushed her hair behind her ears. "Is too much talking for first time," she said. "I am thinking now that you should sleep. In one hour, I will bring you soup. You must return your strength, because we have little time to do very many things."

"What things?" he asked.

She maneuvered her way to the trapdoor.

"I must make you ready to leave," she said.

January 16, 17, and 18, 1944

THE DUSK A CAMOUFLAGE. HIDING IN THE TREES. OAK, beech. Bracken on the forest floor. He stood at the edge of the field and waited for his own eyes, which were sharp, to make out the shape of the fallen plane. The pneumatic jacks that had long since deflated lay discarded under the wings. In the near dark, the broken plane looked tired and sad — already a relic. On the other side of the fuselage, smoke rose.

His own mission, secret, self-ordered. A test of will, and already he was worried he would fail. His body trembled, and in his vision he saw spots at the periphery. He made himself move forward to gain a better view. Two men, one sleeping in a roll of blankets near the fire. Yes, he thought, it might work. A sleeping guard, trapped as he was, would not be able to reach his weapon quickly, even if he awakened. The other guard sat hunched by the fire. The German soldier had wrapped his greatcoat over his head and around his shoulders. To trap the heat. Like an old woman with a shawl bent over her cooking fire. The hunched German moved slightly. A flicker of a knife blade, a long sausage, a movement of the knife blade from the sausage to the mouth. Of course, there would be only the two, he thought, three to rotate at staggered hours. A lonely watch far from town. He saw now a bicycle at the other side of the field, perhaps a second — the light was fading fast. He would have to take the hunched old woman first.

He pulled his own knife from his coat pocket, held it at the ready. His hand shook so badly he was afraid the guards would see a shimmery reflection. Retracing his steps so that he was looking at the plane from behind the guards. How casual they were, he thought — how lazy, inept. He also thought: *Now. It must be now.*

He crossed the matted field until he reached the cold metal of the plane. In a shadow he stood, listening for sounds above the rush of blood in his ears. The snoring of the sleeping German, a small shuffle. To reach the squatting guard first, he would have to circle the plane by its nose.

For days now he had been imagining the quick gestures, the snap of the head, the clean cut, so that when the moment finally came he wouldn't falter, wouldn't panic. Only seconds left now. As one man against two, he could not afford to sacrifice the element of surprise.

He cleared the nose of the B-17. He was certain he had not made a sound, but the hunched German turned slightly, cocking his ear, as though he might have sensed a presence. In the firelight, the Belgian saw the wet gray bristles of the guard's mustache, the knifepoint with its morsel of sausage in the open mouth.

In one swift movement, he reached the guard's back. The German turned, and in doing so lowered his knife. The cloak slipped from his head. Before the guard could cry out, the Belgian slapped his hand over the guard's mouth, heard him choke once on the piece of sausage. He jerked the German's head and slit the bare throat above the collar of the hated uniform. The guard in the bedroll opened his eyes, fought in a panic to free himself. Kneeling quickly then over the frightened German, executing the same cut from left to right on bare skin. Blood spurting in an arc. The Belgian reared away and stood.

His body shuddered and his bowels loosened. Stunned, he watched the German in the bedroll drown. The knife and his hand were covered with a blood that seemed black in the firelight. He thought then that he would throw the knife into the fire, burn the blood from its surface, but the fingers of his hand refused to relax their grip. He stood for a moment paralyzed, as if the knife had been welded, grafted, to his body.

And then he heard the small sound of metal chafing metal.

He turned and saw a third German, his face dazed and creased with sleep, a revolver in his hand, emerging from the belly of the plane. Panicky now and flailing wildly, the Belgian knocked the revolver from the old man's hand, twisted the frightened face away from him, and dispatched this guard as he had the others. The German, his feet still pinned inside the fuselage, fell backwards over the lip of the door, toward the ground.

The Belgian began to shake violently. An awful sound came from his body. He threw down the knife, as if it had a life of its own, as if it might turn itself against him. Then, thinking better of this gesture, he picked it up again. He bent and wiped the blood from the blade as best he could on the coat of the guard who had been eating sausage. How was it they had posted all three guards at once? Or had the old soldiers simply been camping out here — a kind of sorry outpost?

He had expected to feel something — if not triumph exactly, then at least success. He had done what he set out to do. So he was confused for a moment to discover that what he felt was a kind of numbness, a terrible hollowness in his bowels, perhaps even a small seed of dread. He moved away from the plane, looking at the work of seconds, the bodies of the three old Germans in the firelight. He turned and stumbled then back to the forest.

Madness.

Antoine shook his head, put his head in his hands. Angrier than Henri had ever seen him. A small lantern, shrouded with a cloth and set in the center of their circle, was the only light in Chimay's barn. Each had been called from sleep. Underneath his coat, Henri still wore his nightshirt. Emilie had not undone the braid she wore to bed. At this unforgiving hour, roused abruptly as if there had been a fire, Emilie, without her lipstick or her hair framing her face, looked years older than Henri had imagined her to be — fifty possibly, perhaps fifty-five. Her face still bore the greasy traces of her night cream.

Léon Balle smoking, coughing quietly into his gloved hand. Dussart hunched, trembling inside his thin coat. Where was the boy's enthusiasm now? Dussart had forgotten his beret, and his hair had separated over the place where he had lost his ear. Henri, who had never really examined the scar, was fascinated.

Antoine trying to control himself. Speaking in this slow, deliberate manner only when he was enraged and was trying to remain calm. He smoked fast, with short pulls and exhales, as if that, too, might contain his anger. Antoine had waited for them all to arrive, had spoken to no one until he made his pronouncement. *Madness,* he had said.

Henri waited. Antoine stubbed out his cigarette on the dirt floor with a sharp twist of his boot heel.

Finally, Antoine's announcement. Someone has killed the three Germans guarding the plane.

A long silence in the barn.

Jesus God. Emilie whispering.

Léon Balle leaning back, looking at the ceiling of the barn. Bastien, a small, pinched man with pointed teeth that reminded Henri of a rodent, shaking his head in disgust. Dussart, the boy, trembling inside his coat. Henri thought he must be ill. The young man rubbing his hands along his arms as if to warm them.

They'll think it was us. Antoine now.

Léon then. There'll be reprisals.

Reprisals. Henri bent over. He felt heat on the surface of his skin.

Emilie spoke as if from a great distance.

The reprisals will be catastrophic, Antoine said slowly, giving weight to each word. The house searches have already begun. They've taken Madame Bossart from her bed.

Mother of God, this is not possible. Emilie shaking her head in bewilderment. Madame Bossart is nearly seventy-five. What could they possibly want with such an old woman?

Her farm is nearest to the plane. They think she may have hidden the assassin, or one of the Americans.

This is insane.

It's what they do. We knew that.

Will it be like Virelles? Bastien talking, but everyone knew the horror of Virelles. Every male in the village, including the boy children, had been rounded up and shot in the village square in front of their wives and mothers. The SS had even worked out an equation: For every German wounded, three Belgians would die; for every German killed, ten Belgians would die.

When were they killed? asked Emilie.

The bodies were found tonight by a sentry delivering the evening meal.

Silence settling upon the circle. The light flickering in the lantern.

Antoine turning to Van der Elst. Adrien. You and Elise should get out at once. The Germans have been suspecting you for some time. Don't return to your apartment. I'm going to put you through the lines tonight.

Elise starting forward at the news. Van der Elst clenching his jaw.

Antoine turned to Henri.

Henri felt his stomach spasm. Unlike Van der Elst and his wife, he knew, he and Claire could not leave Delahaut. They had the American. He thought suddenly of Jean Burnay of nearby Florennes. The Belgian had sheltered five British aviators in his home. One of the aviators was caught further down the line in France and talked. Burnay and his wife were beheaded by the Gestapo.

Henri, your risk is probably less than Adrien's. But if they can take Madame Bossart, they can take anyone. Emilie will go to Claire, tell her to hide herself inside the house.

Henri nodded. But he wondered why Antoine was not sending himself, Henri, to tell Claire. His mouth felt dry. He ran his tongue over his lips. He felt another severe spasm in his gut; he needed badly to find a toilet. He thought of Claire, alone at home with the injured American. Perhaps even now the Gestapo were raiding the house, dragging Claire from her bed.

Are there always reprisals? Dussart asked in a thin voice from his seat. It was the first the young man had spoken.

Antoine looking at Dussart. There are always reprisals, he

said slowly. And it's worse. Tonight I have received additional intelligence that the escape routes are now the primary focus of the Germans in southern Belgium.

Thérèse must be told, said Emilie.

And Dolane.

And Dolane. And Hainaert. And Duceour.

In Charleroi, at least they have the tablets. Léon talking, his head in his hands.

A stillness in the barn. Henri felt a throbbing in his right temple. They all knew what Léon meant. In the cities, where the Maquis was better organized and had more funds, more access to matériel, each Resistance fighter was given a single tablet of cyanide. To contain the damage in the event of torture. Few men or women, no matter how brave, could withstand the prolonged and creative torture of the Gestapo — he'd heard it all — the electric prods and needles to the testicles, the gouging of the eyes. Without the cyanide, every man was a tràitor.

Henri put his hands against the hay bale on which he sat, to give him leverage, to help him stand. His legs felt weak, and he did not want to stumble in front of the others.

Léon Balle looking up. White-faced with anger. Who gave a shit about the three guards? Was there a reason? Was anything taken from the plane?

Antoine answering. There was nothing on the plane of any real value. The guns had been seized long ago.

Léon shaking his head as though he could not process this unthinkable information. Coughing suddenly and violently, and reaching for a handkerchief in his pocket.

Antoine turning to Henri, who had managed to stand. I'm sorry, Henri, Antoine was saying. It's not safe to move the American. There's a chance it could blow the whole Eva line.

Henri nodding stiffly. If the Eva line were blown, the denunciations, like a lit fuse that ran out from Delahaut in two directions — north to Charleroi and south to France — would be massive. Dozens, maybe hundreds, might be arrested and executed.

You'll stay here with me, Antoine was saying now. There's a lot to do.

Antoine himself, for the first time Henri could remember, looking afraid. Despite the cold, his thinning white-blond hair lay matted with sweat against his pink scalp.

We won't meet again for a while. Antoine speaking, looking away from Henri, then to each of the others in turn. Henri realizing then, with the shock of an absolute truth, that before they met again, some of their number would be dead.

Antoine bending down, removing the cloth shroud and the glass from the lantern. Blowing out the light. Léon Balle asked a question in the darkness.

Did someone really imagine that killing three old impotent men would change the course of the war?

<hr />

She awoke feeling better than she had for days, perhaps weeks. The sun, which they had not seen since before the day the plane fell on the Heights, shone through the lace at the windows, making a filigree on the polished floor. Claire turned in the bed, felt immediately its emptiness, and remembered that Antoine, sometime in the night, had come for Henri.

She thought of the American beyond the flower-papered wall — a silent, sleeping prisoner. Or perhaps he wasn't sleeping. Possibly he was already sitting, waiting for her to greet him with his breakfast. Yes, the sunlight had doubtless wakened him as well, she decided, shining as it must be through the rectangle.

She slipped from the bed and knocked on the wall that separated them. He knocked back and said, in a voice that was surprisingly distinct, even through the wall, "Bonjour Madame."

She shook her head. His accent was atrocious.

"Bonjour Monsieur. Je pars au village pour chercher de l'eau potable à la fontaine. Je reviens tout de suite. Pouvez-vous attendre?"

She smiled and waited.

"I never had a chance," he said finally.

"I am going to the village for drinking water from the fountain. Can you wait? I am not being long."

"Sure. But hurry. I'm starved."

Claire dressed quickly, saw to the fire in the stove, and collected her bicycle. She wondered again where Henri was, when
he would arrive home. His hours lately had become increasingly
erratic. She seldom knew when to prepare a meal for him, or even
if he would spend the night. The two of them were all right as
long as it was winter, when there was less to do about the farm.
But when spring came, he would be needed. Claire wondered how
they would manage then.

Most of the ice along the rue St. Laurent had melted or had
been scuffed with dirt so that the ride to the village was not as
hazardous as it had been in days past. Before she got the drinking
water, she would stop at Madame Omloop's for the flour and
potatoes and sugar and salt. With each day, the American's appetite had increased. It was not even the middle of the month yet,
and it was clear Claire's stamps would not extend until the thirty-
first. Madame Rosenthal had barely eaten at all and had not taxed
the Daussois rations.

It was exhilarating, the sun. Odd how it could lift the spirits,
she thought. She passed the Marchal farm and the Mailleux. The
stone was pale in the early light, and though there were no people
about yet, it was just possible to imagine that there was no war,
had never been, that soon the narcissus and hyacinth would pop
above the soil and that the man in her attic was merely a conva-
lescing visitor.

She reached the outskirts of the village proper, began to pedal
along the rue de Florennes. And it was somewhere along that
narrow street, with its uneven cobblestones, that she realized something was different, amiss. She stopped before she reached the
corner, before she would then turn into the rue Cerfontaine, and
then at the following corner, into the public square. She listened
closely. Yes, that was it: There were no sounds. No voices, no
shouting of schoolchildren, no doors opening and closing, no clatter of bicycles, no vehicles negotiating the narrow side streets,
sending cyclists careening into the brick walls. No cursing from
those cyclists.

Something was wrong, but she didn't know what. Had a curfew been imposed, and she and Henri, so far from the village,

failed to hear of it? On foot, she pushed her bicycle, hugging the wall. The water jugs rattled in the pannier. She peered around the corner and saw nothing. She would have to advance to yet another corner to see into the village square.

Instinct warned her to retrace her steps and her ride, to pedal back to the house as quickly as she could. But she had no water! Surely there would be activity at the fountain. Or at Omloop's. The Flemish woman never closed her shop, not even on the saints' days.

She walked her bicycle to the next corner and, standing as close to the wall as she could, bent her head and looked into the village square. Now there could be no mistake. The square, with its steepled church, its village hall with the wide stone steps, and the old monastery that was now a school, was barren. Not even the pigeons, huddled in the eaves of the church, had bothered to descend to its cobblestones. The fountain bubbled unattended.

A chill settled low in her back. Fumbling with her bicycle and pannier, she turned around, intending now to return home. She hoped only that she would not be seen. There must have been a curfew imposed: No other explanation seemed plausible. She would have to wait for information, wait for Henri to return. Perhaps she could get food, enough for the three of them, from the Marchal farm, if Marie-Louise would open her door to her.

She was nearly to the corner of the rue de Florennes when she heard a faint sound. She stopped, stood astride her bicycle. It was the unmistakable hum of a motor — but from which direction? She listened again, knowing she might be wasting precious moments. The motor — a car? a truck? — was coming from the direction in which she wished to go.

Chancing a sighting, she pulled her scarf forward over her head to hide her face, bent low over her handlebars and pedaled as fast as she could past the rue de Florennes. She knew the back streets and alleys of Delahaut well. If she could make it to the rue de Canard, she knew of an alley there that permitted a bicycle, but not a four-wheeled vehicle. It wouldn't prevent a sentry from noticing her and requiring her to halt, but she would be free of the motor. For to Claire, in the eerie silence of the village, the motor suggested only one thing: Germans.

Having not dared to look up, she didn't know if she had been spotted. Surely, she thought, a lone cyclist would be observed from behind the ubiquitous lace curtains at every window. Why did no one call to her, allow her to hide herself and her bicycle in one of the stone vestibules found behind each streetfront door?

When she reached the alley, she was struggling for breath. She had not pedaled so hard since she was a girl. Still astride her bicycle, she allowed herself to rest a moment, leaning against the back brick wall of a villager's terraced house. The icy air, taken in large gulps, hurt her lungs.

Perhaps, she thought, as she rested, she could reach Omloop's via the same kind of twisting route by which she had reached the safety of the alley. Even more than food now, Claire needed information and possibly somewhere to hide. Madame Omloop could not fail to help Claire, even in the extraordinary event that the shop was not open for business.

More cautiously now, Claire proceeded, listening hard at each blind turn, sticking to the alleys and to the narrow pathway that ran behind the cemetery. Once she saw a figure, not a soldier, run from one side of the street to the other, then disappear.

Her journey took her fifteen minutes, and when she reached Madame Omloop's, she was no longer surprised to see its door shut tight. Along her way, Claire had not observed a single open shop. Looking up and down the narrow lane on which Omloop's was located, Claire quickly rapped on the glass pane of the door. In the distance she could hear again the sound of a motor.

She rapped again — short, fast taps on the stained glass.

She rapped a third time.

There was a minute movement of the door's lace panel.

Claire bent close to the glass. "Madame Omloop," she whispered as loudly as she dared, "it's Claire Daussois."

The door opened quickly. Madame Omloop tugged sharply at Claire's coat sleeve, pulled her inside, and shut the door.

"Are you crazy?" Madame Omloop asked angrily. "You cannot come here. Can you not see the shop is closed? Go home at once."

"I don't know what has happened," Claire said.

"The reprisals! My God! Do you not know about the reprisals?"

Reprisals. Claire now understood the eerie silence of the village. She thought at once of Henri.

"Reprisals for what?" Claire asked.

"Someone has killed the German guards who were by the plane. The Gestapo have taken nearly the entire village," said Madame Omloop. "They have put everyone in the school. All the men and boys, and they are even taking women and babies."

Madame Omloop's fear was electric, contagious.

"God save us," Madame Omloop said. "It was a terrible day when that plane fell on our village. You must go at once back to your house, lock yourself in. Hide if you can."

"Henri," Claire said. "Henri has not come home."

Madame Omloop looked at the younger woman. "Wait here," she said.

In less than a minute the Flemish shopkeeper returned with three rashers of bacon, a large wedge of cheese wrapped in cloth.

"I have this food, and now it cannot all be eaten. Take this and go. Quickly."

The alley past the cemetery led, Claire knew, to a footpath that soon entered the wood on its eastern side. It was a footpath she had sometimes taken as a schoolgirl — a shortcut between the village and the river, but normally a roundabout way to reach her house. It would mean that she would have to push the bicycle the entire way and that it might take as long as two hours to get home. But it would keep her off the main road. She walked briskly, trying to stifle her fear. The American would wonder what was taking her so long. She prayed that when she got back, Henri would be there to help her.

———

He waited as long as he could. He thought he might be able to manage it. He wanted to try.

He dragged himself through the attic opening and then through the armoire. Alone, on the floor of Claire's bedroom, taking in its contents for the first time, he turned and rose to the one good knee, looked for something upon which to brace himself. The footboard of the bed would work, he thought.

Not only was his right leg useless, he discovered, but his arms were also weak. He managed a standing position, holding himself against the slanted roof of the room. Gingerly, he put some weight on the bad leg, was answered immediately with a jolt of hot pain that made him dizzy. Hopping with the good leg and bracing with his hands, he made his way to the top of the stairs, and then with the aid of the bannister to the floor below. He leaned against the wall and rested. He felt momentarily light-headed. How was he supposed to plan an escape — or participate in an escape plan — if he couldn't even limp?

He made his way into the kitchen. There were details of this room he remembered. The stove, the wooden table. The cold of the tile floor. She had a radio here, he was certain. He'd heard it through the floorboards. Ought he to try to find it? Did it have a transmitter? On the table now was a loaf of bread. He was starving. What was taking her so long in the village?

He made his way to the privy and then returned to the kitchen, where he washed himself and enjoyed it, despite the cold. He wanted to linger in the kitchen, but he knew it wasn't safe. He took a slice of bread with him back to the attic room.

Whatever strength he had hoarded in all the days he had lain in the crawl space now was spent. He drifted between sleep and waking, surprised anew each time he opened his eyes and saw the sunshine in the attic garret. When he dozed, he laid his head back against the surface of the wall, almost spongy from its many layers of wallpaper. How old was the house? he wondered. A hundred years? Two hundred? He still had not got used to the idea that in Europe — in the English village where the bomb group was billeted, and now here in this tiny Belgian town — there were houses and churches, many in fact, that were centuries older than the oldest buildings in America. He thought of Mount Gilead, his hometown in Ohio, and of the farmhouse there where he once lived with his family, which was, at best, what? — a hundred years old? This building, the Daussois farmhouse, was ancient by comparison. The layers of wallpaper and paint told a story of their own. Whose stories? he wondered. What stories? Who had been hidden here?

She had left him a book, and sometimes he opened it and read a line or two of English poetry. She had asked him to explain some of the words and phrases to her, and had been perplexed when he had not known their meaning — not even in the context of the lines. "For rose-moles all in stipple . . ." He knew neither *rose-moles* nor *stipple*. He had tried to explain to her that his education had been interrupted by the war, though he privately doubted that even if he'd finished college, the words *rose-mole* and *stipple* would have come his way. His field was engineering. He had taken only one English course: a freshman composition class with a professor whose skin looked as dry as dust, and whose breath smelled of whiskey when he moved along the rows of students.

It seemed to Ted that his years in college occurred infinitely long ago — as though lived, experienced, in another lifetime, another age, or distantly in childhood.

Even Stella was fading in her detail. He could no longer summon the sound of her voice or her scent, and the image he had of her had gradually reduced itself to the single pose in the creased and worn photograph that Claire had placed in the palm of his hand. He fumbled for the picture, beside him on the floor. Dexterity had returned to his fingers; he could slide his nails under the photograph, lift it up.

Stella was sitting at a table in a restaurant. In the picture, it was always her smile he noticed first, no matter how many times he looked at the photograph. No one, he reflected, not a single person since he left America and entered the war, had had such an open and uncomplicated smile. She had her elbows resting on the table, and in front of her were several empty beer bottles — his and hers. She was wearing a white dress that was high at the neck and had short sleeves that seemed to flutter from her shoulders. Her hair was glossy, pulled back tightly at the top, with the sides long and curly. He studied the photograph and felt a sudden despair. Stella did not know where he was; whether he was alive or dead. No one back home knew. Already his mother would have received the telegram with the words *missing in action,* and she wouldn't know if her son was alive and in a German prison camp, or had been blown to bits in the air by a burst of flak. Bill Simmons, the postman, would have come with the telegram, his steps slow and deliberate, so that someone watching at the window would know even before he got to the door that he had a telegram. When the war had first begun, Ted himself, twice or three times, had watched Bill, in his uniform, make the long, slow journey to a fated front door. Curious, Ted had slowed his own steps, waiting for the reaction at the doorway. First the hand to the mouth, and then the wail the hand could not stop.

Now Ted would not slow his steps, would avoid at all costs seeing such a scene. He had witnessed enough benumbed and grief-stricken reactions to last ten lifetimes. And he now knew what was on the other side of those telegrams — events the recipients couldn't see, couldn't even imagine, for they had no vocabulary, no internal photographs, with which to perceive such horrors. A gunner, alive, shot from his ball turret, falling to the ground, the arms flailing like a windmill; another gunner, his own, fumbling with oily fingers for the flesh of his body that was no longer there.

He put the picture facedown on the floor, lay back against the wall, and closed his eyes. Once a man had seen such things, he asked himself, how did he then erase them from his memory? He thought of the men who returned from missions seemingly unscathed — their footsteps still jaunty, eager for whatever small pleasures the base or the town could provide them, wisecracks spinning around their heads. Somehow these men had done what he had failed to do: They had had the same visions and had dismissed them. Or did they, too, have visitations in the night?

His stomach felt hollow. How long had Claire been gone? He had no watch, couldn't accurately even guess the time. The light had changed in the attic room. The sun now cast a brighter rectangle on the unslanted wall. He estimated the size of his lair to be seven feet wide and about eight feet long. He could lie down fully extended, but just. When Claire came, she had to wind her long legs beneath her skirt in order to sit beside him without touching him. He remembered the first day she came to him when he was alert and fully conscious, and her surprise at that, her awkwardness. Her legs were bare and thin; she folded them under her as though to hide them. She wore white ankle socks, odd-looking men's shoes he had not seen since. Her hair, he remembered, was falling from its pins, and there was flour on her apron and on her throat, just under her chin. She brushed the flour from her apron, but was unaware of the white dusting on her skin, and he found that somehow charming, mesmerizing — as though he had caught her, unsuspecting, in the middle of a private domestic act. There was, that day, no artifice about her, and as she talked — haltingly, nervously — he could not take his eyes from that white dust.

Her visits punctuated his days. He sensed, but couldn't be certain, that she came less frequently than she had when he was still not fully alert or well. Now she came only on missions — with a meal, with medicine, and sometimes to teach him simple French phrases, which he seemed to be particularly inept at mastering. No longer did she sit by him for indefinite periods of time, knitting or reading. He wished that she would. He could not define it precisely, but he knew that when he was drifting in and out of consciousness, and she was simply there, beside him, sometimes holding his hand, he felt safe.

Certainly she was different from any woman he had ever known. It wasn't just her accent, or the strange cut of her clothes, or her mouth with its upper lip that rose to a single point and her lower lip with its natural pout. It was a kind of self-containment. Oddly, she seldom smiled, and he was quite sure he had never heard her laugh.

Once or twice, her husband, Henri, had come with the meal, and these visits had been, because of their mutual inability to communicate, awkward and sometimes comical. Henri, on his hands and knees, pushing the tray forward, wanting, out of politeness, to greet the aviator in some way, reduced finally to gestures to the obvious tray; and Ted, embarrassed and feeling faintly emasculated, reduced as well to exaggerated nodding and smiling to convey his gratitude. Henri, he guessed, was in his early thirties. He often smelled strongly of beer and tobacco. And though Henri was never unpleasant, Ted had the distinct sense that Henri did not want him there in the attic room, that the pilot's presence was a burden he'd happily have done without. Henri's visits, mercifully, were brief.

He had now learned to distinguish Claire's footsteps from Henri's on the bedroom floor outside his lair. Many nights, Ted could tell, Henri did not come to the bedroom. He had never heard the couple making love, though he had imagined it in the way one did when one first saw the two partners of a marriage. He was relieved that he had not had to listen to such an intimate act. Perhaps his own presence just beyond their bedroom wall had inhibited them. Or possibly Claire and Henri no longer came together in that way. Ted had heard that in Europe arranged marriages or marriages of convenience were not uncommon. Or maybe Henri had a lover and that explained why he sometimes didn't return home at night to sleep with his wife.

But why was this his concern? He shook it off, feeling mildly prurient. What his hosts did, or didn't do, was their affair, certainly not his. It was the idleness, he reflected, the long hours without company or activity that had led his thoughts in such an unproductive direction. He needed to get outside, to regain his strength, to set off for France and make it back to England. Others had done it, he knew; it was not impossible.

He was aware now of a door somewhere below him opening and closing. Two muffled sounds, distant but audible. His hopes rose. He listened intently for footfalls on the stairway, for the opening of the armoire and the slip of coat hangers on the rod.

She was running on the stairs. He heard the tray set down, the outer door open. He saw, briefly, after she had opened the false back of the armoire, the dropping of a coat to the floor, an impatient swirl of headscarf. When she entered, her face was reddened — flushed, but also from the cold — and her hair was disheveled.

"I am apologizing," she said quickly. "Madame Omloop was ill today, and I am having to find the sausage and the cheese in other places. And when I am returning home, the tire on my bicycle is lying down."

"Flat."

"Yes."

He knew that she was lying. Her eyes slid off his face in an evasive manner. Her hands were shaking so badly he wanted to reach out and hold them still. He picked up the bowl of milk and brought it to his lips, all the while examining her. He put the bowl down.

"What is it?" he asked.

He watched her compose her face, that effort.

She shook her head. "I am not understanding you," she said. She picked an imaginary piece of lint off her skirt. She was wearing a cotton blouse with a deep neckline, along which was a lace border. Her high color, however she had come by it, made her features particularly vivid.

"Something's wrong," he said. "I can smell it."

She looked up at him, puzzled. "Smell?"

"I can sense it."

She shook her head again. "I am only being late, and is not good to have a bicycle that will not do what you want it to do. Is hard work in the cold, no? I am having to walk the bicycle much of the way."

He reached for her hand in her lap. She snatched it away before he could touch her. She laid it at the bodice of her blouse.

"You're trembling," he said. "You've had a bad experience. Tell me what's happened. You're beginning to scare me too."

Her silence was so long he was certain he would have to repeat his demand. He hesitated, however, not wanting to drive her away. She seemed tightly wound, poised to flee, like the small animals he once captured and held in his palm. Her hand still rested on her blouse, and nervously, unaware of what she was doing, she worked one pearllike button — so much so that he wondered if she wouldn't inadvertently unbutton her blouse. Not once did she look up at him.

"You must — "

"I'm sorry — "

They spoke simultaneously. She raised her eyes to his.

"The situation in the village is very grave," she said finally. She stopped fingering the button, put both of her hands in her lap, calmer now that she had made the decision to tell him.

"For all the days since your plane is falling, there are German soldiers surrounding the village, and three of them are watching the plane. And these are old men, harmless. I think it is not very important to be watching this plane, yes? We have spoke of this already."

Ted nodded.

"But there is some person who is killing these old men. An assassin. And the Germans, they are very angry. It is their punishment in Belgium and in other countries to make the reprisals. I have heard of this."

"Reprisals," he repeated.

"The Gestapo have come into the village and they are taking people from their houses, even old men and children, and putting them in the school. And everyone is thinking that the Gestapo will kill a precise number of Belgians for the punishment. It is for the fear. To make the fear."

He nodded slowly.

"And in the village, there is no one. Everyone is hiding in his house or is taken already, and there is a silence I have never heard."

He waited. She put her hand to her temple, let her fingers comb her hair behind her ear.

"Where is Henri?" he asked.

She lowered her head. "Henri is not coming since the night. He is sent for in the night by the Maquis, and I do not know where he is."

Ted closed his eyes and laid his head back against the wall.

One moment of indecision, a single moment of indecision, and how many deaths?

If only he had not throttled back.

Two dead immediately. And who stood innocently beneath the bomb load? Then three old Germans, and now what would the total be? A precise number, she had said. Of hostages.

"Tell me where the bombs fell," he said. He instinctively doubted that now she would lie to him.

She looked away for a moment, then returned her gaze. "They are falling in Gilles, forty kilometers east."

"In Belgium?"

"Yes."

"A village?"

"Yes."

"In the village?"

She was silent.

"What if . . . ," he asked, thinking. "What if you took me to the school and offered to exchange me for the hostages. It might work. They want the pilots. It's common knowledge."

She seemed to think for a long time, as though searching for the words she wanted.

"In this war," she said slowly, "there is no bargains. They will take you and also the others. You are not living with them as I am. And then they will come for me as well, and Henri."

"No," he said, forming a plan. "You'll leave me somewhere. Somewhere exposed, and they'll find me and take me to the school, and I'll persuade them."

"You will be tortured," she said.

"I don't think so. They want the officers out of combat, but they don't kill them. They'll send me to a prison camp in Germany. Trust me. They treat officers differently."

"You will be tortured," she repeated knowingly. "And you will not be able to stand up in the torture, and you will have to tell them of me and Henri, and if we are denounced, perhaps we will have to speak of others. . . ."

He raised his hand to silence her, put a finger to his lips. Below him he could hear footsteps, a low voice calling.

Someone is here, he said silently. He mouthed the words in an exaggerated manner, hoping she would understand him.

She listened herself, heard the muffled voice. It sounded male, but not like Henri's.

She scrambled at once to the opening of the armoire. He heard footsteps on the stairs, then a tentative voice.

"Claire?"

Claire, he could tell, had crossed to the other side of the room, doubtless to draw the visitor's eyes away from the armoire.

"Bastien," Claire said with surprise.

Ted heard the rapid French of the visitor. Claire interrupted him, and spoke herself. There was another exchange, as though Bastien were giving instructions. Ted heard the opening and closing of drawers. Then he heard what seemed to be a series of questions on Claire's part, and Bastien's answers. The next sound Ted perceived was that of Bastien's footsteps moving away from Claire, out of the room and down the wooden stairs.

The bedspring creaked with weight. Either she was sitting on the bed or was lying down. He strained to discern her movements, her breathing. He wanted to call to her, but he sensed that she would come to him when she was ready. For ten minutes, perhaps more, she seemed to be motionless. Then he heard the bed creaking again, footsteps coming toward him.

She opened the armoire, spoke through the wall. He couldn't see her, but he could hear her well. Immediately he noticed that her voice was huskier. She had been crying.

"That was Bastien," she said. She cleared her throat.

"I heard his voice."

"He is telling me that there is a woman who is coming here to tell me of the reprisals, but the Germans are capturing her."

"I'm sorry."

"And Henri is not returning for some days yet."

"Claire, I — "

"And we are being very careful not to be found," she said sharply, as though intending to end any further discussion about trading him for the hostages. "You will not be leaving here. The . . ." She seemed to be searching for a word. "The threads of escaping are too dangerous now."

He smiled at the phrase, despite the import of her message. He wished he could tell her that he would take care of her, but both of them knew that he was useless — worse than useless, a burden. Were it not for him, he knew, she could flee the village. It seemed hideously ironic that her life should be in jeopardy because of him. Oughtn't he to be protecting her, rather than harming her?

"What was in the drawers?" he asked.

"Clothes for Henri. Bastien is taking them to Henri."

"What will you do now?" he asked.

She was a long time in answering him.

"We are waiting," she said finally.

———•———

There was a name for it, *balustrade*, Monsieur Dauvin once said, but the boy thought of it simply as a covered walkway, with stone pillars and mosaic archways and long views down into the village square. It reminded him of pictures he had seen in the rectory, drawings of balustrades in walled gardens in Italian cloisters, hushed places where hooded monks walked and thought in silence. But this covered walkway, the boy's covered walkway, was at the top of the school, once a monastery, and access could be gained only from the deserted fourth floor. It was forbidden to go up to the attic, as the fourth story was referred to, because the floor and the ceiling were in such disrepair that the teachers worried for the safety of the children. The covered walkway, which was open to the square, was thought to be even more dangerous than the attic. The stones of the pillars and the graceful arches had worked themselves loose over the centuries. Merely leaning on the railing, which reached to the middle of Jean's chest, might cause the structure to give altogether. Several years ago, some fuss had been made over whether to repair the fourth story or raze the school altogether, but then the war had come, and all the laborers in the village had been immediately otherwise engaged.

Jean thought of the balustrade as his.

He came to this place often. He had removed the crosspieces that barred the door so many times now that the nails slid effortlessly in and out of their holes. He knew the route across the attic floor as a sapper might a minefield — which boards would give way even under a boy's weight, where to avoid the crumbling plaster chunks that dangled from the ceiling. He came here as often as he could manage. It was, within the school, his sanctuary. As was the wood when he was not in school.

All forays here meant some risk. At the least, a flogging by Monsieur Dauvin should Jean be discovered; an injury or a fall should he not be careful where he stepped or rested his weight. But this journey today was, by far, the most dangerous of all.

For the building was no longer a school. Nor was the church any longer a church. The sisters, in their white-winged cornettes, had fled to the adjacent convent to pray; Father Guillaume had not appeared since the Gestapo had entered the village. The classrooms of the school were now interrogation rooms; the school was a prison. All day, from his perch, the boy watched them come and go, heard, even through the three floors that separated him from the ground-floor classrooms, the muffled screams, followed abruptly by an uncommon silence, as though silence were the only way to survive.

The boy had known this all his life.

Earlier that morning, Jean had ridden his bicycle to school as he always did, but Marcel, whose house he daily passed en route, whispered frantically to him from an open window. Marcel, who was still in his nightshirt and who had not yet combed his hair, told Jean of the assassinations and of the reprisals, and that the school had been closed indefinitely. *Go home,* Marcel had whispered fiercely. It was rumored, Marcel added, that the Germans had brought in reinforcements from Florennes. The Gestapo were everywhere, like cockroaches. Jean, who had taken all of this in, thought it must have been Marcel's father who had said that, who had made the image of the cockroaches. Marcel was loyal, but he lacked imagination.

Jean left Marcel and rode to the dark safety of an alleyway. He was considerably closer to the school than he was to home; the ride to his father's farmhouse might, in fact, be more dangerous than remaining in the village. He could, he thought, seek shelter with Marcel: Madame Delizée would not refuse him. But the thought of being trapped all day (and all night?) in Marcel's cluttered and claustrophobic three-room apartment, where the indoor toilet seemed continuously to be backed up, made Jean shake his head quickly.

He hid his bicycle behind a pair of dustbins, hugged the backs of the terraced houses, and ventured to peer into the village square, bordered on the north by the old school. The shades at the class-room windows had been drawn. Two armed and uniformed sentries stood at the door where normally Monsieur Dauvin waited to reprimand the tardiest of the students.

All the boys knew of the basement entrance. It was where the older boys went to smoke; the younger to play cards for centimes. From the basement, there was the back staircase, filthy and always smelling of stale cigarette smoke. The teachers never used the back staircase; they complained to Monsieur Chabotaux, the old caretaker, that dust caught at their trousers.

Jean crept into the darkness of the basement, heard from the floor above the occasional tread of heavy boots. Behind the boiler, the staircase began; it encountered on each level a heavy metal door. When he had climbed to the ground floor, Jean hesitated, put his ear to the door. There was behind the green-painted metal an odd sound, the low murmur of many voices, as though he were eavesdropping on the waiting room of the railway station at St. Laurent. The sound seemed benign and gave Jean the courage to continue up the stairs, but as he put his foot on the first step, he jerked his body. A scream had come at him through the door. Paralyzed, the boy listened as the terrible voice, a woman's, trailed off and was followed once again by the uncommon silence.

He reached the walkway without much trouble, but needed immediately to piss in the corner. He crouched into the opposite corner, where there was a bit of solid wall, perhaps three feet long, before the balustrade began. He pulled his coat around him. It was cold, but not as cold as it had been, and besides, Jean knew, the sun, which was bright today and unobscured, would soon warm this southern wall of the school.

He crouched or sat all day, peering around the wall only when he heard the clatter of a truck on the cobblestones of the square. First there were the Gestapo, who sprang with their machine guns from the truck. Then the back panels were opened, and one or five or twelve men and women, and sometimes children, stepped or were dragged from the interior compartment. Mostly the prisoners were silent, particularly the men, but occasionally a woman was crying, and sometimes the children were whimpering. Only Madame Gosset, who was, Jean knew, elderly and deaf, would not get out of the truck, possibly because she did not hear the commands, possibly because she refused, even in her frailty, to cooperate; and Jean was horrified to watch the Gestapo grab her by her hair, her bun uncoiling like a thin white rope as the pins popped and fell to the cobblestones. A guard jabbed her between her shoulder blades with the butt of his machine gun. Madame Gosset fell to the cobblestones on her knees and couldn't — or wouldn't — rise. She was dragged in that position by two Gestapo, who hoisted her weightless body by her armpits.

In all, he counted sixty-seven villagers who were taken into the school. In his bookbag he found a notebook and a pencil, and he recorded the names of all those he could recognize, so that he had entries that read this way: "Pierre Squevin and his family: his wife Marie, and a sister of the wife (?) don't know her name; and Georges, 17, from the pensionale."

Fourteen villagers had left the school. Ten young men (Georges among them) were marched out, their hands behind their heads, and herded into the back of a van. The van left the square with two guards, but Jean could not hear from four stories up their destination. Three women had been let go — one was a woman with a baby. He watched the woman stand, dazed, at the bottom of the schoolhouse steps, then begin to scurry, hunching her back as if she might conceal herself and her baby, across the square to her house.

It had been an hour, at least, since anyone else had been brought to the school or anyone had left. Jean estimated the time at about three P.M. He was glad that soon it would be dark and he could retrace his steps to his bicycle. He had seen enough, recorded enough. He had not eaten since breakfast — a hard roll, a cup of bitter tea — though, in truth, the scenes he had witnessed and the sounds he had heard had intermittently stolen his appetite. The sun slanted over the village hall opposite — in another hour, it would fall behind the slate roof. When the sun set, his corner would lose whatever small warmth the stones had harbored through the day, and he would want even more urgently to leave.

Idly he looked again at the names in his notebook, thinking he might be able to fill in the blank spaces, remember a name that had so far escaped him, when he heard a new sound in the square.

Six men, one with a tall ladder, the others with shorter ladders, stepladders, two apiece, entered the square. Two uniformed guards followed the men, the guards' arms weighted down not with machine guns but with coils of rope. The Belgians were workers, laborers from the village. Marcel's father (Marcel's father?) was the man carrying the longest of the ladders. He was dressed as Jean had often seen him — in a blue overall, a pair of clogs, and his navy cap. Monsieur Delizée walked with the ladder to the eastern side of the square, along which were terraced buildings, with shops on the ground floor, apartments on the first story. All along the front of these apartments were shallow, wrought-iron balconies — wide enough for a woman to hang out a wash to dry, wide enough in summer for tubs of begonias and geraniums. The ironwork of these balconies, intricate and detailed, was thought in the village to be among the town's better features.

Marcel's father stopped, his ladder horizontal. A guard gave a command in German, then in French. Reluctantly, Marcel's father slowly righted the ladder, leaned it carefully against the ironwork of the first balcony. The guard spoke to Monsieur Delizée, handed him a heavy coil of rope.

With growing comprehension and horror, Jean watched the father of his best friend climb the long ladder with the coil of rope.

———•———

We were near the signal crossing when they picked us up. We had nothing on us. Twenty minutes earlier, Antoine had delivered a package of propaganda leaflets to . . . well, you don't need to know to who. They were after Léon, really — and he knew it. We knew it. I think they've thought for a while now that he was, you know, leaking things he heard at the hotel. They put us in a truck. We knew the guards — all of us. They were all right with Antoine and me, you know, because we have the livestock, and they've had our meat, and perhaps they were thinking there might be, in this, a favor somewhere, but Léon, what did he have to offer? Léon was coughing badly, he does this when he gets nervous, and besides he hasn't been well, hasn't been well at all, and Antoine and me were looking at each other over his head, and I knew we were thinking the same thing. Léon was not going to get out of this.

"So then we were driven to the school. Inside the school there was . . . it was . . . In the classrooms, there were the children's drawings and their papers up on the walls, and on the floor and on the desks there was blood, spatters of it, the way it spatters when you've hit a calf before slitting its throat. In some rooms, there were old women huddling with their husbands, Monsieur Claussin and Monsieur Clouet. I saw Risa with her baby. But I could catch only glimpses, because they hurried us to a separate classroom — even though you could hear. It made you want to shit what you were hearing.

"And then an officer introduced himself — he was known to Léon and to Antoine, but not to myself, and while he was telling us his name, a guard, from behind, hit Léon such a blow, a whack with his truncheon, that Léon fell over sideways and one of the lenses of his glasses shattered. So I reached over to get him, and I was hit, too, but I was bending, and the stick hit me on the side of my face, but it didn't knock me down. So I stood up. And they started on Léon first; he was the weakest of the three of us and would break first, they reasoned, and they told him they knew he was with the Maquis, and they wanted to know what we were doing at the signal crossing, where we had been and were going and so on, and Léon, who was sitting at a child's desk, put on the glasses with the shattered lens and looked up. I'll never forget this. He began to read the signs that the teacher had put on the walls for the children. 'Jean is eating an apple.' 'Michelle is playing with the cat.' He spoke the words very slowly and distinctly, like a student learning to read. This made the officer furious. He yelled at Léon to stop, and Léon did, but as soon as he was asked a question, he would begin to read the signs again in the same voice. 'Jean is eating an apple.' 'Michelle is playing with the cat.'

"Antoine, who was frightened for Léon, said *Léon*. There were ways to answer questions without making the Gestapo angry. We'd talked about this before. But Léon, you see, he knew he was going to die, he'd seen it as we'd seen it, and he hated them so much he wouldn't even give his *own* name when, of course, they knew it.

"So the officer, his face was purple, he couldn't stand what Léon was doing. It was suicide on Léon's part, but it was beautiful in a way, too. And the officer screamed at the guards to tie our hands and take us to another room and then return, at least that's what I think he was saying, it was in German, but Antoine thought so, too, and we knew that if we were taken out, Léon would be tortured and killed right there. The guards began tying our hands behind our backs. Léon, who was coughing badly, looked up at us briefly and shook his head, as if to say, don't worry about me, don't think of me.

"And that was the last we saw of Léon.

"We got pushed out the door and down a hallway and shoved into an empty room, a smaller classroom with bigger desks, Monsieur Parmentier's room it was when I was a student there, and they tied us to the desks and left us.

"Antoine was on one side of the room, and I was on the other. He said, 'Léon will die,' and I said, 'Maybe they'll just scare him,' and Antoine shook his head. Then we struggled with the ropes for a bit, but I could not get free and neither could Antoine, but Antoine, who barely fit into the space between the chair and the desk, discovered something while he was struggling, and that was that two of the three bolts on the desk's pedestal had loosened. Later he said it was probably the work of a bored student. So Antoine began rocking back and forth violently and thrashing about, he knew we only had minutes at best, and after a time the third bolt popped, and he was free. So he slid and walked his desk over to where I sat — it would have been funny maybe if it hadn't been so frightening, and actually I was so close to panic I did almost laugh, Antoine's face was bright pink and he was huffing and puffing like a pig — it has to be said — but he got himself at right angles to me, and we fumbled with each other's ropes from behind, both at once, then Antoine said to stop, it wasn't working, he said he'd get me free first. And that's what happened.

"When we were both free, Antoine put the desk back where

it was supposed to be and put the bolts in and we took the ropes, so there wouldn't be any obvious evidence of an escape. Antoine was counting on the right hand not knowing what the left was doing in all the confusion, and that maybe the guards when they returned would think we'd been taken by other guards to another classroom. In any event, we opened a window and dropped out. I stood on Antoine's shoulders and closed the window."

Henri shivered beside her in the bed in the dark. He was naked, but the shivering was from shock. He spoke nearly in a monotone, yet his voice was unsteady because of his shaking. She had put blankets on him and was holding him in the bed, but she couldn't stop his trembling. He had come into the kitchen just as the sun was beginning to set. She had put her hand to her mouth and cried out when she saw the bruise on his face. He had stripped off all his clothes and bathed himself at the pump, waving her away when she tried to tend to the bruise. Naked, he had walked up to the bedroom, drawn the curtains and climbed into the bed.

"I can only stay a few minutes," he said when he had told her his story. It was the most he had ever revealed of his experiences in the underground. "I'm going to have to go into hiding with Antoine for a while, until this thing with the reprisals is over. I've come for my papers and some money."

She heard what he said, held him, and said nothing.

"You should know that they are taking women," he said. "They have taken Emilie and Thérèse. And even Madame Bossart."

"It's all right," she said. "They won't come for me."

"Claire . . ."

Henri began suddenly to make a deep, heaving, gutteral sound — an awful, rough sound — that frightened Claire and made her sit up in the bed. She thought her husband was about to be sick. Henri coughed into the pillow to muffle the terrible sounds of the crying. Claire, who had never heard her husband cry, lay down again and held him more tightly and thought of the pilot who was so near them, just beyond the wall. He must be hearing this, she thought.

"It's all right, Henri," she said quietly. "It's all right."

"No," he said, stopping his crying nearly as quickly as he'd begun, wiping his nose on a pillow slip. "It's not all right." His voice was thick and full of congestion.

He felt then with his hand for the hem of her skirt, raising it beneath the comforter so that he could put his fingers between her thighs. Without waiting for a sign from her, he snapped the garters of her stockings, rubbed his free hand hard along the length of her legs, rolling down the stockings to her ankles. He pulled down her underwear, so that it, too, was tangled at her feet. Raising himself onto his knees, he climbed over her. She looked for his face, but when it passed near hers, the room was so dark, she couldn't see him clearly. He bent his head into her neck, held the skin of her neck lightly with his teeth.

When she felt him coming, she shifted slightly, jerked her hips. He spilled himself onto her thigh.

He did not move or ask why.

She thought of the pilot beyond the wall. He must be hearing this, she was thinking.

———————

Ten nooses hung from the balconies, ten stepladders beneath them. The boy watched Marcel's father drape the rope through the ironwork, expertly fashioning the nooses, as if this, and not carpentry, were his trade. The villagers who had been inside the school were brought out into the square to be witnesses. From corners and doorways, a few other curious villagers joined the witnesses, so that by the time the German officer entered the square, there were perhaps fifty men and women on the cobblestones. There was among the villagers a quiet and anxious murmur. It was not clear yet who would be executed — but some of the women who had been inside the school and who had been let out and who could not now find their sons or husbands began to grow panicky, moving rapidly through the crowd, asking questions, receiving small, embarrassed shakes of the head in reply. The officer, whose name Jean did not know, stepped up on the small stone wall that surrounded the fountain in the center of the square. He read, in Walloon (for what good were reprisals if the people did not understand the reason?), the names of those who would be executed as payment for the assassinations of the three German soldiers. Jean was stunned to hear the name of the village Burghermaster, Jauquet, among the condemned, as well as a woman's name, Emilie Boccart. Several women in the crowd screamed and began to claw their way forward, but were held back by their neighbors, who knew that to confront the Gestapo was to invite a certain death for oneself. Jean watched as two Belgians led an elderly woman, who seemed overcome, quickly from the square.

The ten prisoners were led out, hatless and coatless, their hands tied behind their backs. Most of the prisoners had been beaten, and some had bloodstains on their clothes. The sun, slanting into the square and into the eyes of the condemned, harshly illuminated the black and purple swellings on the faces. Monsieur Balle, who looked to Jean odd and somehow naked without his spectacles and beret, had to be carried under the arms by two guards. The mother of one of the men rushed forward, screaming, to embrace her son. A guard hastily beat her back with his machine gun. She grasped the arm of another woman, then half fell, half staggered, to the cobblestones.

Jean picked up his pencil and tried to record the names of the ten condemned prisoners in his notebook: Sylvain Jacquemart, Emilie Boccart, Philippe Jauquet, Léon Balle, Roger Doumont . . . But Jean's hand began to shake so badly his penmanship became nearly illegible. Looking down at his violently shaking hand, the boy was suddenly afraid he might drop the pencil altogether, that it would slip through the pillars of the balustrade and clatter to the cobblestones, giving away his perch and catching the eye of one of the two dozen sentries surrounding the crowd with machine guns at the ready. Carefully, he put the pencil and notebook down, then slowly rose once more to peer around the wall.

The ten condemned were led to the stepladders, ordered to climb the steps. Monsieur Balle presented a problem, however, as he could not stand on his own. He was hoisted up the stepladder by an irritated guard, who held him in place like a marionette. The boy's eyes widened in disbelief as he saw that Jacquemart, in a bizarre twist of fate, would be hanged from his own balcony.

Father Guillaume, his broad priest's hat hiding his face, the skirts of his long robes sweeping over the cobblestones, stood before each of the condemned and made the sign of the cross. Only Balle, though he could not stand, summoned the will to resist this tainted blessing and spat at the priest.

At a signal from the officer in charge, sentries mounted each stepladder to place the nooses around the necks of the prisoners. Each guard then descended the stepladder and retrieved his machine gun. Jacquemart was looking for his wife in the crowd and calling her name; Doumont and Jauquet had their heads bent. Léon Balle was held up only by the noose itself. He seemed already to have lost consciousness. Emilie Boccart, startling the crowd, called out in her raspy voice, *Vive la Belgique!* The officer gave a command. At the signal, each guard jerked away a stepladder. There were gasps and wails from the villagers. The nine men and one woman were simultaneously hanged.

Jean watched as several of the bodies twisted and twitched. Shit ran down the trouser leg of Jacquemart and soiled his sock and shoe. Jean felt light-headed; he was certain he would be sick. The men who continued to twitch were beaten with machine guns by the guards. Jauquet's guard, infuriated by the Burghermaster's refusal to die quickly, sprayed the man with a burst of bullets, nearly severing the body.

The world, which for Jean Benoît had always held its share of treachery, now spun out of control beneath him. He fainted to the cold floor of the covered walkway, bruising his face in the fall, and dislodging a small brick that clattered onto the cobblestones.

A silence had settled over the house and, perhaps, she thought, the entire village. It was the deep hush of a heavy snowfall, a snowfall such as she had sometimes experienced as a girl in the Ardennes. Once, on a holiday, her father borrowed two pairs of skis, and together she and her father made long trails in the snowy woods.

The silence seemed so profound that even the usual ghosts

were silent tonight: She could not summon the voices of the young men and the old women who had stayed in her attic, could no longer hear Madame Rosenthal calling for her lost husband.

Henri had been gone — how long? Eight, nine hours? Was it two in the morning? Three? She had no idea. There was still moonlight through the window, but it told her nothing. Was it possible, she asked herself, that she would never see Henri again? She tried to absorb that fact, feel it, but the blanket of silence had enveloped and cocooned her as well.

Earlier, after Henri had gone, Claire had gotten up from the bed, washed herself and fixed her clothes, and prepared, as she knew she must, an evening meal for the pilot. It was much the same meal as before — the bread and cheese and terrible coffee — and she found herself longing for a piece of fruit, an apple or a pear or, more exotic, an orange or a mango. When she took the tray up to the pilot, he accepted it, but for the first time since he had regained consciousness, he would not meet her eyes. He announced that he would eat the meal in the kitchen — with or without her help, with or without her permission. Normally, she'd have protested: Of all the days or nights to be outside the hiding place, surely this was the most risky. But she no longer felt the desire or the strength to resist him.

She helped the pilot to crawl out of the attic and, once in the bedroom, to stand. He used the armoire and her shoulder to brace himself, and he stood carefully, in increments, as might an old man getting up from a chair. His head grazed the slanted ceiling, and the top of her own head barely reached the collar of his shirt. His features had altered as well since she had seen him last — or rather, she thought, her perception of his features. His eyes were more deep-set than she'd thought them before, the shape of his mouth more distinct and pronounced: the straight lower lip, the full and curved upper lip. He bore the beginnings of a mustache and beard, and with his longish hair, needing a wash and combed with the fingers behind his ears, and his ill-fitting civilian clothes, he looked not like an American aviator, but rather more like a laborer. His right leg had atrophied — she had seen and bathed the pale shin — and he could barely put his weight on it. He worked his way to the top of the stairs and, using the bannister, he hopped down the first step. She realized then the distance he had already put between them: He did not want her help.

She followed him down the stairs — he hopping on the good leg, resting all his weight on the bannister. In the kitchen, she gathered a towel, Henri's razor, and a basin, and set them by the stove. She boiled water, and from the deepest recesses of a drawer in the cupboard, she collected a parcel: clean, newly tailored clothes that had been made for his escape. She put them on the table.

She left him alone then and went up to the bedroom. She removed all the bedding from the attic, swept and cleaned the tiny area, lay clean bedding on the floor, and replaced the photograph of the pilot's fiancée and the book of English poetry. Leaving the door to the attic ajar, she opened the two windows in the bedroom. The room filled immediately with cold, clean air that she hoped would wash out the stale air of the attic as well.

When all of these tasks had been accomplished, and she thought she had given the American enough time, she carried the old bedding down to the kitchen. There she found the pilot, his hair still wet, his face newly shaved, sitting at the kitchen table. The trousers that had been made for him nearly hid the bandaged calf. The cotton shirt, collarless as yet, was opened two or three buttons at the neck. He sat with one leg draped over the other, one arm resting on the table. She paused at the doorway. He no longer looked like a laborer. With his thumbnail, he was tracing the grooves on the old oak table.

He heard her and looked up. He met her eyes for the first time that evening.

"Is your husband all right?" he asked.

She dropped the bedding into the laundry basket. "He is going into the hiding," she said.

There was a long silence between them as she stood near one end of the table.

"And you'd have gone with him if it hadn't been for me," he said.

"No. Is safer for me here. If I go with him, I am a" — she searched for the word — "heavier package?"

"I doubt it," he said, turning away. "Anyway, I'll be leaving tomorrow. I'll need a warm coat if you can spare it."

"No," she said quickly. "You cannot be leaving this house until the escape is made ready. And it will not be tomorrow or the next day or the next day. Is for my safety, too, that you are remaining here."

"Well, we'll see," he said quietly.

"Your dinner is growing old on the floor upstairs."

"I'm not hungry." He turned his face back toward her. He smiled slightly. "But I'd love a cigarette."

She sighed. "My cigarettes are finished."

She thought for a minute, then took her coat from the hook.

"Where are you going?" he asked.

"I have something," she said.

The night air was frigid and hurt her chest. She was glad, however, to be beyond the American's gaze. She had felt herself to be shy in front of him and was angry with herself for succumbing to shyness. It was evident the pilot had overheard Henri in the bedroom, heard the awful coughs of the crying, perhaps even the gruff sounds of the lovemaking. Yet that was not the word, she knew, for what had passed between Henri and herself in the bedroom. It had possibly been an act of love on her part, or more precisely an act of generosity, but for Henri it was a necessary act to forget what he had seen, to move beyond what he had seen. She thought of the way an animal shook another in its teeth; the way a cat, in a sudden burst of animal frenzy, climbed the bark of a tree.

The moon was rising and luminous. Her father had said that under certain moons one could read a newspaper at midnight. When she reached the barn, she left the wide door open so that she could see her way. She found what she had come for in the wooden boxes. She took three brown glass bottles — all she could easily carry on her own.

On her way back to the kitchen, she was alarmed by the thin threads of light around the edges of the blackout curtains. Once inside, after she had taken off her coat and set the bottles down, she switched off the light, fumbled in the dark for the curtains and drew them open. A rectangle of blue light fell across the floor and the table. "We are being safer when I am turning out the light," she said. "The moon is very much bright tonight, and we will be able to see."

She handed a bottle to the pilot.

"Is beer my husband is making. Is for me" — she made a gesture with her hand — "very strong. Is better with the cheese and bread."

She went upstairs to retrieve the tray of food, and when she'd returned, the American had removed the wire fasteners and corks of two of the bottles. She placed the bread and cheese on the table, tore the bread into four pieces, cut slices from the cheese. She felt safer, more comfortable, in the relative darkness of the kitchen. It was difficult to see the American's eyes now, even more difficult to see if he was watching her. She brought two glasses to the table, but he ignored his and drank straight from the bottle. She poured herself a glass of the dark beer, waited for the foam to subside.

"Very good," he said, raising the bottle.

"Yes."

He ate from the tray of cheese and bread. The moonlight, in its way, made the American seem blue, translucent. She was hungry herself, ate from the tray as well and took a swallow of beer.

"I think you have a radio, don't you?"

The question surprised her. Perhaps he had heard the radio on other nights, through the floorboards. "Yes, I have it," she said.

"Can we listen to it?"

She thought for a while. His voice was rich and easy, and had a kind of lilt. Though the accent was different, it was not unlike that of a Welsh flyer she'd once sheltered. It would be risky to listen to the radio with the Gestapo in the village. But perhaps they could if they kept the sound low; and perhaps just for a minute or two.

She got up from the table, worked the bricks loose. She brought the large, heavy radio to the table and set it down. She unwound the thick brown cord and plugged the radio in. When she turned it on, the sudden static shocked her, and she quickly turned down the volume. Unable to read the tiny dial in the moonlight, she turned it slowly through a variety of languages: Parisian French, Walloon French, which was her own tongue, Flemish, Dutch, German, Danish. Then the BBC in English. She sat down and inclined her head toward the radio.

They listened intently. The Germans, besieged at Stalingrad, were ignoring an appeal to surrender. A busload of children, being taken to the English countryside from London in order to escape the bombs there, had overturned into a ditch just outside Oxford. Then, seemingly in a non sequitur, the BBC announcer spoke about a man who had enjoyed a rabbit, cooked in a red-wine sauce, and who would like to thank his hosts.

"There," she said. "Is the code."

"Code?"

"Sometimes I am listening and writing this down for . . . for others. When the aviators . . . mmmm . . . when the aviators are returning to England from Belgium, from falling from their planes, they are telling their . . . superiors, yes? . . . the name of their last meal with their hosts . . . and this information is being told to the BBC, who say it over the radio — 'The rabbit in the wine tasted good tonight' — and that is how the Maquis are knowing the aviator is making it home."

The pilot pondered this. "So if I were to leave tomorrow and make it back safely, you would one day hear on the radio, 'The beer was heavy and delicious.'"

She smiled.

The announcer stopped talking. A tune was played on the radio.

"Glenn Miller," the pilot said.

They listened to the music in silence. He had sat back in his chair so that his face was in darkness beyond the reach of the moonlight. He drank two bottles of the beer. She drank half of the third bottle. They listened to Aaron Copland and Irving Berlin. Each time he told her, before the announcer did, the name of the song and the composer.

"Do you like to dance?" he asked.

"Is a very long time since I am dancing," she said finally.

"Did you go to dances before the war?"

"Not so many. Once in Charleroi, my husband is taking me to a dance hall, but here in Delahaut? We have the dancing when we have the weddings or the festivals. But you? Do you have the dances?"

"In school," he said. "And there were a few in England at the base. There was one just before Christmas. There was supposed to be another the day after we crashed. New Year's Eve."

"You are missing your plane?"

"The plane? No."

"No, I am meaning, are you missing the flying?"

He took a long swallow, set the bottle on the table. "I suppose I miss flying. I enjoy that. But what we were doing up there" — he gestured toward the ceiling — "that wasn't really flying, at least not to me it wasn't. It was, I don't know, a kind of engineering job. An engineering job under pretty awful conditions."

"Yes."

"When I get back, they'll probably put me in another bomber. Perhaps one day, I'll fly right over here again."

"And not fall."

"And not fall."

"I think you should be preparing yourself for the long waiting. Is probable that the escaping will not be soon. My husband is telling me that. And now is not safe at all for any strangers in Delahaut."

"These reprisals," he said. "What will happen to the villagers who have been taken?"

"I am not knowing this. Is usual in the reprisals . . ." She stopped.

"Go on."

"Is usual in the reprisals, there are the executions."

He made small circles with the bottle on the tabletop. "Have there been reprisals here before?"

"No, not in this village, but in other villages, yes."

"Maybe there won't be executions this time," he said.

She was silent.

He lifted the bottle from the table, held it for a moment, then brought it down hard. She thought that it might break.

He saw that she was watching him. He shifted in his chair.

"You haven't wanted children?" he asked, changing the subject. "I'm sorry, that's none of my business."

"No, is all right. I am not wanting children. Not during the war."

"And after?"

"I am not knowing."

There was an awkward silence between them.

"And you?" she asked finally. "You are being married to the woman in the picture after the war?"

He leaned forward into the light. "I suppose so. That's what we planned. Seems like an awfully long time ago. It bothers me that no one back home knows what has happened. I don't like to think of them worrying."

"When is safe, I will write your fiancée."

"Yes, thank you. Actually, I'd rather you wrote my sister."

"Your sister?"

"Frances, yes. It was she who brought me up, acted as my mother, I mean. I think she'll be worrying the most."

"Then is done," she said. "I will be writing to Frances. Before you are going, you will give to me the address, yes?"

"Yes, of course."

"And when you get safely home, you must write to me to tell me that you are safe, yes? But maybe is not safe to write me here until after the war is over."

He nodded slightly.

She stood up and turned off the radio. She rewound the plug. She listened for sounds outside the house, heard nothing. She carried the heavy radio to its hiding place, carefully replaced the bricks.

"You are finished?" she asked beside him.

"I love your voice," he said. "It's very deep for a woman, but it's beautiful."

She held the bottles in her arms. It didn't matter the language, she thought; there was a line one couldn't cross, and he was straying too close to it. There could be no reply to what he had said. She took the three empty bottles to the pantry.

"The name of your plane . . . ," she said from the pantry.

"*Woman's Home Companion,*" he called in to her.

"On the side of the plane," she said, "is a picture that is making the men laugh, and when I am asking, they are not telling me."

When she returned to the kitchen, the pilot was smiling to himself. "Someday I'll tell you," he said. "But not tonight."

"Before you are leaving?"

"Yes. All right."

She cleaned away all traces of the meal, put the razor and the soap in a drawer, hid the dirty clothes and the towel beneath the bedding in the basket. She scattered the remaining coals in the hearth. She took her coat from the hook, then drew the blackout curtains so that they were in total darkness.

"You do this every night?"

"I am being careful every night, but this night my husband is telling me to be the best careful."

"The coat is . . ."

"So they are thinking I am leaving."

"Have already left. That's why you don't lock the door?"

"Yes."

"And if they come?"

"They are not come."

"Then why . . . ?"

"Is habit."

She stood beside him in the darkness.

"I am putting my hand here," she said, touching him lightly on the elbow. "I am seeing the house even in the dark, yes?"

She guided him through the rooms to the staircase. He felt his way up, maneuvered his way into the bedroom. The moonlight through the open windows gave them some light.

"Chilly in here," he said.

"I am having the windows open before so the air is clean."

He stood over her, a large presence in the small room. He had braced himself with one arm against the slanted ceiling.

"Claire . . ."

Instinctively, she stepped back, felt with her own hand for the post of the footboard of the bed. The bed was now painful to her. Too intimate, too reminiscent of the acts the American had overheard just hours before.

"Claire, you shouldn't put yourself at risk for me," he said.

She shook her head and turned away. She laid her coat over the footboard.

"I am doing this many times," she said as casually as she could, folding and then refolding the coat. "Is nothing."

She watched him turn, move aside the coat hangers, open the false back of the armoire.

When she was certain that the small trapdoor was shut, she walked to the armoire and leaned her head against it.

The beer had made her not sleepy, but rather restless. What sleep she had managed to get since she undressed and slid into the bed was fitful. Her dreams fled behind heavy doors before she could catch them.

Perhaps she was afraid. Alone in this house. She wondered where Henri was at this very moment. Was he cold? Had he eaten? Did he have a bed to sleep in, or was he, too, hiding on the floor of someone's attic? Ought she to have gone with Henri? she asked herself. But wouldn't he be more at risk with a woman in tow?

She pulled the comforters up around her bare shoulders. Henri gave off heat. When he was not in the bed, she needed extra blankets. She thought of Léon with his shattered glasses. Was he dead now? Beaten to death and taken away? What was it like, precisely, to be beaten to death? Which blow actually caused the death, or was it that the whole body, at one particular instant, simply gave up? And what of Thérèse and Emilie? Would they be sent to Ravensbrück, where she had heard they sent the women? No one really seemed to know for certain. If a villager was taken away, it was never officially stated where he or she had gone. And Claire personally had never heard of anyone returning from the concentration camps. Although if that were true, how then did any of them know there was a Ravensbrück, a Buchenwald, except for the stories that came down the line? There must be paperwork, of course, but the paperwork would not tell the stories she had heard — terrible stories she could barely take in. Being sent east to Germany was to be sent into a fog, a terrible, thick fog in which no one was ever recognized and from which no one ever seemed to return.

The fast crunch of tires on the gravel made her sit up quickly in the bed. She felt the tight, unnatural beat of her heart. She heard four doors open, precisely, then the slam of two.

At the first German voice, she catapulted from the bed, drew the covers over the pillow in one swoop, then frantically opened the armoire door. A small cry of panic escaped her. She swept aside the clothes, opened the trapdoor. Abruptly she stepped into the attic, startling the American, who sat up. She put a finger to her lips. His face showed his confusion, as if he thought he was still dreaming. She heard footsteps on the gravel, a knock, a shout in German. Sickeningly, she realized she had left the coat still folded at the foot of the bed. Scrambling in her nightgown, she crawled through the armoire into the bedroom, seized the coat, dragged it to the crawl space, hurled it inside. He pulled the armoire door shut, rearranged the hangers. She heard footsteps in the kitchen now — a murmur of voices, of commands.

He stepped back into the attic room, silently shut the false door. He lay down, rolled onto his back. Claire, sitting against the wall, had her fist to her mouth. She and the pilot watched each other as they listened to the raid outside their hiding place.

She closed her eyes only once — when she heard the first footsteps on the stairs. The Gestapo were making no attempt at stealth — their boots were rapid on the stairs, as if they were running. She heard one man, then another, in the bedroom. A *whomp* as something hard smacked down on the bed. The whoosh of comforters and sheets being thrown back. If they felt the sheets, she thought, they would know. A dresser drawer wrenched open. Clothes flung to the floor. She heard the clatter of her rosary beads. A man on his knees, shuffling — peering under the bed? Then another was at the armoire, his boots not two feet away through the wall from the pilot's head. Claire heard the opening of the door, the sweeping of linens and garments to the floor, the poke of metal on wood, testing it. If the man saw, in the shadows of the armoire, the demarcations of the false back, Claire and the American would be found within seconds.

A tired voice. From the other, a note of weariness and frustration. The two voices sounded surprisingly young, not boys exactly, but young men nevertheless. She heard the bed creaking as if a man had just sat on it. A joke about falling asleep. A gruff voice from below with a question. A quick submissive answer. Again, the creaking of the bed as a man stood up. The retreat of boots. She waited. Only one pair of footfalls down the stairs. Why was the other man not descending as well? Was he looking for something? Could he see, from the head of the stairs, the outline of the attic door in the sliver of space behind the wardrobe? She heard the boots return to the bedroom, bit her knuckles hard to keep from making a sound. The man picked up an item of clothing from the floor. She could hear the swish of fabric — a faint and silken sound. Perhaps it was a slip, she thought, or her dressing gown. She did not hear the garment drop to the floor. Finally, footfalls on the stairs.

The American raised his head a fraction. She put a finger to her lips, left it there. He studied her face. A chair scraped in the kitchen. Water ran at the pump. The tread of boot heels on the stone. She heard the distinctive sound of a man pissing into a metal pot. Then the rattle of the glass panel in the kitchen door as it was shut to. She counted carefully now. Two car doors opened; four closed. Unless they were trying to trick her, they had not left anyone behind.

Again, the crunch of tires on gravel.

She dropped her head and rested it on her knees. She hugged her legs.

"There were four of them?"

"Yes."

"They've gone?"

"Yes."

"You're positive?"

"No."

"They were Gestapo?"

"Yes."

"How can you tell?"

"Only the Germans have automobiles."

"What did they say?"

"I am not hearing all of it."

"Anything?"

"They are saying I might be in hiding with Henri."

"And?"

"One of them is saying he wants to climb into my bed."

"That was when they were laughing?"

"Yes."

"Will they come back?"

"Is possible."

"Should we leave? Get out of here?"

"No."

"Why not?"

"Is safer here."

"Are you all right?"

"Yes."

"You're trembling."

"Is cold."

"Here, put your coat around you."

She looked up. He was sitting, holding her coat open for her. She slid one arm into a cool sleeve, wrapped the coat around her nightgown, slipped the other arm in. She tugged her hair loose from the collar. His face was very near to hers.

"Stay inside here," he said, putting a hand on her shoulder. "Sleep here. They might come back."

"I cannot do this. Is not right."

"What's right is for you to be careful. Listen to me. You might not be so lucky next time."

She thought about that. If she hadn't already been awake, would she have heard the car as soon as she did? *Could* she have reacted as quickly?

"I am just sitting here for a while. But you sleep."

"Maybe we should sleep in shifts."

She tilted her head. "I am not understanding you."

"Taking turns. I sleep for a while. Then I wake you and you sleep for a while."

She pondered this. "Yes, all right. You are sleeping first."

He shook his head. "Claire, I've been doing nothing *but* sleeping for days. Let's exchange places. You lie down, and I'll keep watch. If I hear anything, I'll wake you."

She looked at him a long time. When he had gone to bed, he had taken his trousers off and folded them in the corner. Now he reached for them, awkwardly maneuvered each foot into the pant legs, pulled the trousers up and buttoned them. He moved away from the bedding, closer to the wall, and indicated she should lie down. When she hesitated, he put his hand on her elbow, to guide her.

Wordlessly, she lay down where he had so recently been. The pallet still held his warmth. She let him pull the comforters over her, and with her coat on as well, she no longer felt cold, and her shivering subsided. The linens smelled wonderfully fresh. From a sitting position, he reached over her and opened the attic trapdoor and then the armoire door a half inch.

"What is this?" she asked.

"I always crack the door a bit for air," he said.

She thought about this, her thoughts floating and not sequential.

"Then you are hearing me in my bedroom," she whispered.

He didn't answer her.

She fell almost at once into a dreamless sleep.

———◦———

There was a stillness in her sleep, and he thought of this stillness as a kind of innocence. He had been watching her for hours. When the moon set, the outline of her face was barely discernible, lost to him. Now, with daybreak approaching, there was the slow seepage of shadowy light into the attic. Her face and mouth were again visible.

Her body was a comma, slightly curled, her hands folded into each other at the bottom of her throat. He sat against the wall, the bad leg outstretched, the good leg bent at the knee, on which he rested his forearm.

The suggestion of innocence had begun, he knew, before the sleeping. It had been there all along in her language — her throaty language with its halting phrases, its ungrammatical sentences, the poetry of her mistakes. Yet her language, he understood, was deceptive, not innocence itself, but an innocent facade. Were he to try to speak in her language, in French, he'd be taken for less than an innocent — an imbecile. And only he knew how deeply uninnocent he was.

Just as she was. He thought of what she had seen, been forced to witness. He thought of the canniness of her judgment, the necessary wisdom of survival. No one in this country, and perhaps in all of Europe — except the smallest of the children — could be counted among the innocent, he thought. Simply to have known what they had been forced to know was already loss of innocence.

He wondered about the boy. The courage of that one particular child. Could he, Ted, at ten or twelve, have accomplished such a rescue, *dared* to attempt such a rescue? He would like to know what had happened to the boy: How would his family have fared in the reprisals? She spoke the word *executions,* and there was no poetic mistake in that word. She had known things from the very beginning, had given them to him sparingly.

He studied her sleeping face. Her hair had fallen across her forehead. Her mouth was slightly open. He had desired her since the first night she brought him to her farmhouse, but he didn't completely understand this desire. Why this woman and not another? The answer couldn't simply be that she and not someone else was here, because there were other women available, in England, when his physical need was keen — and yet he had not then felt such desire, not as he was feeling it now. He knew only that it was a strong, physical attraction, not entirely sexual, a desire to be attached to her, touch her. He desired all of this woman, particularly those aspects of her he didn't even know about yet. It wasn't simply her face, though he understood already he would never tire of her mouth; nor was it merely her body, which he had seen in her nightgown in the candlelight, saw just hours ago through the cotton of a similar nightdress before he offered her the coat. Nor was it only the timbre of her voice, rich and throaty, a voice that sometimes mesmerized him, that he could hear in his mind even now. Nor, even, could it be merely a combination of these physical attributes. (Or could it be? Was it possible that one particular constellation of features produced in another an unavoidable chemistry?) But his desire was more than physical — he understood that already. It embraced what she had not given him yet. He wanted more than just the halting phrases. It was as though he had been teased by the mystery of her language, by the very fact of this barrier, and now was destined to pursue a woman who could never be fully known, and thus would remain forever desirable.

The seeping light brought to the surface, like a photographic image emerging in its emulsion, the outline of Stella and her smile in the wrinkled picture on the floor. He had betrayed his fiancée already, he knew, even though he had not touched this Belgian woman lying beside him. Simply to have admitted to his desire for this woman was to have betrayed Stella.

But he must force himself now to think of Stella — who *was* innocent — and of Henri Daussois as well. And he couldn't think of Henri without hearing the chilling sounds through the wall just hours ago — twelve hours ago? — when Henri and his wife were in the bed. He could not understand the story Henri told, but the meaning of the odd, choking sound and the coughing was unmistakable, as were the other sounds that followed, sounds that he would like to erase forever from his memory.

It was bad enough to think of betraying Stella, but the betrayal of Henri would be even worse. For all that Ted wished that Claire's husband would disappear, the inescapable truth was that Henri Daussois was someone who had helped to save his life and the lives of other airmen, who might even, at that moment, be risking his own life so as not to reveal Ted's whereabouts. To touch Claire, or even to have told her, as he did in the kitchen, that her voice was beautiful, was to have trespassed against her husband

and, indeed, against all the people who had conspired to try to save him.

He looked again at the small space in which he had been hidden for nineteen days. He heard again the German voices, the footsteps just beyond his head. At this moment, this attic was the only world that existed — a world he might be content to remain in forever. She had said *there are no bargains*. And he himself knew that the war itself had changed the rules, twisted them beyond all recognition.

He lowered his knee, shifted his weight slightly. He reached over for the photograph of Stella, tucked it between the pages of the poetry book. He closed the book. He leaned onto his side, propped up on his forearm. His face was inches from Claire's. He studied her face, the shape of her head. With his finger, he traced the unusual outline of her mouth. The touch wakened her, and she opened her eyes. He put a finger to her lips — an echo of the warning she had made to him twice before.

She looked at him, didn't move.

"Do you understand?" he asked.

She hesitated, then nodded slightly.

He bent and put his lips to the skin of her throat. He rested his face there, inhaling her. Moving his arm, he reached for her hair, her heavy, dark blond hair, and, as he had wanted to do for so long, he lost his hand inside its weight. After a time, he sensed a small movement, then felt her fingers at the back of his neck.

He sat up then and opened her coat. He lifted a strap of her nightgown away from her skin. In doing so, he felt a strange mixture of peace and excitement. He had then an image of the hallucination he had experienced in the woods. He was on his knees, and he was unwinding a woman.

February 8, 1944

H‌E PEERED THROUGH THE GLASS, UNFASTENED THE
metal rod, and opened the window. Though the air was still cool,
he could smell the earth. He remembered spring in Ohio, when
farmers emerged after long winters to till the soil, transforming a
rocky, gray landscape into a rich, humpy black. But this, he knew,
was merely a false spring, a tease. It was still only February.

He made his fiftieth circuit — past the door, rounding the
table by the stove, over by the pump, past the dresser and the coat
pegs, along the other side of the table, and back to the door. He
estimated the circuit at twenty-eight feet. A hundred times, roughly
half a mile. If she didn't return soon, he would start on the stairs.

He had been here more than a month now, twenty days since
the house had been raided by Gestapo. Twenty days since Henri left
and went into hiding with the Maquis. Twenty days that Ted and
Claire had made love. Stopped in his circuit, as he was stopped
every time he thought of them together, he believed he could
remember distinctly every single day of the twenty, every time he
had touched her.

The first was the most tentative, the most chaste, neither
knowing the other. All around them there was a sense of urgency,
as though they might have only that one time, as though any
minute they might be found in their lair. He remembered having
watched her all through the night, waking her with the touch of
his finger outlining her mouth. Oddly, she seemed already to know
that he would touch her. She pulled his neck slightly toward her,

and he knew by that small gesture that they would make love. Beneath the coat, she was wearing the ivory nightgown. He slipped the thin straps from her shoulders and looked at her breasts. She wouldn't touch his clothes (was that because they had once belonged to someone she knew?), and waited for him to half undress himself. He remembered that there was nothing coy or hesitant about her. He kissed her, and he knew he would never forget the relief the kissing brought him. Her skin was smooth — buttery was what he kept thinking — and he felt, under the nightgown, the nightgown raised now to her hips, the wonderful curve of her side, her rib cage to her legs. She never spoke. It had been a long time since he had been with a woman, and he was afraid that he might ruin it for her, but together they had found each other. He recalled the exquisite mix of fear and happiness, an odd sensation he had never experienced before. Just a few hours earlier, they had nearly been caught by the Gestapo. He was never so keenly aware of time as he was that night, of separate minutes, seconds, and all that could be felt during each. Afterward, he didn't want to sleep. He had the sensation that if he did, he might miss something important. He wrapped her again in her coat, a kind of cocoon. Her hair was tangled, and her bare feet protruded from the hem. He held her while she slept. He remembered clearly that when she opened her eyes and saw him with her, she smiled. Before he could speak, she took his hand and, unexpectedly and thrillingly, put her mouth on his fingers. It was the most sexual thing that had ever happened to him, and even now the image had power over him: He couldn't picture her mouth on his fingers without almost immediately wanting to make love to her. As he did then, again, before he himself finally slept.

He had memories now, a hundred memories in twenty days. It seemed extraordinary to him that the happiest days of his life, all twenty of them, had occurred within this house, within this war. He thought it possible these had been Claire's happiest days as well. He knew he made her happy, he was certain of that. Though she seldom spoke to him of what it was they were doing, there was now a contented gesture she made of arching her back, running her fingers up through her hair and shaking it out. Sometimes when she did this, she turned to him and smiled. He loved watching her do this when she was naked, her breasts rising with her arms.

For two days after the Gestapo came, they hid in the attic room, emerging only briefly for necessities. Most of that time he held her against him under the comforters. She seemed to have a great need to sleep. They spoke little, sensing perhaps that this interlude was fragile, and that anything, the wrong word, the wrong memory, might shatter it. On the third day, when they had not eaten in twenty-four hours, he could see that Claire was feeling light-headed, stumbling almost imperceptibly as she got up from the floor to put on her dress. He caught her by the arm. He told her he would go out to get them food and water. She shook her head and asked him, Are you mad?, and said she would go, she'd been planning it. With his leg still a handicap, he could not argue. He remembered the hours she was gone as an agony. Every new sound, every creak in the old farmhouse, made him think they had her. Using the forest route she'd relied on earlier, she had reached Madame Omloop's. She'd returned to the house, finally, with meager rations and horrifying news: Ten villagers had been hanged; thirty-seven had been deported east to prison camps. Many had been beaten, including Jean Benoît, the boy who had found Ted in the woods.

Ted held her as she wept. "I know these people they are hanging," she said quietly. "I am knowing them all my life."

He put his hand at the back of her head and pressed her face into his shoulder. His own anger made his chest tight. He had hated the Nazis, had sometimes been terrified by them in the air. But even then he had not truly understood the ugliness that was at the core of this war. Apart from a brief glimpse of a face behind a cockpit window, he had never really been forced to see the enemy. The planes provided a kind of buffer. It wasn't just the metal; it was the deceptive sense that the air war was a game — a game of skill and wits. He knew pilots who spoke almost reverently about the German aviators with whom they skirmished. In the air, it was easy to be lulled into thinking that like-minded men were fighting with one another. But here, on Belgian soil, in a village where ten innocent hostages had been hanged, there was no buffer, no illusion.

"I think we should get out of here as soon as possible," he said. "I think we should try to get across the border."

She drew away from him, averted her eyes. "No," she said, "is not possible now." She wiped her cheeks with her fingers and shook her hair out. "And also," she said, clearing her throat, "I am hearing that it is not me the Gestapo are wanting. It is Henri. Is better for us if we stay here and are quiet."

He couldn't persuade her, and with his leg still badly weakened he couldn't force her to leave. She was stronger than he was. Even so, it was five days before she dared to venture out again. This time they lay together and talked.

"Do you have other family in Delahaut?" he asked her one morning.

"They are moving just before the war to Charleroi. My mother is frail now, and I am last of eleven babies."

"Eleven children?" In his family, there had only been the three: Frances, Ted, and Matt, and at times that had seemed a lot.

"Yes, is crowded with many children when I am growing up, but some, they are already old and having children of their own and I am aunt to persons who are older than me."

"Complicated."

"In Delahaut, the family is . . . mmm . . . superior? Yes? Family is most important. Our festivals are in the family. And many of us are relations to each other. I am cousin to Henri."

Ted, who had been lying by her side, propped himself up on his elbow. "Cousin? Is that allowed?"

"Is far cousin, so is all right." She looked away from him. She was naked under the comforter. He traced her hairline to her temple, then her ear, trying to think of how to ask this next question casually. He licked the whorls in her ear. In the end, he simply asked it.

"Did you marry Henri for love? Do you love him now?" The words came out more hurried than he had hoped.

She looked back at him. They had never used the word *love*

between them. Once she had said to him that she adored his face. But not love.

"I know from very small child I am marrying Henri. It is not arranged, like in the old days, but is known. So I think that love is not so important in such a marriage, yes?"

He almost smiled. Perhaps he did smile.

"Someday, maybe, my mother is coming to my house and you are meeting her. She is *marraine de guerre*."

"What is that?"

"She is godmother of the war."

"I don't understand."

"My mother, she writes to the Belgian soldiers who are in German prisons because they do not have anyone else to write to them. And when she does, after a time, they fall in love with her, and they are sending her love letters, and she is not young woman, seventy-three. I am loving to read these letters. Very sweet, no?"

They talked about her childhood and his, about his Frances and her mother, about what it was like for him in England, about how she had hoped to go to university. They seldom spoke of the war itself except when it intruded upon them. And after the five days, she had to go out again. They had run out of food and water. That time she came back with the information that the Gestapo had retreated to St. Laurent, the extra reinforcements to Florennes. A strange kind of normalcy, she said, had settled over the village. Even the school had reopened, though she could not imagine how the teachers had managed to remove the bloodstains from the classrooms.

He rounded the corner again, looked out the open window for Claire. He had promised her he would not leave the house. Sometimes at the doorstep she found packages of food: cheese, carrots, onions, sausage, loaves of bread, and other items — a bar of soap, a pair of socks, once even a pack of cigarettes they vowed to ration and then smoked ravenously in one day. These packages, Claire had explained, were offerings from villagers who, though they themselves were not within the Maquis, were nevertheless supportive of the Resistance.

"They know I'm here?" he asked. "That you're hiding me?"

"Yes," she said. "Some."

"And aren't you worried about that? That you might be betrayed?"

"Yes," she said evenly. "I am always worrying about the denunciations. Is every day I am thinking this. But these people who are leaving the packages? I am believing that they are good people and are wanting to help us."

"Why would they do that?" he asked her.

"You don't understand," she said. "The Belgians, we think the Americans are . . . saving us. Are our saviours, no? The French" — she flip-flopped her hand — "maybe they are not so sure, but in Belgium we are sure."

He remembered being confused by this information. "But Claire," he said, "how could you or anyone else possibly think me a saviour when I've been responsible for all these deaths?"

"You are not responsible."

"Of course I am. There must be people in the village who *hate* the day the plane fell. Ten hanged? Thirty-seven deported?"

"You are again not understanding. Sometimes in Belgium we are receiving . . . sometimes the English and American bombs fall on Belgium villages by . . . mmm . . . mistake? Or villages are bombed directly because there is German military base nearly to them, but the Belgians, we are understanding this. Without the aviators, Belgium is not ever returning." Her hand fluttered and trailed away.

Sometimes, within the packages, there were references to Henri: A bridge blown in Florennes; saboteurs at the dam in St. Laurent. There was never any message *from* Henri. Ted watched Claire carefully when she read these bulletins. She translated them for him and explained what they meant, but beyond discussing those few scraps of paper, they never spoke of her husband. Ted assumed that she had made a secret truce within herself, and he could only guess at its price. As for himself, he tried not to think of Henri at all.

In the twenty days, the leg had continued to heal. Twice she had taken him outside at night, when there was no moon, and they walked together from the house to the barn and back again, exhilarating journeys for a man who had been kept in an attic. On the second night they did this, Claire found a message (in a precious tin of cocoa) that said the escape line had been partially blown. Claire was tight-lipped and frightened, and at first Ted didn't understand the full import of the message. That the local section of the main escape route was exposed and Ted would have to wait until another was put together struck him initially and selfishly as a wonderful and miraculous thing. He would be content, he knew, to remain with this woman for months, for years even, and he sometimes allowed himself to invent this as his future. But when she explained to him the significance of a blown line — the denunciations, the arrests, the torture, the further denunciations — he immediately regretted his earlier selfishness and became fearful for Claire. If Claire and Henri were a cog in the escape line, wasn't she, too, at risk of being denounced?

For two days they had hovered near the attic, were cautious in all their movements, listened to every sound outside the house, waiting for another raid. In the subsequent days, however, he noticed that they had become less careful, talking long into the night at the kitchen table, the candle between them. Every evening, they listened to the BBC, a clandestine activity in itself, but even more dangerous since it prevented them from monitoring any unusual sounds outside the house. One night, he made her dance with him, despite his limp, in what he knew would be a comical spectacle had there been anyone to watch them. But it was enough just to hold her in that way and pretend that one day they might dance together in Paris or New York.

"I'm supposed to be teaching you French," she said.

"I'm learning other things," he said.

In the daylight hours, he sometimes read to her from the book of English poetry or told her stories of the war as he had known it in the air. He tried to make these stories amazing or funny to please her and to make her smile. He was sometimes moved by how physically difficult her life was. When they thought it was safe and that the Gestapo were not, after all, watching the farm, he went with her to the barn and helped her with her chores: the milking, feeding the small herd, mucking out after them. Just washing the clothes took her nearly a day. He marveled at the large oak tub with the flame underneath it to boil the water, the wooden T-shaped fixture in the tub with which she agitated the clothes, the way she lay the clothes full of soap on the grass to bleach them in the light, and then rinsed them and pulled them through the wooden wringers. He watched her bake bread every day and was intrigued by the way she sliced the large round loaves: cradling the bread in her arm and slicing toward herself.

And when she was not working or they were not reading or talking or listening to the radio or performing the tasks necessary for their survival, they made love. It pleased him how often they made love, and sometimes it frightened him. It was as though they both knew that what they had could not last. When he touched her, she never demurred, never pulled away from him. She seemed to have the same need as he, a need he did not now think of as physical, or purely physical. He thought of it rather as the desire to be known — the desire to know and to be known by the one person. Sometimes he was truly baffled that the one person should be a Belgian woman who was married to another man, a man critical to his own survival — and yet at other times he made himself believe that their loving was fated, as the fall of the plane itself may have been fated.

Over the pump there was a small mirror in a painted frame (Henri's mirror for shaving, he imagined), and in his circuit, he stopped now to peer into it. He had lost perhaps ten pounds, and his face was too lean, almost hollow. He looked considerably older than he used to. He saw the foreign collar of the cotton shirt and looked down at the clothes he had become accustomed to wearing. His uniform had been burned; his dog tags buried. There was now no trace of Lieutenant Theodore Aidan Brice, except for the creased photograph of Stella, still within the pages of the poetry book. A picture he had not looked at in twenty days. He wondered if there were, in Belgium or France, American aviators who, stripped of their uniforms, had decided to remain missing, who might never emerge, even when the war was over. He thought of his navigator, AWOL in a hotel room in Cambridge. Would it be possible never to return? To meld somehow into a life here, assume a new identity — Pierre, or Jacques, or even Theo? The possibility of anonymity, of assuming another identity entirely, was momentarily delicious, and he toyed with it.

But what then of Stella? Or of Frances?

He heard her bicycle on the gravel.

Her shoulder was just inside the door, and already he had his hand between her coat and her blouse, lifting the coat up and off her shoulder. Balancing on the good leg, he had another hand behind her neck. Impatiently he kissed her mouth, her ears, her hair. The packages she carried made sharp points in his ribs. He pulled away to see her face, and as he did so, he lost his precarious footing and fell with her against the kitchen door. The glass pane rattled so sharply he thought it would break.

"You are surprising me," she said breathlessly.

Her face was flushed, the right side of her lipstick smudged into the corner of her mouth. He took her heavy hair into both hands and raised it up behind her head.

"I worry for you every time you leave," he said.

Her eyes dropped, and he was instantly sorry he had said this, for he had caused the very thing he always hoped to forestall: the inevitable moment of fear or remorse that entered her thoughts and realigned the features of her face, that took away the joy he knew he briefly gave her. She made a small movement with the packages, slipped out from under the fragile hold he had on her hair.

He knew the route Claire had taken to Omloop's, could picture it clearly even though he had never been there, had never even seen the village, except fleetingly from the air. The long dirt road through the woods to the edge of the village, the high walls of the cemetery and the cobblestone alleyways, the village square with its fountain, the shop where Claire purchased food with her stamps, sometimes received messages.

He studied the back of her coat as she took her parcels from the string bag.

Something was wrong.

He could see it: an indefinable stiffness in her movements; just as he could hear, in the hum of an engine, a catch, a misfire.

"What was happening in the village?" he asked, keeping his words as casual as he could.

"Is very . . ." She seemed to be searching for a word. ". . . quiet."

"Something's wrong," he said quickly.

She was silent, methodically removing and unwrapping the parcels from the bag. He stood by the door.

"Claire . . ."

Still she didn't answer him. Turning once, avoiding his eyes, she removed her coat, hung it on its peg. She bent to put the cheese and sausage in the icebox. She lifted a pear, a single pear, from the table.

"Is *poire* . . ."

"Pear."

"Yes."

"Is very rare, from Madame Omloop."

"Claire."

"Is Friday they are taking you."

She was wearing his favorite dress — a brown silklike fabric that drew the eye to her waist. The dress had shoulder pads and narrow sleeves, and the neckline was like that of a blouse, with covered buttons. Her hair had come loose on the right side, the careful roll of dark blond hair sliding lower over her ear.

He closed his eyes.

Friday. Four days away.

"I won't go," he heard himself saying. He had not known until that moment that he would say that.

"They are coming for you in the evening," she said in reply, as if she had not heard him.

"Then you'll go with me." In his stomach, he felt the beginnings of a knot of dread.

"Is not possible."

"You have to come with me," he insisted.

He moved toward her, but she put a hand up.

"Is not possible. I have not the papers."

"Then we'll get you some. If they can — "

"No." She interrupted him. "They will not be making me the

papers. I am waiting here for my husband." She took a step backwards, felt for the table behind her with her hands. "I am waiting here, because if I am leaving, it is the same as to denounce my husband. He is not being able to come out of hiding then. Ever. Not until the war is ending."

He stood motionless by the door. In the harsh light, even from this distance, he could see the fine lines of her face. It occurred to him suddenly that he must memorize this face. The urgency that he felt with her the first time they made love now withered in comparison with the urgency he felt at this moment: four days in which to love this woman.

"I'm not going," he said.

Her face was noncommittal. She had already made her argument. Later, he knew, she would take it up again, make her quiet pronouncements.

He took a step toward her. "When the war is over, you can leave Henri. It will be all right then."

She didn't move.

"You don't love him, do you?"

She raised her head, looked away. She made a small movement with her mouth, a tightening, as if she were biting the inside of her lip, making a decision.

"Is war," she said, turning to face him.

Inexplicably he wanted to kneel.

"Please, we are not speaking of this anymore," she said.

He walked to where she was standing, looped his arms around her. Her hair gave off a rich scent — a combination, he had always thought, of animal and soap.

He closed his eyes. He ran his hands along the length of her back. He had seen the bones there, the run of her vertebrae. He had seen the white skin at the inside of her thighs. He had tasted her — the salt of the skin above her breasts. Hadn't these acts, the most intimate acts of his life, bound them together?

It was the knowing they had only four days that was the worst, he thought. It would have been better to have been taken quickly, even if there were no time for goodbyes. As in death. The worst was *to know* you were going down, he believed, not the act of going down itself. He thought of the gunner who fell out of the sky, hoped the man blacked out as soon as he hit freefall. He thought of the villagers, taken into the square to be hanged. Those moments of anguish. Only a minute, two minutes, to make it right. And the inevitable futility of ever making it right.

Just as this could not be made right.

He wondered what would happen to her after he was gone. He could not imagine now her life here without him. Would she tend to other aviators like himself? Would she return with Henri to their bed?

If only he could persuade her to escape with him.

He heard again her sentence: *I am waiting here for my husband.*

Through the old glass at the far window, he could see the sun on the matted grasses, the spongy soil.

With his right arm, he reached for her coat on the peg, wrapped it around her shoulders. She drew back; there was a look of puzzlement on her face.

———•———

She thought that he might try to walk with her all the way to France. He took her hand, led her out of the kitchen to the barn, then behind the barn into the fields. She knew they were exposed, that he had not, in all the time he had been with her, been as visible as he was now. He limped badly, but she could see that day by day his strength was returning. She suspected that he would have this limp all his life; one leg seemed to be shorter than the other.

They walked slowly without speaking. She knew that what they were doing was madness. At any moment someone might bicycle along the road and see them. With his height, his sand-colored hair, his limp, he would never be mistaken for a Belgian. Yet she could not bring herself to refuse him this walk, just as she could not withdraw her hand from his. For a moment she closed her eyes. Ever since she had seen Madame Omloop and received the message that the escape line had been repaired and that the

American was to be moved on Friday, she had felt light-headed, dizzy. She knew that it was true, that there would not be a reprieve. And it surprised her that that was how she thought of it — a death sentence. Four more days.

He would go, and she would not know what had happened to him. He would be taken across the border, and that night she would not know where he was sleeping. And within days, or even hours, another man or woman would be brought to her to occupy the hiding place. She shook her head quickly. It was not possible that another man would come and sleep where he had slept. Where they had made love.

Sometimes, when she was with him, she prayed that Henri would not come back. She knew she would be damned for such a prayer, but she could not help herself. In all her life, she had not thought that she would love a man in the way that she loved this American. Ted. Such a short, abrupt name. A boy's name. Not a name for a grown man. She thought of the contours of his face above her, his face grown thinner in the days that he had been with her. Would there come a time when she would not be able to remember that face?

She felt the dry, hard skin of his fingertips. Perhaps he *would* take her all the way to France, where she had once imagined there would be color; and if he kept walking, she was not sure now that she would be able to ask him to stop. A wind came up across the fields. It stung her eyes.

"You're shivering," he said.

His face was slightly reddened from the wind. He released her hand and, with his fingers, pushed her hair off her face. She knew that even if a lone cyclist appeared on the distant road, she would not stop him or pull away.

He slid his hands down between her coat and her shoulders. She let herself go — what was there to lose now? He caught her weight at her back and lowered her to the ground. Sharp, dead straw stalks dug into her neck and pricked the back of her head. She was aware of heavy clothes, an awkwardness, of a sharp wind on her thighs. He put his mouth against her ear, pressed her hard. She thought that possibly he was speaking to her, but she wasn't sure. He tried to shield her with Henri's long coat. It was a kind of tent, she thought. She hoped that he would bury her, that he would cover her with himself, that he would stay there with her for days while the clouds moved.

———•———

In the end, she risked the truck. They tried the bicycle, he maneuvering with the one good foot, pulling the pedal up with his toe when he lost his momentum, but the going was slow and cumbersome.

Returning to the house, they had been overtaken by a kind of recklessness. He wanted to go out, he said — just this once, to be with her, however briefly, in a public place. As if there were not a war, and they were just a normal couple. She could not refuse him — his mood was infectious — but she would not go into Delahaut, she told him. If he wanted to venture into a village, she would drive him through the woods to a neighboring town where they would not be as conspicuous as in her own.

Henri's long, threadbare coat made him feel as though he were hiding more than just his nationality; it cloaked him, he felt, in an awkward and unattractive guilt. He wished he had his khakis on. The pallor of his skin and the beret Claire gave him to cover his light hair made him look, he knew, years older than he was. He supposed this was a good thing. Claire sat forward on the torn leather seat, with its tufts of stuffing and wire coils. He liked watching the way the inside of her left knee was exposed under her skirt. A flowered kerchief was poised at the crown of her head and tied hastily around the heavy mass of her hair.

In the woods, the road was uneven and sometimes treacherous. Occasionally the ruts in the road made the cab of the truck bounce violently from side to side; reflexively, Ted put his full weight on his bad leg, and winced. The muscles and tendons were still raw. Even though the day was cold, he couldn't stop himself from rolling down the window. The fresh air was delicious.

"I had a woods like this near my home when I was growing

up," he said when they were well inside the forest. "I used to spend a lot of time there."

"Alone?" she asked. "You are playing?"

"Usually alone. Sometimes with a friend. I had a BB gun — do you know what that is? — and I used to shoot squirrels and then skin them. Pretty awful, now that I think about it. Frances hated it. She used to squeal when I brought the skins back. I was twelve, thirteen maybe."

"I am also," she said. "I am playing in these woods as small child. Very many hours I am alone here. But I am not hunting." She smiled. "I am playing in . . . old stories?"

"Fairy tales?" he asked.

"Yes, fairy tale." She smiled again. "Beautiful stories of princess and bad wolves. You know these stories?"

He loved her smile.

"These stories," she said. "I am never thinking of this before, but is not true, these stories. Yes, there are wolves, and they are eating children and women and men, but the ends are not happy. We cannot tell children these stories now. Is wrong."

"We don't know that yet," he said quietly, looking away from her and out the window.

"But, yes, we are knowing this. The old woman I am telling you they are beating and sending away? Is happy ending for this woman?"

She stopped the truck, the engine still running. "Is there," she said, pointing to her left into the woods.

"What is?" he asked.

"Is there you are found. The boy is telling me."

Ted leaned toward her window, straining to see beyond the fencelike wall of trees. There was a small clearing fifty feet away, where the light seemed slightly brighter.

"I hid underneath a bush," he said. "The boy found me there. He followed my tracks, I suppose. I was delirious. I remember opening my eyes and seeing his face. I had no idea where I was. Not even what country I was in. It's funny. When I was his age, I can remember tracking animals in the woods. Deer. I wonder if he thought it was an adventure. Tracking a soldier."

"I think he is frightened," she said.

"Yes," he said, sitting back.

They emerged from the woods. The road was better here — past fields and some farmhouses.

"Where are we?" he asked.

"The village where I am taking you is Rance. Is not Gestapo in this village now, but still is very dangerous. In Belgium we have the people who are helping the Germans, and we are not certain what persons are good and what are not. Is like the old stories, no? The animal in the sheep's skin?"

"Wolf."

"So you are being very careful and not speaking any word."

"I promise," he said, smiling slightly as if he had been scolded. He reached along the back of the seat, put his hand inside the collar of her coat. He touched the skin at the back of her neck. The gesture caused her kerchief to slip back over her hair. He leaned toward her, kissed the shoulder of her coat. Moving her arm, she gently nudged him away. She stopped the truck for the second time and turned to him.

"We are going back?" she asked.

"No."

"In one hour," she said haltingly, "the village is empty, and there are no people in the café. If we are making this journey, we are making it now, or is . . ." She stopped, searching for a word. ". . . *Fou.*"

"*Fou?*"

"Madness," she said.

He moved his body away from hers, but kept his hand on her sleeve. Anything to be touching her.

Rounding the corner of an alley, poised to enter the village square, Ted had his first misgivings. They had been walking as though Claire were on his arm, as though this were merely a midday stroll, but it was he who leaned his weight on her at each footfall of the bad leg. They were in shadow from a church, and he made her wait. He couldn't tell if she was frightened or not — nothing in her breathing or the touch of her arm betrayed her.

Across the cobblestones of this unfamiliar village was a row of shops with foreign words in beautiful script painted on the glass fronts. To the left was a school, with children's paper snowflakes still taped to paned windows. Just to the right of the shops was the café, where several green metal tables were scattered about near the door. Some of the tables were occupied with pairs of older women and pairs of men. He noticed that there were no couples, nor any young men. He tried to imagine how this café might have looked a few years ago, but this thought, inextricably woven as it was with the possibility of having known Claire before the war, before she married, caused a painful tug inside his chest. Perhaps there'd have been a table of young men and women, drinking red wine, some rowdiness, a few songs badly sung. The café owner himself might have come out and joined the crowd. Someone would be clowning, trying to attract the attention of a certain girl. And he and Claire would be with them or apart, and would be touching, sharing the noon meal.

He took a step forward and kept his face averted when a stranger crossed his path. Even so, in the short journey from the alley across the square to the café, he sensed scrutiny. What was it that gave him away? he wondered. Was it his height? At the table, Claire gestured for him to sit sideways, so that his face was not in full view. He couldn't touch her, or even look at her for very long, and she had told him not to speak. A waiter came to the table as Ted was arranging his leg beneath it. The waiter spoke in rapid French to Claire, who answered him almost curtly. Ted's chair wobbled on uneven legs.

He allowed his eyes to meet hers — that watchful, lovely gray. A gray, he realized, he had seen before: the gray of the sun breaking through a low stratus. Looking past Claire, he noticed at the next table two elderly women dressed nearly identically in black cloth coats, black scarves, and sturdy shoes. Beside them, on the cobblestones, each had a string bag of parcels. One of the women, who had a large and livid bump at the end of her nose, raised her face and caught Ted's eye. Her neck was wattled and fell in a fold above the collar of her coat. Slowly, so as not to appear to be evasive, he slid his eyes from hers and studied the shops opposite. When Ted looked back toward Claire, he observed that the old woman was still looking at him. Worse, she was also talking to her companion.

Ted looked down at the table.

The waiter brought a cup of coffee for Claire, a tall glass of thin beer for Ted. He took a thirsty swallow and set the glass down. "I think we've been seen," he said. "I'm sorry. This was a terrible idea."

She made a small surprised movement with her hand. Her eyes, however, were expressionless.

Ted watched as the two old women gathered their possessions and slowly, leaning for support on the table, rose to a standing position. To his horror, the woman with the bump at the end of her nose approached Claire.

Leaning over Claire's shoulder, the woman in black murmured a few words. Claire kept her eyes focused on Ted and nodded, but said nothing. The woman straightened her back and, with her companion, made her way slowly across the uneven cobblestones. Claire waited until she was gone.

"The woman is wishing me the luck," she said finally in an almost inaudible voice. Ted could hear the quaver in her words. "And to you, she is expressing gratitude."

She took a sip of coffee. Her hand was shaking. His glass was already empty, he realized. He wanted another drink. Badly. How could he have been spotted so quickly?

"We should go," he said urgently.

She shook her head. "No. Is important we sit here calm."

"How can it be so obvious?" he asked. "I felt it all across the square. Is it my height?"

"Yes," she said, considering him for a time. "That and other things I am seeing here and not in the house. See now, you are sitting sideways to the table, and your leg is folded over the other at your knee. Is very . . . elegant? But not so Belgian, I think. And your hands here." She drew a line along one of his fingers with her own. She let her fingertip linger on his hand. "I am loving your hands, but they are not Belgian also." She studied him. "And the sitting. Your back is bent in its chair." She made a curve with her hand. "Relaxed, yes?"

"But not Belgian."

"No, is not even the English. Just the American, I think. Even in the old coat and hat, you are looking American. And is your eyes also. Maybe now I think is your eyes first they are seeing."

"Have you known many Americans?" he asked.

"Only one," she said.

He felt a small worm of jealousy. "Was he a soldier? A pilot?"

She looked away from him. "Is two Americans the Maquis is finding with their parachutes in the north. They are being sent to me, and I am making the room ready. And then there is mistake, and the Americans coming to me are betrayed. One is shot in the head by Germans, and I have never see him. The other one I see. He is shot in leg. Not like you. Here." She pointed to her thigh. "And the bleeding is terrible. And the American is dying that night in my house."

Ted nodded slowly. He let the worm crawl back into its hole.

He turned his head and examined a row of baguettes inside the café window. What if the woman in black was a collaborator? He and Claire might even now be under arrest. The thought of Claire arrested and interrogated made him ill.

"Have you seen many people die?" he asked her.

She took a slow sip of coffee, replaced the cup in its saucer. "Some," she said.

"Three, four years ago, would you have believed this?"

"Believed . . .?"

"This." He gestured to encompass the entire square. "The deaths. The fear. The not knowing if the guy sitting next to you is a traitor or a friend. The fact that one morning you can be talking to a neighbor, and that afternoon she is hanged — for no reason other than that she lived in your village."

"We are knowing this war is coming for many years," she said.

"The unthinkable becomes the thinkable."

"Pardon?"

"One day, getting shot at in a B-17, or watching a friend die, or going without food is no longer the horror it used to be. In a way, it even becomes romantic."

"No," she said, shaking her head firmly. "Is never the romance. We are never forgetting what is for. You, perhaps, you come so far and is not war in America, is hard to know why we are wanting to fight so much."

No, he thought, there wasn't a war *in* America, but Americans were dying all the same. He thought of his gunner — that awful, gaping wound. You could spend the entire war just thinking of that wound. The man's body, the center of the man, gone. And if you were the man's wife and remembered the man's body, how did you stand it?

But of course the wife would never know how her husband had died. She'd be told only that he'd gone quickly and hadn't suffered. If Ted were back in England, he'd be writing the letter himself.

One letter out of thousands.

One story out of thousands.

"I want to ask you a question," he said. "It was a kind of test they put to us in flight training." Her face, he thought as she cocked her head slightly, was intelligent, canny even, but essentially trusting.

"You're driving along a coast road in a jeep. You've got to get your crew to another base in order to fly a mission. It's a narrow road, one lane only, not wide enough for two vehicles. On one side, it's a sheer drop over a cliff. On the other is a solid rock wall."

She nodded.

"You go around a corner, and suddenly you see that a schoolbus full of children is coming right at you. There's no time to stop, and the bus has nowhere to go except through the space where you are. One of you has to go over the cliff."

She nodded again.

"What do you do?" he asked.

She rested her chin on her hand. She seemed to be staring at a point just over his left shoulder. He didn't know if she had entirely understood the question, but just as he was about to repeat it, she answered him.

"Is terrible question," she said, shaking her head. "And is

terrible answer. But I am understanding the answer in the war. The bus is going over the cliff, no?"

"You'd let the children go over the cliff?" he asked, alarmed by her answer.

"The crew is for the war, yes? To fly the planes. And you have job to get crew to planes."

"But what's the point of getting the crew to a plane to go up in the air to theoretically save the lives of people in another country if in the process you kill twenty children?"

"Is obligation," she said. "In war is no choice."

He shook his head slowly, unwilling to concede her point — even though he knew that she, too, was part of a military operation. One with very different equipment and personnel, perhaps, but a military operation all the same.

"I didn't do it," he said. "I couldn't do it. I was supposed to ditch in the Channel, try to make it if I could. But I had two wounded on board, and I couldn't make the decision to kill them outright. As it happened, they died anyway. And a lot more besides."

"Is like the triage," she said quietly. "I am sometimes doing the triage."

As he looked at her, he saw a boy coming from the opposite side of the square on a bicycle. The figure barely registered; but then something, the hand-knit cap perhaps, made Ted turn his head. The boy, sensing this movement, looked at Ted and, with a brief expression of astonishment, recognized the tall stranger in the woolen coat. Possibly the boy's hand came up off the handlebars. The front tire hit an uneven stone. The bicycle stopped short; the boy was catapulted over the handlebars and onto the stone square.

Ted began to rise. Claire, with pressure on his arm, stopped him. Ted watched as Claire ran to the boy. When she lifted the boy's head, Ted could see a bloody scrape on the forehead — but the boy was conscious and able to speak.

Several other people were at Claire's side. With attention now focused on the boy, Ted stood, limped quickly to the side of the café, rounded the corner into a dark alleyway. He flattened his body against the side of the building, raised his head. Above him was a slit of sky, of light.

From somewhere he could hear the drone of a plane. An engine, it seemed to him, was straining. He waited for the plane to cross his narrow window. The engine was in trouble, he decided, listening to its stutter. A bomber. But the plane did not cross his vision, and he could no longer hear it. Some poor son of a bitch lost and going down? Trying to make it to the Channel?

He knew he had to leave her. Now. His presence was for her a death sentence. Twice in ten minutes he had been identified. And even if the two sightings were benign (one, the boy's, he was almost certain of), what of others in the square who might have seen him? A man, perhaps, whom Ted never even noticed?

She would have the truck, but she would search the village first. He had to try to remember the route back to the woods — then head southwest, toward France. With luck, he'd be found again by friendly French or Belgians, sent quickly across the border.

His head hurt from the knowledge that he had to leave her. There was never a future for them together, and she had understood that all along, just as she had known all along that the schoolbus had to go over the cliff. And he was certain they would both go mad if they had to listen to the clock tick away the minutes until Friday. Far better to leave now — swiftly and without words.

He found himself, after wandering alleyways and lanes, at the edge of the village, exposed. Some hundred yards away was the beginning of the wood, a small cottage in between. A dog — a short, fast, yipping terrier — came running from behind the cottage and barked at Ted's heels, creating a sudden commotion in the silence. Frozen, Ted waited for a face at a window, a door opening. But there was nothing; the mutt must be alone. More quickly now, Ted dragged the leg into the forest. He thought that he would give his other leg for another pint of that Belgian beer.

He had been using the sun as an imperfect compass, and was aware that if he didn't make better progress, he'd be spending the night in the wood. He had been avoiding the old logging road, even though the muck and brambles of the wood made the journey difficult, because he knew she would have to stick to the logging road in the truck. But when he saw the road off to the left, he told himself he'd take it for just a few minutes, give the leg a rest.

From the angle of the sun, he estimated the time now at about three o'clock. He realized he couldn't now go back to Claire's even if he wanted to. He had no idea where her house was. With his free hand, he clutched the front of his coat. He wished he'd thought to wear a sweater. As it was, he had on only an open-necked shirt and Henri's inadequate coat. He was aware of a hollow sensation in the wake of the beer without food. He wondered if it would end as it was meant to. With himself crawling under a bush for warmth and dying there.

She would know why he had gone. And if she were in his position, he knew, she'd have done the same. He was sure of that. Always, from the very beginning, she had known that what there was between them was the story of a few days and nights within a larger drama — one over which they had no control. She would go on riding to Madame Omloop's, making the white sausage with no meat, listening to the BBC at night. She would stand at the window as she did, smoking, one arm cradled under her breasts. And himself? America seemed almost incomprehensible, something experienced in a distant childhood. Six months ago he was in Texas, waiting to be sent overseas. Now it seemed that all the important events of his life were behind him.

He rounded a bend and saw the truck, with its mottle of black and rust. It was parked in the middle of the logging road. The engine was not running. There was no one in the cab. Where the hell was she?

He moved as fast as his leg would allow. He called her name once sharply, pulled himself up onto the running board of the passenger side. Startled at the sudden sound, she looked up at him through the window. She had been bent over, her head against the steering wheel. Her face was wet.

He swung open the door, climbed up onto the leather seat,

heard the door close behind him. He reached for her head and kissed her. She could not get her breath. Her hands rose to his face.

"I am so frightened. I cannot find you," she said.

He repeated her name. The Germans or the Belgians would have to shoot him — he would not leave her now. Their embrace, inside the truck, was clumsy, like that of two teenagers. He bent her head into his chest, held her tightly against him. Her hair fell in sheets at the sides of her face, and he remembered this, from the first time he ever saw her. He lifted her chin with his hand and traced the outline of her mouth with his fingertip. Her upper lip was wet. He used his thumb then to wipe away the tears under her eyes, but his hands were dirty from his trek in the woods, and he made half-moon smudges on her cheekbones.

"The boy is all right?" he asked.

She nodded.

"We'll take the truck now," he said. "To France."

She averted her eyes and kissed him. "No," she whispered, sliding off his mouth.

"You know the way. We'll stop at the border. Go on foot."

Another whisper, the same word.

"People in France will hide us. We'll make it to Spain. Gibraltar. Hundreds have done it."

She could no longer say the word to him, but she shook her head. He kissed the top of her head, her hair warm under his mouth. He leaned his head back, closed his eyes. The comfort of holding her was exquisite. He could not imagine now a life without her.

"Claire, listen to me."

She pulled away slightly and turned her head as if to speak to him, and instantly her face changed. He felt the shudder that traveled the length of her body. She was perfectly still, as if she had been shot. She was not even breathing.

He tried to focus on her face. He twisted around to discover what it was she had seen outside the back window.

At the bend in the road, not a hundred feet behind them, was a man. His face was obscured by dirt, his hair grown long over his ears. He was standing with his hands in his pockets, staring at the truck.

"Henri," Claire said.

———◆———

Monsieur Gillian, the owner of the café, had made him put his bicycle in the back of the small van. Jean had protested. He was fine, he said; he could easily walk the bicycle home. But even he, looking at the mangled front wheel, knew that it would be a journey of hours, that it would be long past dark, long past the evening meal, perhaps even near to midnight, before he made it to the farmhouse. He'd had to accept the ride in the van then, his confusion making him nearly mute no matter how much Monsieur Gillian tried to coax him into a bit of conversation.

Everyone, it seemed, knew about the flogging by the Gestapo. Adults were no better than his friends when it came to wanting all the facts, he thought. Even when it was a terrible story, one they knew shamed you or caused you pain, they wanted the details: How had he been discovered? Had he really fainted? Had he tried to flee? How many lashes? Did he still have scars?

Oh, yes, he still had scars, he could tell them. Sometimes in the morning, when he rose from the bed under the eave, he saw thin stripes of blood on the sheets. He would remember the pain then and wonder when the wounds would heal. And then he would turn the sheet over or, if he had time, try to wash out the stains so that his mother would not see.

Madame Daussois had lifted his head from the street. His vision was blurry, and there was blood in his eye. She held his head gently with her hands and, as she was calling for help, turned his face to her chest. The gesture left a bloodstain on the front of her coat.

He was dizzy, disoriented. He tried to tell her once, just before Monsieur Gillian carried him into the café, that he wouldn't tell about the pilot. But she shook her head quickly to silence him.

How fast does such a thing happen? he wondered. He was crossing the square, thinking of beginning the long journey back to school, when the face turned toward him, and he knew at once. It wasn't possible ever to forget those eyes — the green with the light behind them. Were it not for the eyes, he might not have recognized the man. A beret that was too large for him hung over the man's ears. The coat was that of a peasant. When he'd last seen the pilot, near death though he was, he'd been in uniform, and a uniform never failed to convey authority — no matter how torn and dirty that uniform was.

Monsieur Gillian asked him what he had been doing in Rance.

"A parcel, sir. For my aunt."

Monsieur Gillian nodded. The truth was that Jean went there every day now, at the noon hour, unable to bear the sight of the center of Delahaut. He could not look at the balconies of the terraced houses without seeing the faces and twitching bodies of the hanged. He saw this even in his dreams. And he could not enter the square without his eyes being drawn, against his will, to the balconies. It was a kind of self-torture.

So he went to Rance every noon hour, and sometimes was late getting back to school for the afternoon classes. If he didn't go to Rance, he'd bicycle to the woods, or even to St. Laurent, though that was riskier since the Germans were still at L'Hôtel de Ville.

"Here, sir. If you please. I can go the rest."

They were on the road to the Benoît farm. Jean did not want to be seen emerging from the van.

"But you are injured, no? I must take you to your house."

"No, please, it's best here. Please." Jean heard the sudden begging in his voice. So be it. Better to humiliate himself now than to excite his father's anger even more than it would be.

Monsieur Gillian stopped the van. Jean quickly hopped out of the passenger side before Monsieur Gillian changed his mind. Reluctantly, the café owner walked to the back of the van and opened the paneled doors.

"You're sure you don't want me to go in with you, speak to your mother?" Monsieur Gillian offered, as he lifted the bicycle to the ground.

"I am certain. Thank you for the ride."

Monsieur Gillian hesitated, looked puzzled.

"You're all right?" he asked.

Jean nodded, tried to smile.

"You're all right at home, I meant," Monsieur Gillian added.

Jean wondered for a moment if Monsieur Gillian knew about his father. Then, to reassure Monsieur Gillian, Jean nodded eagerly, quickly. He was anxious to be gone now.

"Well then, I'll be off. But I can't say I like this."

The boy watched the café owner climb up into the driver's side, shut the door, and reverse the van into a turn. Jean waited until the van was on its way back to Rance, and then waved. A hand shot out of the window and waved back at him.

Slowly he turned in the direction of his house. It would become visible around the next corner. The wayward front wheel of the bicycle made forward progress impossible. Jean had to lift the front wheel, then guide the back wheel as if it were a unicycle. He was glad now that he'd accepted Monsieur Gillian's offer to drive him home.

She'd put the plaster on his forehead. Monsieur Gillian had given her iodine for the cut. After the forehead was tended to, she'd ordered milk for him and a roll.

"I have to go now," she'd whispered to him when Monsieur Gillian had gone to fetch the milk. "You understand?"

He understood she meant the pilot. She had to go to him. He badly wanted to ask her so many questions: How was the American? How was the wounded leg? Did the American remember the night in the forest and in the barn? When was he leaving? How were they getting him out of the country? But he asked her nothing.

Then she'd done a strange and wonderful thing. She'd bent forward and kissed him. The kiss landed somewhere between his left eye and cheek. His face flushed. She said thank you to him — twice quickly, in a whisper — when it was he, really, he thought, who ought to be thanking her.

He brought a hand up now to touch the place where she had kissed him.

He left the bicycle in the gloomy barn, out of sight. His father would go on about his carelessness when he saw it. Tentatively, he pushed open the kitchen door. His mother, at the sink, had her back to him.

She turned, her eyes widening at the sight of him. And what amazed him, even then, was how her face went from boredom, to surprise, to alarm when she saw the plaster, and then immediately to fear as her eyes darted sideways to the door of the parlor. It meant his father was home. It meant there would have to be questions and explanations — questions that would be confusing and impossible to answer; explanations that would be inadequate no matter how hard he tried, how careful he was. He took a step forward, and she looked at him again. He knew what she was thinking. If only they could hide the plaster.

The smell of cigarette smoke hung in the air. He saw his father in the doorway.

"I fell," the boy said at once. "It was an accident."

His father was unshaven. The man didn't shave but twice a week. He was wearing a grease-stained blue workshirt that opened midchest.

"What accident?"

"On my bicycle. I fell off my bicycle."

His father leaned forward to look out the window. "Where's the bicycle now?"

"In the barn."

"So why aren't you in school? School's not out yet."

"They thought I should come home," he lied.

His father's eyes narrowed. He seemed to smell the lie. He always did. Jean's mother wiped her hands on the dishtowel. She took a step toward him. "I'd better see to that plaster," she said.

"Leave him be."

His mother stopped.

"Where'd you get the plaster?"

Jean hesitated. He'd better leave the school out of this. That was shaky ground. "It was in the square. The accident. And Madame Daussois fixed it."

"Madame Daussois?"

Jean winced, cursing himself silently.

"What were you doing with Madame Daussois?"

"I wasn't exactly. It's just that she ran to me when I fell, and it was she who put the plaster on."

"Madame Daussois was in the square?"

Jean looked down. His mind raced. Where was this going? Where would he trip himself up? How could he have been so foolish as to mention Madame Daussois's name?

His father moved closer to him. Jean could smell once again the stale breath of the drinking.

"Madame Daussois was in the square?" his father repeated more loudly.

"Yes, yes," the boy stammered.

"The square of Delahaut?" His father was almost shouting.

In his thoughts, the boy panicked. He could not mention Rance — he would never be able satisfactorily to explain why he went to Rance. Oh God, why had he mentioned the name Daussois?

Always later, when Jean was alone, he tried to reconstruct the argument, tried to figure out where the trigger was, what it was that had set his father off. But it was like an endlessly repeatable science experiment that never produced the same results.

The hand to the side of his face came sooner than he'd expected. He heard his mother exclaim. He put his hands up over his head. In doing so, he fell back against the wall, couldn't keep his balance, slid to the floor. His father stood over him.

"You think this is a game? You think I don't know what you're doing sniffing around Madame Daussois? You want to be with the Maquis, maybe? The Partisans?"

Jean brought his knees up, sheltered his head with his hands. It was always the same.

His father pointed a finger and shook it. "You want to fight the Germans, do you? You want to be a hero? A Resistance fighter?"

Jean was silent. It was no good shaking his head no. That would only further enflame his father.

"Well, I'll tell you something, you sniveling little shit, you're going to get yourself killed. That's what's going to happen. I ever catch you near the Daussoises' again, I'll beat you to a bloody pulp."

Jean wanted to laugh. If you don't get killed first, I'll kill you. His father kicked him. His father's rages often ended with a kick.

But the toe of his father's boot connected only with the wooden sole of Jean's shoe, and the boy didn't feel the blow. For a minute he was afraid that, having missed, his father would kick him again.

Instead, mercifully, his father went out the kitchen door, slammed it.

Jean brought his hand to his cheek. It was the same cheek she had kissed. He felt the skin with his fingers.

———•———

Claire brought her hand to her mouth. Ted didn't know if the gesture was for having been seen together, or if it was simply horror for the state Henri was in.

Ted thought of the Depression bums and the hoboes who had sometimes come to the back door of the house in Mount Gilead. He remembered how Frances would make cheese sandwiches and wrap them in wax paper and give them to the men who knocked at all hours of the day. It was seldom the same man, but the word seemed to have gone out: You can get a sandwich and a cup of hot coffee in that kitchen. Ted, barely a teenage boy, would watch in fascination, trying to imagine such a life. At the time, the thought of sleeping by the tracks and riding on railroad cars, not knowing one's destination, was a promise of infinite adventure.

Henri had grown a beard. His hair lay in greasy strands across his forehead. His eyes seemed sunken in hollows that might have been caused by grime or by lack of sleep. His trousers were frayed at the hems, and his coat no longer had buttons. His shoes had given out. Ted wondered what had happened to the man. He wondered how he could walk.

Claire got down from the truck, her kerchief untying itself and fluttering to the ground. He watched her walk toward her husband, put a hand on his arm, speak to him. He felt the touch of Claire's hand on her husband's arm like the blow of a baseball bat to his gut. Barely aware of what he was doing, he opened the passenger door of the truck and stumbled down. He walked to the other side of the truck and picked up Claire's scarf. He held it loosely in his fingers, staring at the pattern, as if he had come upon an important artifact and did not know what it meant. Then he folded the scarf and put it in his pocket.

When he looked up, Henri and Claire were approaching him. She was not touching her husband now. Henri studied Ted, then said, remarkably, "Bonjour." He removed from his pocket a crumpled pack of cigarettes, shook one loose, offered it to Ted. Ted, anxious to break the tension, to have something to do, took the proffered cigarette and bent his head as Henri lit a match. The man smelled foul, as if he had not bathed in weeks, and Ted supposed he hadn't. Cupping his hands around the flame in Henri's hand, Ted glanced up at Henri's face. Within the sunken sockets, Henri's gaze was steady — not sullen, not wounded — and yet there was an unmistakable sense of deep exhaustion, an exhaustion that puts a man beyond the range of normal feelings. Henri looked at Ted's face, then examined the length of him to his feet. Claire stood with her hands in the pockets of her coat. She bit the inside of her cheek. Her hair was loose over the shoulders of her coat. Oddly, Henri lit a cigarette for himself, but did not offer one to his wife. Ted watched as Henri put the packet away inside his buttonless coat.

Ted took a long pull, turned his face, and blew the smoke away. He caught Claire's eye as he turned. Henri, who held his cigarette between his thumb and forefinger, took a quick drag, looked again at Ted. Ted left them then and walked to the truck bed. He climbed onto the back, leaned against the metal side. He rested the hand with the cigarette on a raised knee. He smoked quietly, a kind of desperate humming in his ears. What was preventing him from taking Claire, putting her in the truck and heading for France? he asked himself. He wanted to tell Henri the truth of what had passed between himself and Claire, but he couldn't even speak to the man without forcing Claire to translate. It would have been laughable, he thought, if it hadn't been so serious.

But Henri, he realized with a sudden jolt, watching the man walk slowly around the truck bed to the passenger side, already knew. He hadn't needed a translation. It was why he'd offered Ted the cigarette, he thought now; it was the cause of the steady gaze, the cause of the prolonged scrutiny from Ted's face to his feet. It was a curious kind of knowledge on Henri's part, Ted thought, a *knowing* without precisely having been told. A knowing not just of the facts, but of what lay behind the facts. Ted had sometimes seen this on Claire's face as well.

Claire drove. The truck bounced over the ruts while Ted hung on to the side to keep from banging helplessly around the back. At the house, Henri went immediately inside. Ted stood by the rear of the truck, unsure of what to do.

Claire came to speak to him. She glanced briefly at him, looked away.

"I am to go for Dussart," she said. "My husband says you will leave this house tonight."

Ted reached forward, caught the sleeve of her coat.

She shook her head quickly.

He released the sleeve.

Ted did not enter the house. Henri was there, somewhere inside, perhaps washing at the pump, perhaps lying on the bed. The image of the latter made Ted almost ill. Or maybe the man was eating. Ted felt a gnawing at the bottom of his stomach that was distinctly not hunger. He had the sense that he had only minutes left, that something was about to happen to him over which he had no control. In the near dark, he looked down at his hands. They were raw from the cold, and shaking. He remembered the half-moon smudges on her cheekbones.

The sun was just setting across the fields. A wind was blowing, making a faint whistle. For a moment, just before it set, the sun lit up the landscape and turned everything — every tree, every matted piece of straw, the barn, the gray stone of the house — to a pink salmon that seemed to have a life of its own, to imbue the world around him with beauty. The straight furrows of the fields, only minutes ago just barren troughs, were luminous arrows pointing toward the west. A large bird overhead was a black silhouette with a golden wing. Even his hands, which had been a mottled red, seemed now to glow with the pink light. He felt exhilarated by the sudden light. It was an exhilaration he'd sometimes known before — in a Tiger Moth 2,000 feet over East Anglia; at 15,000 feet at dawn, leaving the Channel behind him. It was impossible to believe, at such moments, in the decay of war or in a world that did not contain the possibility of joy. He imagined then the search after the war for Claire, their reunion. He saw this as a certainty. He shut his eyes to contain the vision, to seal it.

When he opened them, the sun, directly west of the house and the stairs on which he sat, sank abruptly — and just as abruptly the pink light was gone. Like a swift cloud, the air around him darkened; color left the landscape. Two bicycles entered the drive, stopped in front of him. An odd-looking man, not much older than a boy, swung a leg over one of the bicycles. Claire dismounted from the other. Ted saw that the man was missing an ear. His name, said Claire, was Dussart. He and Henri were taking Ted that night to meet with two other aviators — not from his own crew, she added quickly; then the three would be transferred to the next stop further down the line. They would leave when it was fully dark, in one hour. Now she would make some food for all of them, she said. She climbed the steps beside Ted. Dussart followed her. She hesitated at the top. She asked Ted to come in to have the meal with Henri and Dussart. Ted shook his head.

For a time he heard muffled sounds emanating through the shut kitchen window. Men speaking. The chink of crockery. He wondered occasionally as he sat on the stoop — shivering badly now from the cold; the beret had been lost in the woods, and he had no gloves — if he ought to go inside, eat the meal that had been offered him. It might be some time before he'd get another. And he wondered, too, if he shouldn't allow himself to watch Claire at the pump and the stove, experience the last few minutes they would have together for some time as well. But the thought of sharing the small room with Henri and the young man with the missing ear stopped him.

He heard the door open. She had her coat on and sat on the step with him. She lay the book between them, the photograph of Stella peeking out of the top. In her hands she held some papers, which she gave to Ted. They were, he saw, his identity cards. He could not read his new name in the darkness.

"I am bringing you these," she said.

He glanced quickly at the book, looked away. He didn't pick it up.

"Has he said anything to you?"

"No."

"I'm sorry."

She nodded.

"He knows, doesn't he?"

She was silent. Again she nodded.

"I love you," he said.

She didn't answer him, and he was momentarily stung by her silence. And then he sensed that she was trying to speak, but couldn't. Was it that she didn't know the precise words, or was it something she simply couldn't say?

He rubbed the toe of his good foot against the hard dirt. She shifted so that she was facing him. He could barely see her in the darkness. She put a hand on the book, and he covered it quickly. Her hand was so warm — his must feel like ice to her, he thought. Neither of them moved. He closed his eyes, concentrated on her hand. He tried to memorize the feel of it — the skin like kid beneath his own. He felt her wedding ring, the hard gold band, left it alone. He felt the tips of her fingers, the short slices of nails.

They heard voices just beyond the door.

"*Non,*" she said quickly, with a kind of strangled cry. She pressed her forehead to his face — a frantic gesture. "I am . . . ," she began, then was stopped.

The door opened noisily, shut against its frame. Henri, after bathing, looked a different man. Claire withdrew her hand and stood up. Ted did likewise. He looked for her face in the darkness. What had she been about to say? *I am . . . loving you? I am . . . afraid?*

Henri spoke to his wife.

Claire put her hands in the pockets of her coat. She said: "They are taking you now. My husband is telling me you are walking between them, and when is time, my husband will say to you *courage. . . .*" She turned to Henri. "*Courage?*" she asked. He nodded. She looked back at Ted. "He will say *courage*, which is to you courage, and you are then walking forward alone to the automobile which will be there. They are not walking with you, because they are not wanting to see the faces of the persons in the next cell, yes?"

Dussart and Henri walked a few feet away and stood waiting for Ted.

He tried to say, "I want to thank you," which was true, and which he could say to Claire in front of Henri and Dussart, but his voice left him. He felt a hand on his arm. She kissed him once on each cheek. She said quietly into his ear, "I am remembering you." He felt her hand linger on his arm. And then the touch was gone.

Ted watched the door close behind her.

He thought then that it was the hardest thing he'd ever done — harder even than the belly landing in the pasture, which had brought him to this place. He looked toward Henri and Dussart. Henri's eyes slid away from Ted's. He realized then, with the shiver of an absolute truth, that not only had Henri known about himself and Claire, but the whole village had also known. The affair, the allowance of the affair, had been a gift to him and to Claire. To him because he was the American. To Claire because she was Resistance.

The wind blew up, and his eyes stung. He shoved the documents into his pocket and felt Claire's scarf. He left the book and the picture on the step where she had put them.

They walked for what seemed like hours, but what must have been, Ted calculated reasonably, not more than forty minutes. It was his leg that distorted time — that and the distance he was creating with each step between himself and Claire. *I am remembering you*, she said. Her throaty, low voice had lodged somewhere deep within him. He knew he would always be able to hear her.

But there was so much he would never know. A year from now, would she think of him? Would she one day have a child, two children — put the war and himself far behind her? Had she begun that process already to keep from going crazy? *Fou*, she had said. He tried to imagine her as a middle-aged woman, an old woman. Her gray eyes, he was certain, would never change. He tried to picture her with Henri — could not, would not.

They were traveling west. Southwest. Impossible to be sure. Perhaps they were walking all the way to France. The fields in the near-perfect dark were full of ruts and holes. Several times Ted stumbled, caught his balance. Occasionally, there were night sounds — the low calls of unfamiliar birds, a sense of creatures scurrying beside him. He began to imagine a small smile of satisfaction on Henri's face as the man took the American aviator farther and farther away from the Belgian farmhouse. Yet Henri too, he thought, had to be nearly comatose with exhaustion. Only Dussart, who had tried unsuccessfully to engage Henri in conversation, whistled tunes from time to time. He wondered why Henri would not chat with Dussart. Was there a kind of hierarchy within the Resistance that did not permit fraternization? Or did they simply have nothing in common except this mission?

The first signal was so brief, Ted thought it was a spot of light the eye had produced, the way straining into cloud could create tiny bright stars. But the second was unmistakable. The flash of a torch in a horizontal line, held at the height of a man's waist. A sole tree intersected the light at each pass. In the brief swathes of the signals, Ted could see finally the lay of the land — the hard furrows, the jutting pieces of straw.

Dussart murmured something to Henri, who answered him. Henri briefly put an arm in front of Ted, slowing his forward progress. They proceeded more cautiously now, inching toward the torch. Fifty feet from the source of the light, Henri called out a name or a word — Ted wasn't sure. A man answered briefly. Henri motioned for Ted to stop. The torch now swung away, cast a swift streak of light across a small, colorless car with a high roof. Dussart, in a quick anxious whisper, asked Henri a question. Henri answered curtly, dismissively. Dussart began to protest. Henri cut him off. In his ears, Ted felt again the desperate drumming. Beside him, Henri was removing an object from his pocket. The object crinkled faintly in the silence. Ted thought it must be cigarettes, and that Henri would offer him one before sending him off to

France. Instead Henri reached for Ted's wrist, placed the object in Ted's palm. The object was flat and thin, wrapped in paper.

"*Chocolat,*" Henri whispered beside him.

Confused, Ted held the bar of chocolate. What was it for?

Then Henri said distinctly the one anticipated word: "*Courage.*"

The shaft of light now made small circles on the ground, a continuous circle toward which Ted had to walk. Where would Claire be now? he wondered. Sitting at the table in the kitchen? Lying in her bed, listening to the night? Henri said again, in a low voice, the single word: "*Courage.*" Ted took a step forward, hesitated, took another. Where were the other aviators? He felt his way over the uneven terrain. Behind him, to his surprise, he heard the sound of retreating footsteps. Ted whirled around, wanted to call out to the fleeing figures. Why were they leaving him so soon? There were so many questions to ask. In the distance he could hear a dog barking. He turned back to look at the spot where the colorless car must still be. The car was his promise of freedom, wasn't it? The promise of a life as it was meant to be lived, on familiar soil? He laughed once in the dark. He looked at the steady movement of an unknown arm — the continuous circle of light on the dark ground. There was nowhere else to go.

April 5, 1944

WHEN SHE PRESSED HER HAND TO THE STONE, THE palm came away wet. Sometimes she thought she could hear the water running down the walls.

A tiny rectangle, the size of a book, had been cut from the stones at the top of the outside wall. She sat on the hinged board that passed for a bed, wrapped her arms about her, and watched the dawn begin to illuminate the cell. She thought the light through the rectangle was different with each passing day — stronger, brighter — and that she could see a hint of color now: the fuzzy, yellow-pear of leaf buds. In the distance, as always, she heard the traffic of Antwerp, as people, miraculously, went about their business, unaware of or indifferent to the activities within these walls.

She heard the outer door to the corridor open noisily and then shut. There was the smart tread of boot heels, two pairs, and the slough of a body along the stone floor. At the sound of the boot heels, the women in the other cells started screaming — screams that were angry, or near madness, or simply trying to attract the attention of the guards. The metallic clatter of keys echoed throughout the block, and beyond the door a woman coughed. There was a sudden harsh light. They brought Odette into the cell.

Claire knelt, lifted the woman's head. Odette appeared to be still unconscious. She coughed once, and a quantity of blood spilled out onto her dirty shift.

Bastards, Claire whispered.

As gently as she could, for she did not know as yet what

Anita Shreve

damage might have been done, she rolled the woman onto a blanket on the stone floor. She would have preferred to lift her onto the hinged bed, but until she regained consciousness that would be impossible.

In the dim light, Claire tried to inspect Odette's body. There were bruises upon bruises now. The mouth was badly cut; Claire put her fingers inside to feel for loose teeth. The woman, who had been rounded up in the raids on Louvain, had been with her for four days now. As best as Claire could tell, Odette had been a courier within the Partisans. She was only eighteen years old.

Odette coughed again, struggled, tried to sit up. Claire put a hand on her chest, pressed her down. "You're safe now. I'm here. Just rest."

"Why are they Belgians?" the young woman from Louvain asked in a hoarse whisper.

That their torturers and interrogators were all Belgians had bewildered Claire, too. She had seen some of this in Delahaut — men who were willing collaborators; women who went with the German soldiers — but she had never seen anything like the insidious brutality that existed within these walls. Perhaps they did it for food and money, or out of fear of being beaten themselves. Many of the guards, she had discovered, were street criminals who'd been let go. Political prisoners were the maggots at the bottom of the pile — of lower status than even thieves and murderers.

Claire supposed that she herself should feel fortunate that her own beatings had not produced as much damage as was apparent on the young woman from Louvain. Claire had suffered several broken ribs, and she was now deaf in one ear, but she was still alive and had not vomited blood. The circular trap slid open. Claire lay Odette's head down on the blanket, went to collect the two cups of cold broth and the two slices of black bread from the tray. She set the food down beside her cellmate.

"Can you eat anything?" Claire asked.

The woman from Louvain shook her head. "But you take mine," she said. "Don't let it go to waste."

Claire carefully pulled her to the wall, propped her into a half-sitting position. She was afraid the woman might choke and drown if she lay on the cold floor much longer. She brought a washrag to the woman's face, wiped off the sweat and dirt there.

"What, what have they done to you?" Claire asked angrily.

Odette shook her head from side to side.

Beside her, Claire raised the tin cup to her own mouth. The broth smelled foul. As always, it was some form of cabbage soup, but other ingredients — chewy, unrecognizable items — were sometimes added. She forced herself to drink the liquid. She was afraid to give Odette anything to eat while the woman was coughing blood; yet Claire knew that if the woman did not eat even the foul rations they were given, she would lose what little strength she still had.

When Claire had finished the broth and bread, she leaned against the wall and held the woman's hand. Her own chest hurt. With her fingers, she massaged her rib cage, where the bones were knitting themselves together without having been properly set. She had not seen a doctor since entering the prison. Her thighs, beneath her thin shift, were only loose skin over bone. Her breasts still swelled slightly, and there was the small round abdomen, but the rest of her was shrinking. She wondered dispassionately — scientifically — if the body of a starving mother would die before the fetus inside her; or if the baby would die first, and then the mother later.

She felt the stiff tufts of Odette's hair. They had hacked off her own, too, and she was glad of this. In the beginning, they had yanked and dragged her by the hair so forcefully she was afraid they'd snap her neck. Now her hair stood out from her scalp in uneven, ragged bits. Bathing with the tiny square washrags and with the small ration of water they were given was difficult. She knew she smelled, as did the woman beside her. She wondered how the guards could stand it: all these foul and retching women; all these screaming women day and night. Perhaps it was a kind of punishment for the guards. She fervently hoped so.

Today they were taking her east to Ravensbrück, but they wouldn't tell her why. The interrogations and the beatings had stopped some weeks ago, and there had been no explanation for that either. Since she had been in the Old Antwerp Prison, she had heard terrible stories about Ravensbrück, but it was hard for her to imagine it could be worse than what she was living through. In any event, she reasoned, they were bound to see daylight on the journey, either en route or when they got there. She badly needed to see the light.

Odette started forward. She seemed to be trying to flee. Claire restrained her, held her arms. "It's all right. You're with me. You're safe now."

The young woman, Claire knew, was terrified of the beatings. There was no respite: When you slept, you had them in your dreams. The first days were the worst.

"Did they tie you to a chair?" the woman asked. Her voice wasn't much above a whisper.

"Yes."

"And they beat you then?"

"Yes."

"No matter how you answered the questions?"

"Yes."

"Why are they still doing this? I've given them all the names."

"I don't know."

They had come for Claire near dawn. SD officers in black coats and peaked caps. A Wehrmacht truck outside. She'd fallen asleep at the kitchen table, and when they broke the door, bellowing loudly in her ears and dragging her across the floor by her hair, there'd been no thought of escape. No thought at all, so great was her disorientation. They shouted questions at her incessantly, toppled tins from their shelves. They kicked her out the door so that she fell onto the dirt. They shoved her into a truck. A convoy to Antwerp. Inside were other villagers, their heads bent, some clutching children. Some weeping. No one dared to speak to her.

That night, when Henri and Dussart had taken Ted, she had sat at the kitchen table, wrapped her arms around herself and finally wept. The unthinkable becomes the thinkable, he'd said. She'd sent the American pilot away as she'd known she must. She did it with her silence.

She remembered walking toward Henri from the truck in a kind of stumbling trance. She'd thought, even before she reached her husband: I'll tell him now. But when she stood in front of Henri, and put her hand on his arm, she'd looked into his eyes. There was something different there. It was Henri, and yet it was not the Henri she had known. And then she'd been frightened.

It was over then, she thought.

He promised her they would get the American out at once. She was urgent, frantic. It had already been arranged, he said. He just needed Dussart. They must not find the American with them, she said to her husband, when what she really meant was: They must not find the American at all.

Ted.

She thought of the color of his eyes, that shimmery green. She thought of the way the small of his back never touched a chair. She remembered his smile and could hear his voice, but she could no longer remember what it felt like to make love with him. She wondered if, as the flesh left you, the pleasurable sensations of the flesh left you as well. Or if this inability to feel was merely protective. That if you could remember, the memory would be intolerable.

That night, they'd taken her in the truck to Antwerp, where the beatings had begun immediately. When she emerged from the convoy into the light, a guard had hit her ear so hard she spun to the ground. She'd been dragged into the prison, where the new arrivals all stood in two lines facing each other — men on one side, women on the other. An officer told them all to undress right there. The shame of that moment still haunted her, despite all that had happened since then.

The days that followed seemed to have no sequence. Fifty days, sixty days — even now she couldn't be sure. No one knew precisely the date. Some thought it March; others thought it already April. In the corridors, with the screams, Claire sometimes heard news: The Partisans in Charleroi had been decimated; the Americans were at Anzio.

At first, there was no night, no day; there were no regular

meals and no events that were at all familiar to her. All that she knew was that she was taken to a room, tied to a chair, and asked the same questions, over and over — asked about the same names, over and over. Except for Antoine's name, and Dussart's, Claire did not truthfully know any others. But as the days wore on, as the beatings became more severe, the names blurred together, and sometimes she said yes when yes was not the correct answer, and sometimes she said no, even to her husband's name. She waited for them to say Ted's name, but they never did. She didn't like to think about what that might mean. Had he been caught? Was he dead already? Oddly, through all of this, they did not ask her about anyone she had hidden in her home. She kept the secret of the attic room.

Sometimes they hit her with a flat hand to the face; sometimes they used fists — on her arms and back and chest. Occasionally there was only one man who beat her; at other times there were three. Always, though, her interrogator was the same: a slim Belgian officer with a sharp chin and an eye that wandered. He was Flemish, from the north. He called her *Liebchen*. He gave the signal for the beatings with one raised, well-manicured finger.

On the last day of the beatings, the interrogator had her tied to the chair but the guards did not hit her. He queried her once again, but with a weariness she had not seen before. He didn't seem to care anymore about her answers.

She risked a question.

She asked where Henri was. The officer didn't answer her. She asked if she could see her husband. He refused her. She asked if Henri was well, or even still alive. He remained silent.

She didn't know if Henri had been taken to Antwerp or to Brussels. Or if he'd been shot resisting arrest. Or if, miraculously, he was free.

Odette stirred beside her. She leaned her face into Claire's chest. "They broke a chair against my head," she said.

Claire smoothed the woman's hair. "It will end soon," she said.

"Why are you here?" she asked.

"It's better for you if you don't know," Claire said.

Suddenly, Odette coughed blood onto her chin and neck. Claire held her arms.

"Am I going to die?" the young woman asked.

"No," Claire said. "Sleep if you can. Whatever is injured inside you needs to heal."

She didn't believe the woman would heal. She believed the woman beside her would die that day. Or if not today, then soon. In some ways, she thought the woman lucky.

"When the war is over, Georges and I are getting married," Odette said. "Were you very happy with your husband?"

"Yes," Claire lied quickly.

"Georges was with me in the Partisans."

"Shhhh," said Claire.

"But I've already said his name. I *had* to say his name."

The woman began to weep quietly.

"We all do it," said Claire. "No one can withstand the torture. And you didn't tell them anything they didn't know already. Your Georges will be all right. I'm sure it's not the first time his name has been given. He's probably more worried about you."

"I was supposed to meet him," she said. "At the house of Barbier. And then they came for me. They took my mother and my father and my grandmother. They dragged my grandmother by her dress. . . ."

"Shhh . . . ," Claire said again. "Try to sleep. It's best."

Sometimes, sitting in her cell, she thought of the twenty days they'd had together. Occasionally it would seem to her that it had not really happened — that such an interval could not have existed simultaneously with the events that occurred on a daily basis just inside this prison — but then a detail would come back to her, and then another, and she would know that what she remembered was true. The details were tiny, seemingly insignificant: a fragment from a tune he had whistled through the wall; his face turning away to the side when he laughed, so that she saw his smile in profile; the way he sat slouched with his hands in his pockets, as if nothing in the world were serious. She could see his skin from his cheekbone to his jawline. She could remember how he looked that first night, wounded and naked by the fire. She could not remember everything, and she could no longer *feel* much, but she knew for certain it had really happened. She tried then to imagine him at his air base, the leg healed, as he walked across a green lawn toward a silver plane, his hands in his uniform pockets. Was it at all possible that, against the odds, he'd really made it back to England?

Abruptly, she became aware of now familiar sounds: the corridor door; the boot heels; the echo of the massive ring of keys. They've come, she thought. She brought a hand up to shield her eyes from the light. A figure stood in the doorway.

In a small room, they moved away from her and asked her to strip. She let her shift fall to the floor. Instinctively she sucked her belly in as best she could.

The bright electric light illuminated the bruises. They looked like purple and yellow spills that had stained her arms and thighs. There was so little flesh on her legs that her knees stood out sharply — knobby, awkward joints. She resisted the temptation to cover herself. A nurse handed her a sliver of soap and a cloth, and pointed to the door to the showers.

"As you have been told, you are being transported to Ravensbrück today," the nurse said. "But first you will see the doctor."

Claire gripped the soap and cloth. She was unable to move. The doctor, she thought.

"What is it?" asked the nurse, turning to Claire with irritation. "Is there something wrong?"

The water was not hot, but it was not cold either. In the showers, there were other women with her. It was the first time she had bathed properly since she'd been taken from her house. She wondered if the showers were a good sign. Perhaps the sanitary conditions were better at Ravensbrück, and the Belgians didn't want to be accused of sending dirty women to the German prisons. She wondered how long they would give her in the shower. She was careful with the sliver of soap — she needed to make it last so that she could wash her hair, too.

Her hands trembled, and she had trouble keeping the soap from sliding out of her grasp and onto the tiled floor. How thorough would the doctor be? Mightn't he miss the signs? Or would he be looking for this very thing in the women he examined?

She herself had almost misinterpreted the symptoms. One month, then another. She thought it was the trauma to the body; the near starvation. Other women, long-timers, told her they hadn't menstruated in months. But then she'd tasted the strange, metallic swallow at the back of her throat, and felt that her breasts were tender in a way the bruises weren't. Tender from the inside out, and swollen. This sudden and absolute knowledge had passed through her with a shiver of unexpected pleasure. There was life inside her — proof of the twenty days.

She dried herself with a small towel. Even the rough nap was luxurious on her clean skin. She was told to comb her hair, and she was given a clean shift. Her anus and her vagina were searched. Then she was told to dress and stand along the corridor with the other women.

As she leaned against the tiles, she heard French and Walloon and Flemish, many dialects. The cleanliness had produced civility and chatter. The women talked among themselves of the upcoming transfer as if they were secretaries in a firm. Would they go by train? she heard a woman ask. No, answered an older woman, it would be the trucks like always. But would it take more than a day? Ravensbrück was deep, said the older woman, deep into Germany. Claire did not know if this was true. It must not be so bad in Ravensbrück, said another woman. They wouldn't have given us the showers.

The line moved briskly forward one woman at a time. A doctor's assistant would open a door and call a name. Claire's feet were cold and lined with blue veins. The shift was too big for her and kept slipping from her shoulders.

She hadn't prayed in nearly two months, not since the first beating. When the beatings continued with no sign of mercy —

indeed grew worse — she stopped the prayers. And even when the beatings ceased, she found she couldn't pray.

Now, leaning against the wall, moving forward in small increments, paper slippers barely covering her toes, she prayed. No matter what else happened to her, she said silently to God, no matter what she was asked to do, she would keep the baby inside her. It was a declaration, a challenge.

The woman in front of her was small and graying. Her back was hunched at the top of her spine. Claire saw the bruises on the woman's naked arms. How strange we all are, she thought. Each of us with the same awful medallions, chatting as if this were merely an outing.

The graying woman's name was called. Claire watched her disappear behind the door. She caught a glimpse of a leather gurney, metal stirrups, a sheet. Somehow, she knew, she had to avoid putting her feet into those stirrups.

She waited for her turn. She wondered what happened on the other side of the doctor's office. Where did the women go? Were they given more clothing for the journey? It was late March or early April. Perhaps there would be a calendar in the doctor's office. But whatever the date, they would all need warmer clothes. They couldn't travel in trucks in cotton shifts. They'd all be frozen before they even got to Germany.

She thought about Henri. She tried to imagine him alive. But if that was so, how had he eluded the Gestapo? He'd have had to flee to another village, perhaps even across the border into France. She did not think it likely she would ever see Henri again, even if he was alive. She fervently hoped that if he were caught he'd be shot and not hanged. She did not feel guilt for what she had done to Henri. It did not seem to her an act of betrayal. It was only twenty days out of a lifetime. She could not bring herself to believe that loving the American was wrong. And then she wondered briefly: If she did not feel guilt, was she entitled to the prayers?

"Daussois."

The doctor's assistant held the door. Claire wanted to say, I too am a nurse. Was a nurse. In a corner, she saw a tall, dark-haired man in a white coat who had his back to her. The doctor.

The room was all white and glass and chrome with the brown leather gurney. Over the movable cabinets were fixed cabinets with paned glass fronts. In some of them she recognized the contents: the instruments, the sizes and shapes of the plasters and dressings. There were two other doors to the room. One was unmarked; the other had a sign: *Contagion.*

The doctor was working with something Claire couldn't see; he seemed irritated and called to his assistant to help him. With a sigh of frustration, he told the assistant he had another syringe in the laboratory. The assistant went quickly through the door marked *Contagion,* closed it behind her.

The doctor seemed to have forgotten Claire's presence altogether. She looked quickly at the unmarked door, wondered where it led, how far she would get. She moved silently a step closer to the door. She watched the doctor raise a small vial to his face, tap it twice with his finger.

The door marked *Contagion* suddenly swung open, and the doctor's assistant walked through, holding a syringe. Through the open door, Claire could see a narrow hallway, and across that, another open door. She could see a doctor with a pince-nez and in front of the doctor, with his back to the door, a man seated at a table.

The man had his shirt off. There were no bruises or cuts on his skin. She saw the back of his neck, the line of his shoulder.

She sucked in her breath and took a step forward. How had he been taken? And when? If he was in Antwerp, didn't that mean he hadn't made it out of Belgium?

Something in her posture — a start, the hand on her abdomen — made the doctor who was examining the man glance briefly up at Claire. Mistaking her stare, he smirked, said something to his patient.

Ted turned around.

He looked at her, but he seemed not to know her. Didn't he recognize her?

She took another step forward, opened her mouth as if to speak. The doctor behind Ted turned away, removed his stethoscope from his neck.

He was thinner in the face and paler. His eyes seemed somehow larger — translucent circles in beautiful shadowy sockets. Seeing him, she could finally remember what it was like to feel the skin on his face. His hair had been badly cut.

He did not turn away, but his face remained expressionless.

She wanted to hear his voice, to have some small indication that he knew it was she. She wanted to say his name.

He sat perfectly still, his body half-turned, his bare arm braced on the back of the chair.

She put her hand to her chest. In all the time since the door had opened, she had not drawn a breath.

Briefly — so briefly it might have been a baby's kiss — she put a finger to her lips, took it away.

Casually, her back to Claire, and remembering the door, the doctor's assistant reached over with her hand and pushed the door shut.

Claire closed her eyes, swayed on her feet. She put a hand on the gurney for balance.

He was gone, and she didn't know if he had *seen* her.

———•———

The trick God plays so that everything won't happen at once. Frances used to say that to him in answer to his endlessly tedious questions about time: How long until my birthday? How many days until Christmas? When will we be there — a long time or a short time? A long time or a short time. Twenty days or a thousand days. Yet an entire lifetime could change in a second. A catch in an engine, the giving of a name. He was not sure he understood time any better now than when he was a kid. Not so long ago, the thought of only four days was an agony. Now the idea of four days more seemed almost intolerable.

From his position on the bed, he could watch the day begin in increments — almost imperceptible degrees of light, until soon he would be able to discern the outline of the objects in the cell. A slop bucket. A chair. A pair of boots by the wall. He shivered on the cot, drew the blanket higher on his chest. He coughed hard, breathed deliberately and slowly to stop the coughing. They had made him wear a khaki shirt and pants. They wanted him to be an American pilot. He could not imagine how Belgian prison officials in Breendonk had come by American military khakis. He didn't like to think about it much.

They called him Lieutenant and asked about his plane and crew, but always he responded the same way — with his rank and his name and his military number. They threatened to beat him, but they never did. They appeared to be holding to a code that Ted could only guess at. At Breendonk, they had kept him in solitary confinement, withheld some meals and all medical attention, and woke him at all hours of the day and night to disorient him. Yet they never touched him except to take him to and from the cell. Indeed, sometimes the Belgian officers seemed almost genial. Occasionally they offered Ted cigarettes and lit them for him and asked him questions about the B-17 or the P-38; not, Ted thought, to elicit information, but rather in the same way two men might smoke and compare the features of a Ford versus a Chevy.

Had he kept track, he would know what the date was. But in the beginning, his anger and confusion were so great that the passage of time meant nothing to him. Now a single hour was among the worst tortures he could imagine — every minute anticipated, painstakingly observed, and noted in the brain. Then that minute passing to the next.

He rolled over onto his side. He thought, as he had thought a thousand times since he had been here, that an excess of time was not the worst torture he could imagine: The worst was not knowing.

Retreating footfalls behind him, he walked forward over rough field. The circle of light spun incessantly, beckoning him. In his hand, he held the chocolate bar. The documents and her scarf were in his pocket. Would he be expected to know his false name? he wondered. Would the promised aviators already be there?

When he was five feet from the circle, the light went out. Immediately, there were two men, one at each elbow. They guided him politely to the car, opened the door to the back seat, gestured for him to get in. In the car, behind the wheel, was another man. Ted saw, just briefly, the glint of a bar on a shirt under a nondescript raincoat. He thought quickly of the boy, Dussart, with his missing ear, his tone of voice with Henri. Ted knew then, processed the information in an instant. The knowledge hit him like a shell — once, hard and deafening. He bent slightly forward, put his head in his hands. He thought he might be sick.

Henri.

And Claire as well?

The man to his right took the chocolate bar from Ted's hand. In perfect, if heavily accented, English, the Belgian said: "You won't be needing this where you're going."

"Where am I going?" Ted asked.

The man cleared his throat. He spoke as if he'd rehearsed his pronouncement.

"Lieutenant Theodore Brice, I am sorry to inform you that you are not going to France. You are being taken to Brussels."

Ted thought he saw a slight smile, as if in satisfaction at having accomplished an important task for a superior.

They rode through the night, first on bad, unpaved roads, then on a smoother highway. The man beside him broke the chocolate bar in pieces, gave some to the driver and to the man at Ted's left. Had there been a sign, a clue? He tried to remember all of it, play it through like a film. He saw Claire's face in the truck, wet from crying, and her obvious relief. But then he saw her hand on Henri's arm, the intimacy of that gesture.

What had it meant, then, her loving him?

And what had she been about to say? *I am . . . not what you think?*

His mind looped and circled, reversed itself, took off. He couldn't put his thoughts into a logical sequence. He started again, played the film through. He saw every hour, searched every gesture. Beside him the two men spoke in a rapid French and sometimes laughed. They seemed relaxed and happy. His head spun, momentarily cleared, spun again. His stomach was hollow and nauseous — the kind of nausea he sometimes had emerging from the plane after a bad mission. It was the aftermath of shock, a shock you couldn't allow yourself to experience in the air. But it always hit you when you landed. Like Case, who got the headaches when his feet touched the tarmac. Where was Case now? Home? Out of the war with a shattered arm?

Had Henri been paid? Or had he done it for a cause, for a belief? Did Henri positively know that Ted and Claire had been lovers? Did he approve? Enjoy the irony of the aviator's guilt?

Along the way to Brussels, the driver stopped the car once so that each man could get out to piss. When the two Belgians guarding him left the car, the driver turned around and pointed a revolver at Ted. It wasn't six inches from his face.

He almost said, Do it.

For weeks he didn't care about his cell or time, in the same way (and yet its opposite) that weeks earlier he'd have been content to remain in the attic room forever. He wanted only to play the film through, over and over, again and again. He minded the interrogations not because he feared them but because they distracted his focus. He tried to remember how much he was supposed to tell his captors, what he was supposed to do to escape. Once, bitterly, he flirted with Henri's name and even with Claire's, stopping himself on the threshold of revenge. Some days he was certain she'd been in on the plan. The details and nuances could be put together just so to construct a plot. At those moments, he would see her canniness and instinct for survival as traits nurtured not by resistance but by pragmatism and opportunity. Then he would remember the way she reached for his hand, put her mouth on his fingers, offered herself. Never again, he knew, would he be able to see something, taste something, and say, This is positively so.

After a time (weeks, a month?) he became ill. He had fevers and soaked the khakis. Then the damp in the cell set in and chilled him and made him shiver so violently he thought he might never get warm. He began to cough, and his chest seized up when he breathed. He felt as though there was something lodged inside his chest, an unfamiliar entity — as anger was, or bitterness.

At Breendonk they said they had no medicines for him and no doctor, but the interrogations stopped, and he was sometimes given dry blankets. He became delirious and spoke aloud to Frances and to the group captain, a man he'd barely known at base. He thought he was in Ohio, then in the air. Once he dreamed of finding Claire tangled in a parachute above the clouds. In another dream, Henri was beside him in the truck, whistling and smiling.

He drifted in and out of consciousness, recovered slightly, relapsed. He thought once he had been visited by an RAF named Bernie, an officer who still had his own uniform and seemed to swallow his vowels. This visitation had about it a quality that was unlike all the others, and so Ted thought it had probably actually happened. The RAF was solicitous and asked Ted what he needed; then he confessed he couldn't help the American much. He, too, was a prisoner. His crew had bailed out over, of all places, Brussels, and he'd been arrested immediately. He seemed fascinated by the story of Ted's crash, and, as the conversation progressed, pressed for more details about the damage to the plane, Ted's night in the woods, and his rescue by the Belgian Resistance. On the verge of confiding the tale of the boy who found him, Ted saw in the RAF's movements (the too-casual way he lit a cigarette, surveyed the cell; and why wasn't the RAF frightened or his uniform dirty?) an overeagerness that set off a faint alarm. Or was he, Ted, becoming more and more paranoid, seeing betrayal everywhere, even where it couldn't be? He feigned sleep, heard the RAF sigh with exasperation, call for a guard. Ted never saw the man again.

He slept again with the blanket up around his ears. His sleep rose to the surface, floated near a state of wakefulness, sank again to a world without dreams, then rose again and dissipated like fog. He sat up finally, remaining still a moment to get his bearings. The cell seemed somewhat lighter now — he estimated the time at near eight A.M. Over at the door, the circular trap had been opened. A mug of tea, once hot, had cooled in its tin cup; two hard rolls were beside it. He bent forward, tested his legs, stood. He collected the food from the tray and returned with it to the bed.

He held a roll in one hand, the tin mug in the other. His

hands seemed overly large on his thin wrists — the hands of a cartoon character. He wondered how much weight he'd lost since the crash — twenty, thirty pounds? He bit into the stale roll. The sun had etched a rectangle against the gray stone. Some days, from his bed in Breendonk, he watched the rectangle descend the entire length of the wall until it folded itself onto the floor.

He coughed, put a fist to his chest. If you loved a woman, and you discovered she was not what you thought she was in one particular detail — one particular important detail — did you no longer love that woman? He could never answer that question. He tried to make himself believe that she had known what Henri was about to do, and when he thought he was thoroughly convinced, he asked himself if he still loved her. And almost as soon as he thought about loving her, the entire construct collapsed, and he could not believe in her guilt. How intimately could a face lie and not, over a period of twenty days and nights, betray itself even once?

He replaced the empty tin and plate on the circular tray, picked up his boots. They were Belgian issue of indeterminate material, too small for him, but still preferable to walking the damp floor in stocking feet. His evasion clothes had been taken from him his first day in prison, and he had been wearing the same shirt and pants and socks for nearly two months. Socks. What he wouldn't give for a clean pair.

He put his hands in his pockets and tried to make a few circuits in the cell. The leg couldn't bear all his weight, and so he still limped. Several days after he arrived at Breendonk, a Belgian officer ordered the bandages removed. A laborer was sent in with industrial scissors and a small saw; Ted was certain the man would sever his foot.

After ten revolutions, he stopped at the bed, lay down flat, stared at the ceiling. He knew he tortured himself with images of Claire and Henri together. Perhaps they even talked about him. Henri must have known, must surely have guessed when he saw Ted and Claire in the truck. Had he forgiven her? Or worse, were the twenty days merely part of Henri's larger plan? He covered his eyes with his arm.

A neat click in the door made him turn his head. He waited for the circular tray to slide the mug and plate to the other side of the door, but instead the door opened. A figure beckoned to him.

He sat up, knowing he had no choice but to comply. With his limp, he left the cell, followed the guard along a series of corridors and into a room. A scrubbed green wall, a three-legged stool. Two large guards stood sentry by the door. The floor was wooden, and on it were bloodstains. An officer was sitting behind a clean metal desk. He gestured for Ted to sit.

The officer took off his peaked cap, put it on the desk. He removed a handkerchief from a trouser pocket, wiped his brow.

"You've come from Breendonk."

"Yes."

"You've been ill."

"Yes."

"You're better now."

"A little."

"You've eaten your rolls."

"Yes."

"You know you're being sent into Germany today. To a Stalag Luft."

"Nope."

"Do you mind if I ask you one or two questions?"

"Yes, I mind."

"Lieutenant Brice. Your resistance and silence in Breendonk were useless. You are not in good health, which I regret."

"Sure."

"I could make your circumstances more comfortable. I could arrange for your release."

"I doubt it."

The stool was short, and Ted felt ungainly sitting on it, with his knees raised above his waist. There was no possible way to assume a dignified position. He wondered how long it would take the guards to get to him if he suddenly lunged at the officer and tried to snap his neck.

"Lieutenant Brice, do you know a" — the officer leaned forward to examine a piece of paper — "Henri Daussois?"

He sat perfectly still, knowing that by his lack of expression and his momentary silence, he was giving himself away. He felt the heat rise to the back of his neck. He put the palms of his hands on his knees to steady himself. He tried for a tone of indifference.

"My name is Lieutenant Theodore Brice. My military identification number is AO 677292."

"Yes, yes." The officer fluttered a hand at Ted, as if having expected this reply, but disappointed even so.

Didn't they know it was Henri who betrayed him? Or did they know him only as a courier, and not as a double agent? Did they have Henri in custody, or were they searching for him?

Blood rushed to Ted's head, sloshed in his ears. He could sink Henri with one sentence — so easy, hardly any effort at all. He remembered how Henri handed him the chocolate bar in the darkness, marking him. It would be a swift and sweet revenge. Almost certainly, Henri would be shot or hanged.

"Let me ask you again, Lieutenant Brice. And bear in mind that I might be able to arrange a release for you. Regardless of what you may have heard of the relatively better conditions at the Stalag Lufts, they are not places you want to be — particularly not with your health as it is."

Ted closed his eyes. He felt his head spin as it sometimes did when he'd had too much to drink. He opened his eyes to stop the spinning, and he saw that one hand on his knee had curled itself into a fist. He extended the fingers and tried to relax the hand, but not before the officer had seen him do this.

"Lieutenant Brice, I do require an answer."

His chest hurt. He coughed, again pressed his fist against his breastbone. He looked up at the officer. Yes, he could betray Henri with a sentence, but he wouldn't be able to stop the fuse once lit.

"My name is Lieutenant Theodore Brice," he said. "My — "

"Please." The officer cut him off. He rubbed his eyes. He put his fingers to the bridge of his nose.

"There is a woman," the officer said wearily, "a Claire Daussois. Did you by chance ever meet her?"

He knew, thought Ted. He didn't want an answer because he already knew the answer. He merely wanted to see Ted's reaction.

And then Ted had another thought, simultaneously, one that made him want to vomit.

They had her.

"Claire Daussois," the officer repeated. "Did you know her?"

Ted didn't trust his voice. He hated the way her name sounded on the man's tongue. He wanted to tell him to shut his fucking mouth. Instead, he sat back, deliberately tried to cross his legs in a casual pose. He stuffed his trembling hands into his pockets. He forced himself to look toward the window and to whistle. Glenn Miller. "In the Mood."

"Let me put the question to you another way, Lieutenant Brice. I think you knew both Monsieur and Madame Daussois rather well."

For the first time since being captured, indeed for the first time in the entire war, Ted felt himself suffused with rage. The heat and the color had now come into his face. He didn't now care what Claire had done or not done. It would not be he who linked her to the escape route, or who confirmed that link.

But the rage quickly gave way to an almost paralyzing ache. He forced himself to whistle another tune. "Hot Chocolate." Duke Ellington. He jiggled his foot nervously to the beat. He sat there, in his trapped nonchalance, desperate for a word of Claire, but he couldn't ask. It was possible he would never know what had happened to her. He thought suddenly of the story Claire had told him of Léon Balle — his recital of the children's reading lessons.

"For skies of couple-colour as a brindled cow," he began. "For rose-moles all in stipple upon trout that swim. . . ."

He could not go on. He folded his arms in front of his chest, pressed his lips together.

The officer looked momentarily confused. Then disgusted. He stood.

"Take him to the doctor," he said quietly to the sentry.

He vomited into the toilet, the first toilet he had seen in weeks. There was no food in his belly now; his body simply wanted to heave itself inside out. He wiped his mouth on the back of his sleeve. Outside the stall, the guard banged impatiently and mumbled something in French.

Ted stood up, opened the stall. They were in a different part of the prison, the infirmary if he had to guess. Beyond the stall, he could hear water falling. Showers. One of the guards handed him a towel, a small bar of soap, pointed in the direction of the rushing water.

Barely knowing what he was doing, he stripped off his clothes, left them on the floor. He entered the shower room, dimly aware of other men who seemed too absorbed in the pleasure of the shower to notice him. He turned on the water, warmed it up to tepid. Performing a set of motions learned long ago, he lathered his body, scrubbed his hair. His right leg, he noted from a far distance, was withered at the shin. With his mouth open and his eyes closed, he let the water cascade over him and down his throat. He stood motionless until another naked man, nudging him aside, pointed to an exit door.

He dried himself, put on the clothes folded neatly on a table. More khakis. Too small. He wondered briefly what had happened to their owner. Shot? Shot down? Escaped to England?

The moist air from the shower room momentarily cleared his chest. He breathed deeply for the first time in weeks. He was led to a long line of men sitting on a narrow bench. Thirty, maybe forty men. At the end of the bench was a door, into which the men, one by one, disappeared.

There was some talk, a ripple along the water (*cat's paws*, Frances used to say). He could not understand any of it.

How many dead now? he wondered. He tried to count. Two in the plane. Three guards. Ten hanged. And who else? Nineteen? Thirty-five? Fifty-five? In the end, didn't it come down to numbers? That was how they tallied it at base: Four planes missing. Twenty-seven dead. Twenty-four missions, one to go. He slid along the bench with the other men.

Today he was going east into Germany. Don't bail out over the Germans, they told you at briefings, you'll never get out. Well, that was all right. He hoped only that some asshole of a group

captain didn't try to get them to dig their way to France. He just
wanted the Germans to park him somewhere, leave him alone. He
needed a deck of cards. He needed a drink. He wondered if the
prisoners at the Stalag would have the means to make a home-
made booze. A hundred and fifty proof. Lethal. Didn't seem likely.
He'd heard the stories: After a while you stopped fantasizing about
sex, started fantasizing about food.

The line moved, and he moved with it. An assembly line to
Germany. He looked down the line; he was the only one in a
uniform. Who were these other men? he wondered. What had
they done? Hidden an Allied aviator? Distributed a few leaflets?
Blown up a bridge?

He heard his name as if from very far away. The accent was
like hers, and, for a second, a painful memory stirred.

He entered a room with a stretcher to one side. In the center
of the room was a desk with a chair in front. Cabinets with medical paraphernalia were attached to the walls. To the right of the
desk was a door open to a corridor.

A man in a white coat, with a stethoscope around his neck, sat
on the edge of the desk. He appeared to be making notations on a
clipboard. He looked up as Ted entered the room and, oddly, smiled.

"Lieutenant," he said in very good, if accented, ·English. The
doctor had a pince-nez at the bridge of his nose. It had been years,
Ted thought, since he'd seen anyone with a pince-nez.

The doctor gestured for him to sit in the chair, which had
been positioned sideways to the desk.

"This is merely routine," the doctor said amiably. "A physical
before sending you off. I see you're headed for a Stalag Luft. You'll
like it better there. More like being in a barracks than in prison.
And you'll be left alone. Pretty much. No more interrogations.
You're the first American I've had in a while. You are American,
I take it."

Ted nodded.

"Here, stick this under your tongue. I'll have a listen to your
chest."

Ted closed his mouth around the thermometer. The doctor
bent to Ted's chest, put the stethoscope against his shirt. The

doctor's mouth was a thin line of concentration. He repositioned the stethoscope. He did this repeatedly, then stopped.

He took the thermometer out of Ted's mouth.

"I think you'd better take that shirt off."

The doctor scrutinized Ted's face and eyes as Ted removed his shirt. Ted laid it on the desk.

The doctor felt his neck, behind his ears.

"You've had some coughing?"

Ted nodded.

"Congestion?"

"Yes."

The doctor bent again to listen to Ted's chest. He moved the stethoscope along the skin. He thumped Ted's back, which made him cough.

The doctor stood up, crossed his arms, studied his patient. "You should have seen a doctor sooner."

"I tried."

"It sounds like pneumonia to me. I'll prepare an injection. Normally, I wouldn't suggest moving you, but I want you out of here. You'll die if you stay here," the doctor added matter-of-factly. "I'm not promising it will be a lot better in the Stalag, but it can't be much worse. Well, look at that. Not bad, even without the hair."

Ted glanced up, followed the doctor's gaze out the door and across the corridor.

Her hair, slightly damp, fell in jagged bits around her face. Her mouth was parted, one hand flat against her stomach. The thin shift she wore outlined the shape of her breasts and nipples. He saw the purple and yellow stains on her legs and arms.

A rush of heat moved from the center of his body to his skin.

Silently, he bellowed her name.

Her face was whiter than he had ever seen it, and so thin he could see the bones beneath the skin. She opened her mouth, and he thought she would speak to him. He willed her to speak, and then instantly willed her to be silent. He hooked an arm around the chair to anchor himself, to keep himself from catapulting across the corridor.

Only two, three seconds had passed.

But in those seconds, he had understood that he could not acknowledge her. For to do so was to convict her of knowing him. A death sentence. She would not be in this infirmary, he told himself, if she had already been sentenced to death.

His decision was immediate and agonizing. He could see she did not understand.

He wanted to cry. Even after all they had done to her, she was more beautiful than any other woman he had ever seen.

She took a step forward, put a finger to her lips.

It was a gesture he would remember all his life.

The door across the corridor slammed with a shudder.

———•———

A steady breeze made the new leaves turn their backs. Underfoot, the green of the pasture was uneven, with the onion grass sending up tall shoots. The boy laid down his bicycle. Bright reflections from the plane hurt his eyes where the metal had been scuffed shiny. With his hands in his pockets, he walked toward the plane, examining it as he went. It seemed to him a broken animal, an old dog, that had lain down to rest. Around the belly, dug into the pasture, weeds and wildflowers grew. The skin of the tail made a rat-a-tat-tat sound as it slapped against its frame.

The rumor was that tomorrow the Germans would come to dismantle the plane. He wondered if they'd hack it to death, and what tools they'd use. Everything that could be removed from the plane had already been taken. Only the carcass — dented, pockmarked, bent — was left. They were going to turn the pasture into a landing strip, it was said. German cargo planes. Jean thought the American pilot would probably shake his head in amazement to think that his emergency landing had led to this development. There was no telling sometimes how one thing led to another.

The pilot was gone, and Jean didn't know where. He'd seen him in the square at Rance, and the next day he'd heard that Madame Daussois had been taken. It wasn't known if the American had been taken with her, or if he'd gotten away. Jean hoped passionately that the aviator, with his ill-fitting beret and peasant's coat, had made it safely to Spain and beyond. Sometimes, when the boy heard the drone of a bomber, he looked up and wondered. Surely if the aviator flew over Delahaut, he would signal them somehow.

When the boy drew closer to the plane, he touched the wing with his hand. So much had happened since the plane had fallen a little over three months ago. He remembered the scar the plane had made that day; it was now just a wide rut covered with a mat of grass. He remembered the search through the woods, the shock of seeing the foreign pilot's boots. He thought it lucky that the crash had happened in the winter. With the new foliage, the boy doubted he'd be able to find a man now.

He rounded the nose, trailing his fingers along the metal. He was worried about Madame Daussois. Where had they taken her? And when would she be back? On most days he made it a point to ride by her house. The grass was beginning to grow over the foundation, and her bicycle leaned against the gray stone. The blackout curtains had not been opened and gave the house a gloomy look. The truck, the one that everyone knew she kept behind the barn, had been taken by the Germans. Jean was surprised they hadn't taken her bicycle as well.

He thought that when the war was over, he would ask Madame Daussois if he could live with her. She didn't have any children of her own, and he could offer to work for his keep. He was a good worker, and he knew she trusted him. Maybe she'd been lonely without any children of her own.

But no matter what happened, he'd already decided, when the war was over, whatever the outcome, he was going to leave his father's home. If the Allies were defeated, living with his father would be intolerable; if they won, his father would be tried as a collaborator and probably shot. Jean couldn't bring himself to actually *hope* that his father would be shot; it was just that he thought he would be. In either case, Jean couldn't stay at home anymore. He'd see the war out, for his mother's sake, but that was all. She couldn't expect more than that from him.

He thought suddenly that the next time he passed the Daussois house he would see if he could find a scythe in the barn, cut the grass for her. Yes, that was a good idea. He'd keep the place up. On his own. She'd see then what a good worker he was. He might even begin today, after school.

He banged against the metal as he circled the plane. He wished the Germans wouldn't hack it up. It was a wonderful thing, the plane. He put his hands together in the shape of a bomber, the thumbs hooked together as a fuselage, the two sets of fingers the wings, and made his imaginary plane fly over Belgium, falter, loop low over the village, and execute a belly landing in a field. He separated his thumbs, put his hands in his pockets, and ducked around the tail. He ought to be getting back to school, he knew. Afternoon classes would begin soon.

But heading out of the pasture to fetch his bicycle, he stopped. He turned for one last look at the plane. He studied the cockpit with its smashed windshield. He thought about the waist with its exposure to the cold and to the German bullets. He tried to imagine being a gunner in that waist, or the pilot in the cockpit. Impulsively, not knowing quite why, he ran back to the plane and hoisted himself up onto the surface of the near wing. He turned, looked out over the pasture and toward the woods. The day was clear, but the young trees bent and dipped in gusts.

Jean carefully made his way to the tip of the wing, unbuttoned his jacket, and closed his eyes. His jacket filled and billowed behind him.

The boy arced his body and spread his wings. He jumped as far as he could go.

December 30, 1993

Her voice lingered long into the night and stopped quietly, like a candle that had been pinched out, and he thought then that he understood, or imagined, how it must have been.

Between them on the table was an empty bottle of red wine, the remains of a simple meal, and an ashtray full of cigarette debris — hers. She had more or less chain-smoked the entire time she talked, and the air around them in her kitchen was faintly tinged with blue. Once or twice she had interrupted her story to leave the room; Tom didn't know where she had gone. And once she had stopped to put together the meal — bread, cheese, sausage, a plate of fruit. On the table there was an ivory lace cloth.

Her voice was easy to listen to — deep and steady and without drama. Most often she sat with her chin resting on the heel of her hand, her fingers and the cigarette held away from her face. She had pushed her sleeves up to her elbows when they sat down; her wrists and forearms were both thin and strong.

But it was her eyes that night that Tom noticed most. Large and pale gray — a gray he thought of as calm. She had ivory skin, and it seemed as though it would be powdery to touch. There were many lines on her face, but beneath the skin, her bone structure was distinctive, and it was not hard to see, as it sometimes was in older people, the younger woman she had been. Her hair was white and drawn back behind her ears. She wore a linen blouse and a gray cardigan that matched her eyes; her skirt fell just below her knees. She wore no jewelry of any kind. Her back was straight, and her posture made her look younger than he knew she had to be.

When he had sought her out just before the ceremony began, he had seen that she was not entirely surprised to see him — even though she started a bit when she first looked into his face. The ceremony was impressive and moving, he thought, particularly the flyby by the Belgian Air Force, and the priest making the sign of the cross on his father's engraved name. After the ceremony, she asked him to come to her house for a cup of coffee. And it was then, in her kitchen, with a weak sun slanting through the windows, that she'd begun her story — with her low voice and her accent.

She'd been talking for hours.

When she finished, it was some minutes before he could speak.

"Why did Henri kill the German guards?" he asked quietly.

She turned sideways in her chair, crossed her legs. She had one elbow on the table still; in her other hand, she held a glass. "I did not know this until after the war. The war was terrible for Henri. He was afraid, as I am telling you. I think he wished to show to himself he had the courage."

She took a small sip of wine.

"After the war," she said, "I am discovering that when Antoine is escaped from the school, Henri is stopped. He is tortured, or I think he is threatened with the torture, and when he is let go and he returns to Antoine, he has . . . turned. Yes?"

"A spy," Tom said. "A double agent."

"Yes. He is making the bargain: His life and my life for the information."

"You said there are no bargains," he said quietly.

"Yes, and I am correct in this. The Germans, they shoot Henri before the war is over, when he has given them the pilot and helped to make the new escape line. And when he is not telling them where the pilot was hidden."

"He never gave them you."

"No."

"But you were picked up."

"Yes. For the interrogation. But I have not the execution."

"You went to Ravensbrück."

She was hard of hearing in her left ear, and when Tom spoke she turned her head so that her good ear was toward him.

"No. That day I am telling you of I am put into a truck. But this truck is last in the convoy, and is something wrong with it, and is not starting. So we are taken off and put back in the Old Antwerp Prison. I was very disappointed that day, but later I see that I am having the luck after all. I stay in Antwerp Prison for three months more, and then I am taken to Antwerp train station for the deportation, and at train station all the women I am with, we are let go. I have never know why."

Tom looked around at the room they were in. The cast-iron stove was still intact, but the cabinets and appliances were white and new and distinctly European; they fit together like an expertly designed puzzle. The stone floor, he guessed, was probably the same as had been there in his father's day, and behind the white cabinets was a wallpaper with small bouquets in a seemingly random pattern. Had that been the paper when his father was in this room? On the marble mantel were a crucifix and two silver candlesticks.

He was sitting with one hand on the lace cloth. He couldn't hide his curiosity. He lifted up the cloth and felt the table with his fingers. He pushed the cloth farther back. The table was oak and scarred.

Across the table, Claire Daussois turned back toward him, put down her glass, and brought her folded hands to her mouth. She seemed to be studying him, making a decision.

After a time, she stood up.

"Would you like to meet my daughter?" she asked.

He sensed it was not really a question. She waited for him to stand, and indicated he should follow her. The narrow corridor into which she led him was darkened, but he was aware of an elaborate wallpaper of street scenes, a crucifix on the wall, and a shallow bookcase with framed photographs. She stopped at the threshold of a room, softly called a name, and said a few words. He heard a television in the background. Gently, Claire pushed open the door. She held the door back and leaned against it, an invitation to him. He turned and looked into the room.

The woman in the chair had his father's face and his eyes. The resemblance was so acute, he felt a stab of pain, as though he'd stumbled into a room and found his father still alive. He put his fist to his mouth.

Her hair was cut short and graying slightly, the way dark blondes tend to do. She was sitting in a rocker, her hands folded in her lap, and when she looked at him, her face melted into a sweet and girlish smile — the smile of a child. Her eyes were guileless with that unique color Tom had seen only in his father; and those eyes, combined with the smile, suggested to him a serene spirit. Though she wore a sweater and a pair of slacks, he had the sense that she was wrapped in a cocoon, and he thought it was perhaps that sense of being surrounded and protected that gave her a nunlike quality.

"This is my daughter, Charmaine. Charmaine . . ." Claire spoke up when she addressed her daughter. "This is Tom Brice."

He walked to where the woman was sitting. The images from the TV screen were flickering in the window beside her. She held a hand up to him, and he took it. He could see, even though she was sitting, that she was nearly as tall as he was. Her face was pale and smooth, untouched by the years.

"Bonjour," he said.

The woman looked a bit flustered.

"She is not speaking very much," Claire said from the doorway.

He held her hand longer than he needed to. He was bewildered to realize that all the years he'd been alive, she had been alive. Here. In this house. She was forty-nine, he quickly calculated. Three years older than himself. His sister. His half-sister. He bent down and kissed her on the cheek.

She colored instantly and shyly withdrew her hand. Like a child might, she put the flat of her palm on the place where he had kissed her. She murmured something he couldn't make out and looked toward her mother.

"They are starving me in the prison," Claire said. "When she is in the womb."

There was a chair behind Tom. He backed up to it and sat

down. Claire came and stood beside him. Charmaine turned her attention back to the silent TV screen.

"I'm . . ." He couldn't continue.

"Yes," said Claire. "I know."

"He never knew he had a daughter," he said slowly.

"When the war is ending, we are trying, all of us, to put those years as far behind us as we can."

"When my father was liberated from the POW camp," Tom said, "they brought him out on a stretcher. They shipped him straight home."

It seemed almost more than Tom could take in. And he knew that if he thought about the sadness of it — of his father never having known he had another child — he would not be able to remain in that room.

"You've been alone all this time?" he asked Madame Daussois.

"Oh no," she said quickly, leaning against the wall. The room was small. It had a daybed, the TV, a lamp, a dark oak armoire, a table that Tom could see doubled as a tray. Another crucifix. "I am raising the boy, Jean, along with Charmaine."

"He never told me, when I met him today at the ceremony, about finding my father in the woods."

"No. He would not. Is not his way. He is beautiful child growing up. His father is shot after the war, and his mother is leaving the village. And then I am meeting a man, a teacher, from Charleroi, and we are married. We are on holiday in Spain this month, and at first I am not coming to the ceremony. There are many bad memories, and there are some persons in Delahaut who remember Henri as traitor. And though I am living here and am well remembered for what I do in the war, is best, I think, I do not come to the ceremony. But then I change my mind. I am wanting too much to see the monument. And to have the chance of meeting you. My husband is still in Spain."

She looked at Tom and then looked down. She wrapped her arms around herself.

"I have something," she said.

She left the room and returned with a photograph in a silver frame. She handed it to him.

It was a picture of his father in a white shirt with a poorly knotted tie. His evasion photo, Tom guessed.

"I am keeping this," she said. "Sometimes I am showing it to Charmaine and telling her the man is her father. I am never holding the truth from her or from anyone."

She took the photograph from him, flipped it over to its back to remove the frame. In the backing was another photograph. She offered this picture to him as well.

"It's my mother," he said with some surprise.

Claire almost smiled and nodded her head. "He is marrying her, then. I am thinking this."

He looked at the young woman in the picture — his mother a half-century ago. Had his father once told her about Claire Daussois? Or had she somehow guessed?

"They are loving each other?" Claire asked.

"Yes," he answered, "I'm sure of it." He gave her back the photograph. "They broke his arm in prison camp," he told her. "After he went back to America, he flew cargo planes for a while, and then worked as a flight instructor at a small airport near where he grew up. It was hard for him to keep a job, though. He had problems with his lungs as a result of the prison camp. He died in 1960 of pneumonia. Actually, his name isn't on a marker anywhere but here."

She held the pictures to her chest with both hands. "I have never know," she said, "if your father is all this time thinking it is me who is betraying him. And I am always sorry about this."

"I'm sure he didn't believe that," Tom said quickly.

She made a small movement toward the door. It was late, nearly midnight. But he didn't want to leave the room.

"I always knew that the war had changed my father," he said, "but I was just a boy when he died, and I never really knew why. My mother died in 1979. Luckily the invitation somehow made its way to me."

"I'm glad."

"May I come back someday?" he asked. "To see . . ." He tilted his head toward the woman in the rocking chair, who, all the time that Claire and he had been speaking, had watched the TV screen. He could not yet say her name.

"Yes, of course," Claire said. "You are welcome always."

Tom stood up and walked to where his half-sister sat. He touched her on the shoulder and said goodbye. She looked up at him and smiled again, but didn't speak. He wanted once again to kiss her, but he didn't.

Outside her room, Claire and Tom made awkward progress toward the door.

"You have children?" she asked.

"Yes, I have two boys. But I'm divorced."

"What do you do?"

"I teach high school English — in the town where my father grew up."

"You don't fly?"

"No."

"When you are coming here next time, you must bring your boys. Charmaine is aunt?"

He nodded.

"Oh," she said suddenly. "I am forgetting. On your father's plane is drawing with the name of the plane, *Woman's Home Companion*. When the plane is crashing, as I am telling you earlier, I am hearing of this drawing, and your father is saying he will tell me what it is, but then he is taken. . . ."

"*Woman's Home Companion*," Tom said. "It was the name of a popular magazine then."

"Yes. And the drawing?"

How was he to describe the drawing to this Belgian woman? His father had told him when he was twelve, and he had blushed furiously at the time.

"Have you ever seen much of the nose art that was on the war planes then?" he asked.

"Yes. I know these drawings. They are like cartoons, yes? And the women, they are not wearing too much clothes."

"Well. Yes. But in this drawing . . ." He stopped, trying to think of a way to put this. "It's a picture of a man's . . ."

He waited.

"Oh," she said suddenly, getting it.

"A very large . . .?"

"Ah, yes," she said, nodding. She looked a bit shocked. *"Woman's Home Companion,"* she repeated thoughtfully. Then she put her hand to her mouth and looked at him. She began to laugh. It was a wonderful laugh — tickled and scandalized at once. The laugh lit up her face, and he saw that she was beautiful.

He laughed with her, but what he was really thinking about was of all the things our fathers couldn't tell us.